IN THE HOLLOW OF HIS HAND

Also by James Purdy

Novels

63: DREAM PALACE

MALCOLM

THE NEPHEW

CABOT WRIGHT BEGINS

EUSTACE CHISHOLM AND THE WORKS

JEREMY'S VERSION

I AM ELIJAH THRUSH

THE HOUSE OF THE SOLITARY MAGGOT

IN A SHALLOW GRAVE

NARROW ROOMS

MOURNERS BELOW

ON GLORY'S COURSE

Poetry

AN OYSTER IS A WEALTHY BEAST

THE RUNNING SUN

SUNSHINE IS AN ONLY CHILD

LESSONS AND COMPLAINTS

Stories and Plays

COLOR OF DARKNESS

CHILDREN IS ALL

A DAY AFTER THE FAIR

PROUD FLESH

IN THE HOLLOW

James Purdy

OF HIS HAND

Weidenfeld & Nicolson New York

Published by Weidenfeld & Nicolson, New York
A Division of Wheatland Corporation.
10 East 53rd Street
New York, NY 10022

LIBRARY OF CONGRESS CATALOGING-IN-PUBLICATION DATA

Purdy, James.
In the hollow of his hand.

I. Title.
PS3531.U42616 1986 813'.54 86-5462
ISBN 1-55584-002-7

Manufactured in the United States of America by
Maple-Vail Book Manufacturing Group
Designed by Helen Barrow
First Edition
10 9 8 7 6 5 4 3 2 1

In Memory of

James Link

and

With Thanks to

Elaine Benton

and

David Granger Carr

PART I

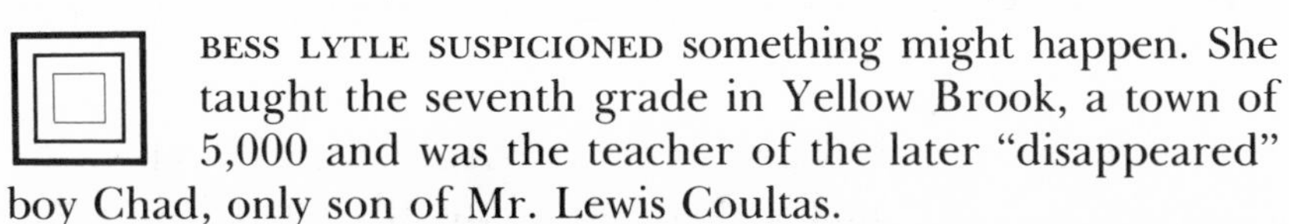

BESS LYTLE SUSPICIONED something might happen. She taught the seventh grade in Yellow Brook, a town of 5,000 and was the teacher of the later "disappeared" boy Chad, only son of Mr. Lewis Coultas.

Bess knew Decatur from when he had gone to school to her, but in actual fact she had known him since he was a small boy. Nowadays he often prowled about the town, but for some days now he had begun to station himself under the biggest of the elms and look over at the schoolhouse. The war had been over for some months, perhaps years, and back came Decatur, from his service overseas, wearing his medals some days.

Then from standing under the elm staring at the schoolhouse, one day he opened the door of the same classroom where she had taught him some fourteen years before. Without saying good morning, how do you do, or even clearing his throat, he went to the back of her classroom and sat down in a vacant seat.

Bess Lytle had the yardstick in her right hand pointing to a map (for they were having a geography lesson) but for the first time in all her teaching career she was speechless, the yardstick held against the map, a surprise or confusion on her face as if the yardstick had turned to dust in her hand.

She turned from the map and stared at Decatur. He was a full-blooded Ojibwa Indian. When he felt like it, as today, he let his hair fall to his shoulders, and his eyes, usually half-closed, made most people look away—they said his eyes made them think of the Northern lights in winter, or a far-off explosion from a city refinery. His skin appeared to get darker each year. He had lied to the recruiting sergeant about his age, and had joined the army when he was only fifteen, in 1912.

One evening a few days after his first visit to her classroom Decatur returned late in the day when she was straightening up the room, washing the blackboard, picking up some of the gum and candy wrappers dropped on the floor.

"Which is Chad Coultas's seat?" he inquired almost before she was aware he had entered the room.

"Decatur!" She stared at him. He looked like a man enveloped in smoke.

"Which is his seat?"

Before she could collect herself she pointed to the third row, fifth seat.

Decatur went over to it and touched it quickly.

"What do you want to know for?" Her voice followed him going to the door.

He turned sideways and stopped. "Ah, I forget." Then he wheeled about after saying this, and his mouth opened showing the teeth which one dentist told him rich folks would give a half million dollars to possess, and look at you, the doctor said, not a penny in your pants pocket.

That was not quite true now, however. Decatur, with his mustering out pay, had been buying up property, old houses deserted by very old people who had died without heirs. He would stay in one of the houses he had purchased for a few days, then tired of it, he would move on to another house he had recently taken possession of. He also bought several used but luxury cars. But in the end, no matter how many houses or cars he had, he always went up the small mountain near Yellow Brook and disappeared—into a tepee he joked. But others said it was a house containing twenty-five rooms which he had built by hand, beginning with the foundation, and only recently the massive roof. He himself called it a tepee.

Bess was turning out the overhead light and beginning to gather up her keys when she thought all of a sudden back to the disgrace at Chad Coultas's maternal great grandma's funeral. The old woman, who was over ninety, had died while opening a box of choice arrowheads she had taken down from the attic. While the elaborate funeral was in progress in her home, a fearful looking and very old Indian man, clothed in a blanket and wearing a kind of headdress of deep red feathers, had tried to gain admittance to the ceremony. He was turned away by an usher, but pushing past him, the terrible old man went directly up to Eva Coultas, Chad's mother, and said to her in a loud voice that the old woman lying in her coffin had Indian blood, and he could not therefore be denied admission. Lewis Coultas, seeing his wife being harangued by the Indian, lost his temper, and struck the man, whereupon the Indian drew a knife. Brandishing it, he said, "Your punishment will come—is already in preparation—both of you!"

He disappeared as quickly as he had come. The old man was Decatur's grandfather, and had reared him on the death of the boy's parents in Canada.

Bess Lytle felt a cold dread come over her. In her troubled state, she forgot to lock the classroom door. And that night she slept hardly more than a few troubled minutes, for she kept hearing Decatur's voice: "Which is his seat?"

Bess Lytle was about forty, but her extreme thinness approaching emaciation made her often appear much younger. She lived in a fourteen-room house inherited from her grandmother, and next door in an even larger house lived her brother Todd. He had been gassed in the war, and for a time could not do any work at all, but then a dairy farmer finally hired him to distribute milk on a horse-drawn truck, and after a few years Todd came to own both the horse and wagon. He began to get his health back, and not being married, he slept most of his free time under Bess's roof. But he liked to think he had his own house to go back to. The town's people criticized both Bess and her brother for keeping such big houses, and permitting so many rooms to lie vacant. People felt they were putting on airs, and trying to be gentry, when Bess was only a poorly paid public school teacher and her brother a delivery-boy for a dairy. But neither of them would give up their property.

"Decatur," her brother Todd repeated the name as Bess told him the day's events. And he would shake his head like a very old man. In fact almost everybody in Yellow Brook pronounced the name the way Todd did tonight. The way people say *cyclone* or *syphilis* or *murder*. Nothing could be done about Decatur. He was the town Indian. They expected bad things of him, but not too bad. He always wore his army medals to remind people he was a hero.

As he ate the Brunswick stew Bess had prepared for him that evening Todd began to give an abbreviated version of a story that went the rounds in the illegal drinking places of town.

Bess held up her right hand to indicate she did not want to hear about something time should have buried.

"But time don't ever bury anything, Bess," Todd said, hurt that she forbade him to tell the story.

But Decatur's visits did not stop. He waited now outside the schoolhouse in his car, which he had cleaned and polished carefully so that it looked brand new. For a while nothing happened. Decatur would wait in the car, and then when all the children had gone home he would drive away.

Then one Friday when she let the children go home a bit early owing to a threatening sky, she saw it happen. Decatur as usual was sitting in one of his cars, this one a Stutz. And before she could rush out of the building to prevent it, she saw Chad Coultas go up to the car, talk to Decatur, and then get inside and Decatur, like a racing man, stepped on the accelerator and they drove off at a breakneck speed.

She stood at the window, almost gasping. Then she remembered that after all Chad knew Decatur. At least his mother Eva knew him, she remembered. Decatur had once worked around the big house in years gone past.

Nonetheless she went to the hall telephone, and called Mrs. Coultas.

Mrs. Coultas was very queer on the phone.

"Did you hear what I said, ma'am," Bess kept repeating. "He got in the car with Decatur."

But there was no real response from the mother for a time, until finally she heard Eva Coultas say: "Thank you for your concern, Miss Lytle." The voice was cold, aristocratic, really cutting, uncivil. "I am sure young Coultas will be all right, Miss Lytle. Your concern is appreciated, but unnecessary."

Forbidden by Mrs. Coultas's voice, Bess did and said no more. She was haunted by Decatur's face. She sometimes recalled during classwork that she had dreamed about him but what she dreamed escaped her in daylight. It was his hair more than anything else, which he kept tied unusually tightly under one of his many hats, which stayed in her mind dreaming or awake. He always wore a very expensive hat, for the express purpose she conjectured of keeping his long hair safely imprisoned in the crown. His hands, too, resembled the paws of an animal, and each nail except that of the middle finger was blackened so that one might have thought someone had beaten his hands with hammers.

Then it began in earnest, the visits. Each afternoon he came, and each afternoon he was almost always in a different auto, waiting outside the school for young Coultas. Sometimes when the boy came to him, they only talked. Chad did not get in the car, though the door was opened, waiting. And then the Indian would drive away with great velocity, his tires screaming. Bess noticed Chad stood watching after Decatur for a long time, sometimes letting one of his schoolbooks drop to the ground, not bothering to pick it up for a long time.

"Oh, I must see Mrs. Coultas," Bess would say each evening to Todd. "Things have gone too far. I must brave her—for him."

"For him?" Todd barked. "You are a fool to see her when she's told you in plain English it's none of your business."

One day in class during an examination there was a loud thump in the room. Something had fallen out of one of the desks.

Bess saw that the object lay beside Chad's feet. She waited, however, until the examination was over, and she was busy collecting the papers, then quickly she stooped down to pick up what had fallen, but just then Chad grabbed the object as she was almost touching it. They wrestled with it, but as they did so the boy's hand closed more resolutely around the object.

Her rule was that pupils who dropped something on the floor from the desk, carelessly, during recitation or examination, would have that object taken away from them and placed in a locked drawer until the year's end.

He would not release the object under any condition but at last her greater stength allowed her to wrest it from him. She let out a funny sigh as she saw what was now in her hand.

"Who gave this to you?" she thundered.

He glared at her.

"Who is the donor?" she cried so that all the pupils watched them. "You'll stay after school, Chad Coultas," she fulminated.

The object she held was marked "Bear Grease."

So he was kept after school that day. Seated close together as she scolded and complained and he refused to speak, they watched the car waiting outside with Decatur in it. He wore an enormous new hat.

"I asked you," Bess went on as they both sat watching the waiting car, "I asked you and I expect an answer. Who gave this disgusting salve to you?"

"Disgust—" he spoke as if coming out of a drowse.

"We will sit here all night until you tell me."

Then perhaps desirous of leaving, despite his pride and rage against her, he mumbled, "Him out there in the car—him."

"And who is him?" she wondered almost deliriously in her pique.

"Decatur. He don't have no other name."

Bess stood up and to her discomfiture the jar of grease fell to her feet. He astonished her by handing it to her.

"What does he come here for all the time, Chad, when you have a father and a mother?" She was almost imploring, beseeching him to explain it. Her hand tightened over the jar of pomade.

"Oh, do I now," Chad replied with a kind of savagery, and all at once he seized the jar of hair oil and removing its lid he took a whiff of the pomade.

"You are insolent," Bess said without force or conviction. "And you are doing so poorly in your schoolwork. You spell like a small child, and you do not even know at this late date the multiplication table."

Not hearing her, he gazed tenaciously at the waiting car.

"I shall therefore have to see your mother."

"She won't care," Chad replied, his gaze never leaving the car. "Won't care about anything. See her!" he commanded, then triumphantly, "I dare you."

"Chad Coultas!"

Wearily, almost sleepily, she let him keep the pomade, though reminding him that the rule had always been that any object carelessly dropped belonged to the teacher until the year's end.

"He'd give me another," he whispered.

She gazed at him, then looked out again at the car. "No civilized person wears bear grease on his hair," she said. "No one!"

She gave him a look of dismissal. Then as he hesitated she almost shouted: "Go, go to him, and take the pomade along with you. I don't want it to stay in my classroom. Go, Chad, leave!"

She stood at the window watching the boy race out toward the car. He did not even greet the man at the steering wheel. As soon as the boy was seated and even before he closed the door, the wheels of the auto were moving, and they sped off like bank robbers.

Then, looking back she saw that he had not taken the bottle. She took off the stopper from the bear grease and smelled.

"Bergamot? Honeysuckle?" she wondered. She took a small daub and put it on her hair.

The day came finally when Eva Coultas agreed she would see Bess concerning Chad's poor grades, and his general inattention in class, his truancy, his daydreaming, his sullen silence. Bess would even mention the bear grease probably. She would mention everything but Decatur. She had promised Todd she would not bring this up.

The big house of the Coultas family with the turret and the mansard roof had been standing as long as Yellow Brook. Mr. Coultas's family went back a long time, much before the Revolution. Mrs. Coultas herself came from across the river, from an even sleepier village. Her mother had spoiled her, people said, hoping she would marry someone worthy of her beauty and refinement, her accomplishments as a singer and performer on the piano and harp, and for a time the flute—she gave up the latter instrument on the grounds it spoiled her good looks. For some years after her marriage the doctor feared she would never be able to have children. After an excruciating delivery, she gave birth to a daughter, Melissa. Then the physician told her she would never have any more children. But after some years, to everyone's astonishment, she gave birth to a boy.

Mrs. Coultas began when Bess entered the front parlor. "Sit over there, why don't you, Miss Lytle, where the light is less glaring on the eyes."

Actually there was almost no light in the room. Mrs. Coultas sat in a small weathered Windsor chair, shading her eyes all the while.

"I suffer miserably from migraine," she reminded Bess. "We have another child in the house. Melissa. She is very close to me—she was my first. She has helped raise Chad because I am so often ill. She looks after the poor boy, more than I, but she has not been devoted enough to his schoolwork, I am afraid. She has so many activities of her own. She is studying to be an actress."

Bess knew of course that Mrs. Coultas wanted to talk of nearly anything but Chad. She reminded the schoolteacher now of a beautifully rich plumaged bird which is trying to escape from an airless room into which it has wandered by accident.

"You couldn't help the boy with his arithmetic—in a special way, Miss Lytle?"

It was Bess's turn now to fidget and feel at a disadvantage.

"I have tried and tried," Bess reviewed her own failure with Chad. "But he so seldom pays any attention when I do give him extra time." She felt at that moment she could smell the bear grease. "I had to give up helping him."

"Oh, I understand. He pays no attention to anything I say. And his . . . father . . . Lewis Coultas is always away on business matters."

A queer almost terrible look came across Eva Coultas's greenish blue eyes.

"But yes," Eva went back to the boy. "His mind is a thousand miles away."

Both women suddenly gave the other a riveting look of understanding as much to admit they both knew where his mind was! And that they had known where it was but no power on earth would draw the secret from them!

Mrs. Coultas had promised herself she would not mention Decatur by name as fervently as Bess Lytle had promised her brother she would not also.

But there it was, the name on her tongue, and clasping and unclasping her beautiful hands adorned today only by one small emerald ring, she heard herself trespassing on territory she had forbidden herself. She caught herself though in time and blurted out:

"Does he . . . daydream a good deal of the time, Miss Lytle?"

Somehow Bess Lytle was positive she had heard Eva mention the name of Decatur, so that, confused, she cried:

"Who, ma'am?"

Relieved by the seeming stupidity of the teacher's question, having escaped saying the dreaded name by so close a call, Eva said:

"Chad does nothing sometimes but daydream at our evening meal. Barely touches his food."

Bess nodded solemnly. Then resigned, steady, knowing she had to come to grips with it, Eva said:

"But he's more restive now that he is visited."

A great hot breath came from Bess's lips, combining relief and strength to go on.

"Yes, he's much worse since they see one another."

"Of course, that stands to reason." Eva pressed a handkerchief soaked in witch hazel against her nostrils.

"And Miss Lytle," Eva steeled herself. "These visits, as we call them, occur with frequency?"

Eva's eyes almost looked black at that moment from the increased width of the pupils.

"Oh, but he comes every day—to see him."

Bess gave the impression at that moment that she did not believe her own words, that what she said had been handed to her by a letter from the postman.

"Every day, I see." Eva's response sounded very far away, and the expression in her voice, if there was any, had no color or emphasis.

"Yes, he comes every day now."

Eva pulled on her ring, raised her hands slightly, and let them fall to her lap.

"It doesn't seem . . . right," the mother spoke too low to be heard, for Bess was going on with:

"In different cars. Each evening in a different auto."

The mention of "different" cars somehow brought Eva out of her languor.

"And you allow Chad to go with him!"

"But no, Mrs. Coultas, of course not," the teacher too came out of her own reverie and confusion. "I cannot run after him, can I? I cannot watch him once he's gone out of the schoolhouse. The road is a good ten rods away from where I teach!"

"I am afraid, Miss Lytle, I am like my boy. I don't know how far a rod is."

"Well, it would take me some haste to reach Chad in time. And I could never force him to not go with him, could I?"

"In a different car each evening! And I was not told of this by anyone!"

The mother looked about the room like one expecting assistance from someone.

"I am sorry I have upset you, Mrs. Coultas. But I felt—"

"If Chad's father were only at home more often." Eva was

now fully awake, and her eyes were brimming over with tears. "He is the one who should deal with it! But I do thank you for coming. It was thoughtful, conscientious, deeply considerate of you. I frankly do not know what to do! He is as wild as . . ."

Both women gave each other a look of something like terror. They must have heard the sentence finished for them as if from another room, by an invisible speaker.

Eva rose then with the sentence not finished, and shook hands with Bess.

"I do not like to cause anyone pain. But Decatur," Bess spoke at last the name and brought to sound the man they had really been speaking of all the time. "Decatur," she repeated as if she had just now learned the name for the first time.

"We can do nothing, Miss Lytle!"

And to the schoolteacher's considerable embarrassment Eva took her in her arms and kissed her.

After the embrace, Eva brought from the table an envelope, and pressed it into Bess's hands.

"But Mrs. Coultas," the teacher protested. "This does not contain money, does it? I would never accept it!"

"Cannot I give someone a gift, if I so choose, Miss Lytle? When we are both in possession of this terrible secret, this terrible man! And when I am so desperate, you have shared my desperation today! You deserve it all!"

Bess Lytle laid the envelope very gently down on the table from which Eva had taken it.

Eva did not seem to notice her gift had been returned to her.

Forgetting all and any resolutions, the mother went on like one carried away.

"You don't know what the very mention of his name does to me, Miss Lytle!"

Taking the teacher again in her arms, she said: "Help me, my dear, if you can. Help my boy, too, as you have in the past. I don't expect the impossible. But I need help and have no one to turn to for it."

Bess felt a kind of fear such as she had never experienced before. She saw there was something here and in Decatur's visits for which she had no clue.

She longed for Todd at that moment even more keenly than Mrs. Coultas longed for her husband.

Bidding Eva another goodbye, she hurried out of the house and almost ran down the street.

Chad and his mother usually took their supper alone in the big gloomy dining room. Mrs. Coultas did not even bother to have the hired girl remove some of the leaves of the huge table for their repast, and so they sat at a board which would have accommodated twenty persons easily. Mother and son sat, Eva thought, perhaps as many rods from one another as Miss Lytle was distant from the daily abduction of her boy. Chad's sister, Melissa, took her supper upstairs more often than not. She was always in preparation, she said, for a dramatic role in the Little Theater Guild.

Chad had already put his napkin in the silver ring and was about to ask his mother to excuse him when Mrs. Coultas said, "I must speak to you, Chad."

"About what, madam."

She flushed at the term. She knew that Chad and his sister got together upstairs and discussed her, and that the *madam* was like a concentrated drop of poison on his tongue.

"Bess has called today about you . . . I mean Miss Lytle." She corrected her own familiarity in calling the teacher by her first name.

"Oh, well, mother, as you always say, what does a dried-up old maid know about anything!"

Stung by the exact reiteration of her own words in his mouth, Eva could think for a moment of nothing to say. The visit of the teacher and the rudeness of Chad reduced her to a kind of moody silence. When she still said nothing, perhaps a bit concerned, he said:

"Well, what?"

"You have failed in your mathematics again, and you withheld your report card from me."

"You only sign it when you are shown it, mother. You never look at my marks or ask anything about my schoolwork. And Melissa is always too busy acting to help me with anything."

"You mean to tell me you have signed my own name to your report card, and handed it back unseen by me to Miss Lytle!"

He grinned at her.

"I think they call that forgery in law," she spoke in a low voice, an octave below her usual range.

He stared at her, unmoved.

"You are being escorted home every evening by a dark-complexioned man," she accused him in her low rather awesome voice.

"An Indian," Chad pretended to be helpful. He noticed his mother color violently.

"This has upset Miss Lytle greatly."

"Oh, so I gathered. She watches me like a whole nest of eagles from the school window."

"I don't know what is to become of you, Chad. I swear I don't!"

She looked about the room in her old helpless manner. "How did you meet this man?"

"Decatur?" He looked at her very sharply then, his mouth compressing itself into a bitter smile.

"What has he said to you?" Mrs. Coultas whispered, watching that smile.

"He has hardly said ten words to me. I supposed," he went on lethargically, "that my dad sent him to see I get home all right."

"Your dad!" Her anger mounted at this patent prevarication. "Your dad knows no such person. Have you looked at this person who escorts you home as if you were some young prince? What on earth do you think you're doing riding about with him in state! Chad, listen to me now, I forbid you to see that man. So does Bess, that is, Miss Lytle."

"Shouldn't my own dad have some say in all this?" Chad's eyes rolled loftily now as his insolence increased.

"Your dad," she said throatily, "is away." She rose now, not bothering to place her own napkin through the solid silver ring. "I warn you, if you go on seeing this . . . Decatur . . . I caution you, Chad, if you go on seeing him . . ."

He pretended to prompt her by looking sympathetic.

"If you see him again, young man, watch out, do you hear? There will be trouble."

"There's already trouble!"

She had turned her back on him before he said this, and now hearing this statement she wheeled about and faced him, her countenance burning.

"What has he said about me?"

"Who?"

"This swarthy companion of yours of course, who else! What has he said to you to make you dare to speak to your own mother in this rude manner! Will you tell me?"

"I told you," he replied brazenly, "he does not say ten words. He probably can only speak Algonquin!" He laughed mischievously, even hatefully.

Mrs. Coultas studied her own son's dark features. Ever since the boy could remember it had seemed his mother only looked at him sideways—while his dad looked him straight in the eye. But now she stared holes through him. As a result of such scrutiny he felt his own left hand slowly touch his face.

"You have always told me," he began somewhat appeasedly, "that my dad was the one who made the rules and shot the orders. Until I hear from him about Decatur I will go on seeing him, go on doing as I please. You have no jurisdiction over me." He almost spat out these last words.

"You don't know what you're doing, or saying. So go to bed. Do you hear? Go to bed!"

"I will see who I please until the King returns."

"The King!" she shouted as if he had blasphemed. "You insolent disrespectful puppy!"

She advanced so quickly he had no time to shield himself. She slapped his face three times resolutely. "You go to bed, do you hear, or I will call for help to put you there!"

Eva Coultas's elder child, Melissa, was so different in appearance from her brother Chad that no one would take them for even distant relations. There was, however, one similarity, which only a careful observer would take note of. Chad's right eye was the same sky-blue as his mother's and Melissa's, while his left eye was a deep intense black. If one looked only at that right eye one would perhaps think Melissa and he were related.

Melissa spent all of her free time studying to be an actress. She lived in front of the nine-foot mirror in her own room and spent countless hours looking at herself in the downstairs hall mirrors. In fact, the Coultas house had more mirrors than many a hall of mirrors described in travel guides to European showplaces.

Melissa and her mother had a controlled but intense relationship. Since there was nobody else to confide in, each found themselves driven into the other's confidence.

Eva's only occupation now was sewing. She made beautiful quilts (some had won prizes at the county fairs), and she was always making dresses for her daughter and for herself. Her one finger, Melissa once pointed out, was worn to the appearance almost of deformity, despite her always using a gold thimble.

"What am I to do with him?" Eva spoke immediately Melissa had entered.

"By him of course you mean Chad?" Melissa leaned down and kissed Eva on the mouth, then stared at her mother's present task, a petticoat so elegant it would have made Marie Antoinette's eyes sparkle.

Eva looked up at her daughter. Melissa was extremely good-looking, but, her mother could not help observing, she would never be so beautiful as she herself had been in her prime.

"Who else, darling, would I mean?" Eva put her sewing down for a moment. "He insulted me tonight at the dinner table."

"Oh, now, mother, a stupid little boy like Chad does not know how to insult."

"It seems," Eva said, picking up her work and then abruptly biting a thread, "I am told, that is, Chad keeps company with an Indian now."

"What Indian?" Melissa's voice was very soft, as if coming from an adjoining room.

"There is only one in Yellow Brook," came her mother's choked reply.

"A few months ago," Melissa kept her voice low, "Decatur came into the house."

Mrs. Coultas's hands froze against the petticoat.

"You say into the house?"

"I was on the third floor—in my little theater room, you know . . . I heard the door open. As Decatur stood immovable at the foot of the stairs, Chad was coming down. Decatur acted as if he had seen . . ."

"Yes what, dear?" Eva's voice was hard and almost mean.

"Well, a ghost then," Melissa'a voice rose in volume.

Eva Coultas almost whipped the petticoat across her lap.

"If Decatur could look pale, he would have been very pale at that moment. But he is almost as black as a Negro, isn't he, mother?"

"I haven't observed him that near."

An odd smile moved over the daughter's face.

"Well, then what happened? If you've gone this far!"

"Decatur began swearing when he saw Chad at the top of the stairs. Or maybe he prayed. Anyhow he got out a whole string of words."

"What words?" Eva sewed with awkward obtuse fingers now.

"Oh, I don't know if I can remember, but he said, I think, 'It's true then! Christ Jesus.' He kept shaking his head, I recall, so that his hair fell down about his shoulders."

Mrs. Coultas waited a moment, then wondered: "And what did Chad do?" She looked directly at her daughter, though her own face was burning.

"He looked queer also." Melissa's whole demeanor had been changing. She seemed to be back upstairs reading some stage part to herself.

"What do you mean, queer?"

"Open-mouthed I guess . . . But I couldn't see Chad too well. He was in the shadow."

Eva put her work down again. "And you never thought to tell me! Melissa, you must talk to Chad about this. Decatur is taking him for drives each evening after school. Who knows if he will begin coming here. And what would your father think of that?"

"He's Chad's father also, dearest," the daughter reminded her.

Eva flashed an angry glance in Melissa's direction.

In the ensuing quiet, Eva drew out the needle from the cloth, and stared at it as if it had wounded her.

"Let's not push one another too far," Eva said after a long pause.

"I will never push you at all, mother. I think you know that." The girl rose and went over to her mother. "I'll do anything you ask of me." She tried not to look at the tears streaming down Eva's face.

"Dearest, if you could go to Chad," she struggled with her sobs. "If you could ask him, my darling, what he is doing with . . . Decatur! What they find in one another's company! What, in fact, do they *know!*"

"What they *know?*"

"Yes," Eva looked up desperately now at her daughter, her face like that of a spent swimmer. "Something is going on between them. It's not right for a young boy to meet a stranger like that every evening after school. Bess Lytle is right for once. I don't know what they are hatching together!"

"Mother!"

"Yes, *mother.* I know you think I'm an hysteric. Very well. But I won't sleep any more until I know what this is all about."

"Oh, you make it sound so sinister, darling."

"Yes, don't I? Well, let me tell you something, dear. It is sinister. Oh, Melissa, your father, should he find out everything," (and she gave Melissa almost a look of terror) "your father is capable of driving me out of the house!"

"Father loves you, dear." Melissa's words were dry, toneless.

"Oh, Melissa."

"Yes, after all these years, all this time, he is very much in love with you. And besides, Father has his ladies, mother."

Eva stopped sewing then.

"But his ladies are not very real, are they, dear? They come and go like the flowers and the little birds, and are gone forever. They don't come back to claim something. They don't come in cars, waiting for something."

"I'll speak to Chad, and bring you his answer."

Melissa took her mother's right hand, the one with the damaged finger, pressed it and went out.

"I do wonder at you so, Chad. I do."

Melissa was seated in a dilapidated but costly rocking chair, placed near her brother's study desk. A day had passed since her painful talk with her mother.

"What are you poring over so hard?" Melissa said when her brother did not answer her. Chad was staring at a book without really concentrating on what was written there.

"Well, I guess I'm trying to do these arithmetic problems for old Bess Lytle," he muttered at last in reply. "I'm failing in math, you know."

"Oh, math, Chad. I could never get through plane geometry. The young man teacher finally took pity on me, and passed me on to the next grade . . . But Bess Lytle! To think she's still alive!"

"What have you been up to, Meliss?" Chad closed the arithmetic book, and came over to her chair and lazily kissed her on the forehead and then on the mouth. She took his hand and pressed it against her breast.

"I was just about to ask *you* that, sweetheart. You're the one who's been up to something."

"So you've talked with Mother."

"I'm afraid Bess Lytle has stirred her up." Melissa smoothed down her dress, which had come far up against her legs, and she tightened one of her rings.

"You always look such a princess, Meliss. You ought to live in a castle, not in Yellow Brook."

He saw that something was bothering her, and her troubled face made him uneasy.

"You have nothing to tell me, your best friend?"

For answer he sat down all at once in her lap and threw his arms around her, then buried his face in her breast.

"I don't think I have," he mumbled against the perfume of her blouse.

"But Chad," she put her hand through his thick black hair. "This man who meets you after school all the time, in different cars. You have nothing to tell me about him?"

"What do you want to know about him?"

"Why does he . . . meet you, Chad?"

"Why, isn't he a friend of mama's?"

"A man . . . who looks like him?" Melissa spoke with her mouth pressed against his hair.

At that moment, as if a bell had sounded to prompt them, they both looked up at the enormous mirror at the far end of the room, and caught the reflection of Chad, his ebony-colored hair and coppery complexion against the paleness of his sister.

Chad's hair had never looked so long or so black. And only his left black eye was visible. Chad rose and moved a distance away from his sister. He looked over at the mathematics book, and then returned to half face Melissa.

"I've grown accustomed to him waiting for me," Chad said at last.

"But perhaps you're not safe with him, Chad, dear?"

He shrugged.

"Chad! You can't go on riding with someone every afternoon and not talk with him. What *do* you two talk about?" she wondered.

"Oh, nothing," he said with his old sulkiness. "We don't say anything to one another except hello and goodbye . . . but he looks at me a lot, sideways."

"I don't like it. I think you should stop it."

They remained moodily silent for a few moments.

"And you say *nothing* to this dark-complexioned man," Melissa summarized their talk. "You wouldn't *story* to me now, would you, darling? There is a mystery to all this, I suppose. But I don't want to know what it is."

Having said this, she held Chad in her arms for a considerable while. Then she kissed him abruptly and abruptly went out.

There came the afternoon, then, when Decatur did not show up for his appointed meeting with Chad. Bess watched the boy waiting under the biggest of the elm trees. A douse of rain began falling, then abated to a sprinkling indifferent wetting. A westerly wind blew the stray leaves over the acre or so of schoolyard where the boys were released for recess.

Bess watched him on and on. Occasionally she would glance at the wall clock, now pointing to five. The factory whistles blew for quitting time. Mechanically she reached for the pile of examination papers she would need to grade that night, and walked out of her classroom.

He fidgeted when he saw her coming toward him, and unaccountably put his satchel down on the ground, and went over to the tree and touched its wet bark assiduously.

"He's not coming, and you know it!" Bess scolded, waiting near him.

Chad hung his head.

"Do you hear what I say? Decatur's not coming this evening."

"You don't know that," he responded without turning away from the tree.

She picked up his satchel for him. "I will drive you to your mother's house."

"No, Miss Lytle, I will wait a bit longer." He was imploring, almost desperate.

She took his face in her hand and brought him before her. He studied the collection of freckles on her partly exposed chest.

"In any case, I can't let you stand here in the rain." She

almost pulled him with her toward her car, then as he made no effort to go back to the tree, she went ahead. He lagged behind almost stumbling.

"This is not a good thing," Bess was speaking to him, as she opened the door of her battered Ford. "It is not a thing which can continue."

Turning to face him again, she said: "What does he tell you when you're together? I mean, you're with him every afternoon. What do you talk about?"

He shook his head.

"I mean," she began again when he made no answer, "what would your father say if he knew?"

"My father?" He spoke in a kind of surprise as if he was astonished to think she thought he had a father. Her own hand trembled on the steering wheel.

"If I didn't know Decatur from times past . . ." she went on with her own thoughts, rather than speaking directly to him. "For I was his teacher too, you must remember. I say if I didn't know him from so far back I would be afraid for you. But I will speak to him certainly. It cannot go on, that's all there is to it. These daily rendezvous." The word, coming out unexpected like this, stopped her.

When she did nothing after she had said the strange word, he stared at her, as he often stared at Eva, with a kind of sullen, contemptuous insolence and hate.

"It is for your own good, Chad, that you don't see him."

They arrived at the gloomy old Coultas house at last. She opened the car door for him, and he rushed out without a word, carrying his little satchel by one finger. As he reached the last of the twelve steps leading to the front door he turned around and waved to Miss Lytle, who went on sitting in the car as if, he thought, she had turned for a moment into Decatur.

Then Chad plunged into the darkness of the great front parlor.

When Bess had returned to her house, night had fallen over Yellow Brook. The rain had stopped, but a chilling sweep of wind had risen from the east.

She fumbled in her large coat pocket for her keys, though the door to her house was seldom locked, and she could have thrown her keys in a ditch and lived out her life without them. As she passed under the heavy gray branches of the wisteria that hung from the roof she heard a sound like that of a katydid or tree toad. She knew at once who had made the sound. She found herself with her hand on the doorknob, not daring to move.

She heard a man's voice say:

"Where was he?"

Decatur stepped forward out of the dark, and handed her her keys which she had dropped.

Instead of giving an answer to Decatur's question, her mind somehow roved back to what people in the town were always saying of her and her brother—that they were two peculiar people living in two large houses all by themselves, and seldom entertaining company. They were accused by the townspeople of being rich and poverty-stricken, miserly and at the same time lavish and living grandly, niggardly and regal.

Decatur's unexpected presence here, and his unexpected return to town, had jarred her into a kind of recollection of her life as if he held her future in his hand. Actually she was not afraid of him in the least. And in any case, he was after all a former pupil of hers, and now he was a war hero.

Seeing the door unlocked as usual, she put her keys away.

"Come in, why don't you?" she asked him. They walked on inside together. She took off her prim little black hat with the long hatpin, and laid it down on a sideboard. Her hair and one hairpin had come slightly loose. She straightened a strand of hair quickly and pushed back the hairpin.

"Come on out into the kitchen, why don't you," she suggested. "I'm going to make myself something hot to drink. Will you join me?"

He barely nodded. She put the teakettle on the broken-down black stove. She measured out the Postum in a pot and poured the hot water on it. Waiting a short while she poured the Postum into two cups arranged on the kitchen table.

Then turning about she faced him directly and boldly for the first time since he had been her pupil some thirteen or fourteen years ago, she had forgotten how many exactly.

A low cry escaped from her.

"Now what is it?" he spoke with throaty intensity.

Decatur standing there in the dim kitchen light was the spitting image of Chad Coultas. Had Decatur been fourteen years old again, and had Chad come into the kitchen and stood beside him, they would be as like as peas in a pod except for the blue cast in Chad's right eye.

He stared at the Postum, then uninvited by her, sat down, and tasted it critically.

"I waited two hours, Miss Lytle," he spoke like someone holding her to account.

She sat down facing him now. "You were late," she reminded him. A thousand disconnected thoughts were rushing through her brain. Her whole life before and after Decatur presented itself to her, why she could not begin to fathom. But this visit made her feel more like herself, made her feel younger and with life still ahead of her.

She watched him drink. He almost sloshed the liquid about in his mouth so that it could be heard across the room.

"Don't you have any sugar or cream for this drink of yours?" he said after a wait.

She began to rise, but he put out his hand and said, "Tell me where they are and I'll fetch them."

"They're in the ice box on the first shelf."

He brought the fresh cream and cubes of sugar to the table, but then he never used them, and went on drinking what he had in his cup.

"You must go away," she said. "Think what Mr. Coultas will do if you go on like this."

"I have the right to see him. Maybe even take him!" His eyes moved toward the high ceiling as he said the last sentence.

"You must not say such a thing, let alone think it. You must leave behind what has been done so long ago. It's too late for you to come between them all!"

He stared in her general direction, then seizing a cube of sugar, he threw it into his mouth and made a loud crunching sound.

"You always used to listen to me," she reminded him.

"This is not a lesson. This is me."

"You cannot drive a wedge into this family!"

"When I come back from from across—from overseas," he said, thinking back as Bess Lytle had thought back a few minutes before, "the first thing I wanted to see was the big house and the staircase in the big house. I opened the door, always unlocked, and went in. I waited at the bottom of the staircase. I thought I called out, but I didn't. I was silent as the dead there. He come then and stood at the top of the stairs, lookin' down. Chad. I must have let out a sound that scared him. Then when he offered to run on up the stairs further, I called after him. 'Don't be afraid,' I said. 'It's your very good friend wants to see you. Maybe your best friend.' "

"Thank God you said friend," she moaned.

"Why thank Him?" Decatur made a spitting sound between his two front teeth.

"I noticed," she changed the subject, "that your middle finger looks as if you had hurt it."

"Oh," he looked at his finger. "Yes, I suppose it does show."

They exchanged looks.

"It happened overseas, along with some damage you don't get to see." He laughed in short little spasms.

"But you're well otherwise?" she wondered.

"Seem to be. *Have* to be."

"But wouldn't it be better, Decatur, if you went away? For your own good."

"I have been away, Miss Lytle. Now I'm back. I belong here more than any of you do. This is where I grew up. This is where my people used to be—all over this territory, the dry land and the water too."

"But there's Mr. Coultas!" she appealed to him. "He has such a fearful disposition. If he found out you are taking his boy away, by stages." She stopped at her own description of the thing. "If he even saw you *once* together, what might happen?"

"That's the least of my worries," he said, staring into his drink. "All I know and care about now is this: there is Chad. And Chad . . . comes from me, not from Lewis Coultas."

"I knew from the very first, I think," Bess Lytle began her own avowal. "When Chad came into my classroom for the first time, I held my breath. I felt I had fallen into the brook in winter. I saw he was . . ."

". . . me," Decatur finished it for her.

"I have been ill ever since," she said.

He drank his Postum from the saucer where he had poured it.

"Ill, huh?"

"You cannot meet him every evening. There's already talk everywhere."

"I can't help myself," he told her.

"That is the worst thing you've said yet . . ."

"I read somewhere while overseas that *the body is the socket of the soul,* and wait," he interrupted a gesture from her, "there is more, *the body is the socket of the soul and borrowed garments never fit well.* Well, Miss Lytle, he has my body and my soul, and he shall one day wear my garments and not those of Lewis Coultas."

"And what of Mrs. Coultas?"

"What of her?"

"Isn't she his mother?"

"And what is that, his mother?" He made as if to empty out the Postum from his mouth.

"You can't take Chad away from her!"

"I can do what my blood tells me to."

Bess Lytle dropped her hands at her side and her head moved forward a little; then she tried to straighten herself up as if she was in her classroom.

"Then be cautious at least, if you can't be anything else," she begged him, and he looked at the tears in her eyes with a kind of bitter outrage.

"Maybe I will act cautious for you, and for the boy. Maybe even for Mrs. Coultas. But caution can't last forever. Not where the boy is concerned."

"You can't undo all that has been done over the years in one night!"

He had risen and gone before these last words rang out. Nonetheless the echo of her words and his retreating footsteps kept on resounding in her kitchen. Her head fell over on the table. All her hairpins, which had been coming loose, fell one by one to the bare floor of the room.

Then one evening, while grading her papers under the lamp, Bess heard the imperious banging on her outside door. She opened it on Decatur's gloomy hulk. He did not speak, made no effort to come in. Then finally she heard him say, "Can I stay under your roof a few days, Miss Lytle?"

He followed her on into the house, for she was too astonished at first to respond to his question.

They sat down at the white ash table in the kitchen.

She watched him chew industriously on his plug of tobacco.

"I'll pay you. I have money. I tell you, I have a lot. I have been buying up property—you may have heard—on Ganglass Mountain."

She nodded, watching the thin trickle of the tobacco at the corners of his very dark red mouth.

To her own annoyance with herself, she found she was glad he had come. But his request to stay worried her.

"I'm too tired to go up there."

"Why should a big strapping fellow like you," she began, thinking back to the way he had filled the threshold of the door, "why should you be tired?"

"My thoughts tire me."

She looked at him chewing.

"Can I stay?"

"Yes," she agreed dolefully. "I suppose so."

"I knew you wouldn't turn me away, Miss Lytle. I'm not a fellow who begs, you know that. And I was your pupil too, like him."

"Yes, that's so." She gave him a faint half-smile.

"Look here, Miss Lytle." He pulled from his breast pocket a huge wallet stuffed with what looked like hundred dollar bills. "Take all of this."

"Put that away, Decatur, and don't let me see it again in any way, shape or form."

He looked down sheepishly at his wallet.

"You can have the big guest room upstairs, on the left as you go up."

But he appeared entangled in his own thoughts, and was silent.

"Do you have anything in the house stronger than Postum?"

She smiled. "I keep a little whiskey for emergencies," she confessed.

"Just a nip would help," he spoke softly. "I have an ache and pain here and there from being across, I guess."

She started on hearing *across,* and got up and opened a little cabinet and brought out a bottle marked "For medicinal purposes only."

"Won't you join me?" he inquired when he saw her pour only one glass full.

"I don't touch it, and can't stand the taste."

He drank the whiskey in two or three sips, and then let out a contented *"Ahh."*

There was a smell coming from her visitor like that from a deer she had once seen in a walk through the woods. It was not unpleasant, but it was strong even in a house as big as hers.

"I have to stay here to think, to come to a decision. I have, then to do something."

"But so many years have gone by, Decatur!"

"What do years matter if he is mine? What if a hundred years went by. Wouldn't he still be mine? Won't he be mine forever?"

"But the proof, Decatur. We're not talking about landed property now, and land."

"All the proof needed in the world is to put us two together, and take a long look. We're as like as . . ."

"And haven't I noticed that these past two years, teaching him," she almost wailed. "So often as he sat there I have at times almost called him Decatur. I swear I almost have. Called him by your name."

"Then you'll back me up?"

"Back you up! Decatur! Who am I? An old-maid schoolteacher as my brother so often reminds me. Can I raise my right hand in a court of law and tell the judge he is yours? They'd think I was touched."

"You mean I can't prove it?"

"I don't know law, Decatur." She kept thinking of the imaginary courtroom proceedings. *They'd say, perhaps, Why didn't you claim him then the day he was born? Or, And where have you kept yourself so long, if he is yours?*

"Yes," he spoke bitterly, "where was I so long?"

"Then they would ask you, wouldn't they, how you came to know so great a lady as Mrs. Coultas. Wouldn't they?"

He stared at her, quit chewing his tobacco, for she actually looked then like some hostile judge in a courtroom.

"Granted," he said open-mouthed.

"And then," she turned to him with her accusing blue eyes, "what would you have gained if you told them the pitiful and exact truth. Think of the misery you would bring to so many people's lives with your truth!"

"Misery?"

"Yes, misery, desperation, actual suffering, and perhaps death."

"Oh, Miss Lytle. Death? After all—"

"Yes, death," she repeated. "I mean it."

"But what about my misery. Am I to have nothing at all?"

"You know Chad is yours. That may have to be enough."

"Enough? Do you know what you are saying? Do you even know what you are talking about at all? So he called you, did he, an old maid? I see perhaps what he meant. *Enough!*"

"Well, what do you expect? You loved her, then, one warm sun-filled afternoon, then you left her, ran off, were gone a lifetime. A boy's lifetime. . . . What do you expect people to do in light of such willfulness on your part, such absence. She must have thought you were dead or that the earth had swallowed you up."

"I don't know what she thought." He bent his head. "Maybe I don't even care. But you must realize that when a man sees he has a son, and can't have him for his own, he is filled with desperation. When a man knows there is his other self and he can't hold him to his heart! Though I have been doing that. I have been holding him to my heart."

"Decatur!" she cried out his name, for the look on his countenance was the most unhallowed thing she had ever seen, and also perhaps the most beautiful.

"Decatur, yes *Decatur,"* he echoed her. "I only came alive when I held him to my heart."

"And have you told him then who you are?" She spoke now like a preacher at prayer meeting.

"I don't think I have to."

"What do you mean by that?"

"Just what I say. I think he knows in his heart, and his blood, I am his dad."

"This is a sorry business," she almost moaned now. "I am stricken by it."

"Not so stricken as me!" Then moving his chair back violently, he went on. "Why on earth did I come back that day? I knew better. One day when my grandad was sober he even warned me about returning. Why couldn't I have died with my outfit in France? That would have solved everything. But to come back and see him. See what I am, and was, and will be. It is too much! That's why I need your quiet guest room to think in."

"It's yours, Decatur, for as long as you need it."

He gave her a kind of famished look of entreaty. "Maybe I will have the strength to leave Yellow Brook, but I don't see how. I could easier cut off my own arm, or plunge a knife in my own throat than leave him now. To know he is my own flesh and blood, and leave him! What is being asked of me?"

"That is why, then, you have done right in coming here to me," she appeased him through her own fear. She touched his hand lightly with hers. "You are in the right place, Decatur. Always trust me. And we have time to think it over."

"Time?" he cried in a kind of outrage.

"Yes, and you are a brave man."

"No, I'm not." He had raised his voice so that the dishes in the china closet vibrated. "Just because I have faced death a score of times! Nothing. Death is nothing. But to see him, to know he is mine and to have to hear he is not! Don't you see that is harder than wounds or death? That is asking too much of flesh and blood, Miss Lytle."

"I believe I understand," she spoke humbly. "Anyhow, my house is yours, Decatur. But let me beg you: don't do anything on the spur of the moment. Be cautious. Think of the other lives which are in jeopardy here, the hearts, too, which can bleed like yours. Think of what might destroy other lives. You are a brave strong man. Now be a cautious, circumspect one, and act slowly. Very slowly."

Todd was open-mouthed, dumbfounded when Bess told him the news.

"Yes, you heard right," she braved him, her voice ringing out as if she was in battle-array. "I said I have taken him in, and I know I did the right thing."

Todd had never looked at her in this fashion before, and she hardly knew where to rest her eyes. Her anger mounted with her feeling she had done something reckless without having asked his advice beforehand.

"I don't know what our neighbors will say," he finally commented lamely.

But all the time Todd was pointing out to her as gently as possible how open to criticism and censure her action was, all her thoughts were on what Decatur had told her. Later, she could not recall whether she had shared Decatur's confidence with him, or whether Decatur's almost rhapsodical words merely kept going round in her imperfect memory.

"Other old maids in Yellow Brook put out a shingle *Rooms to Let,* and their houses are filled with young men, and nobody says boo!"

"But you are hardly just an old maid, Bess. You are a public servant, an instructor of youth. You stand for something."

But the whirlwind of Decatur's recollections, indeed his "confessions," were all that occupied her mind now. She could barely prepare Todd's supper that evening.

"He's out at the moment," she told her brother, "so you can speak freely." A fearful silence had come over Todd. His thoughts, his words were all muffled, as though he were now speaking to her through a blanket of falling snow. He let her talk on, but it is doubtful if he listened.

"You see," she was going forward, "he compares it to when he received this letter while he was in the army overseas. The letter was from his aunt, informing him that his mother had just died in Canada, when all the while his grandfather had told him that his mother had died just a short time after he was born. And so finding out, he said, while he was dressed in Uncle Sam's clothes, that she had only now just died when he had thought of her for so long as already dead, this strange news had hurt him more deeply than the hurt he had always borne that she was dead (so to speak) from his 'beginning.' For all the years he had thought of her as dead she was actually alive, and had he only known it he would have gone to her! So the same thing occurred, though so very different, when he came home to Yellow Brook. He came to the realization he was the father of a young boy—Chad. For he had never suspected he was a father or that this handsome, very winsome boy was his. And to come home to see him, to know he was his, and to know he had been his in fact all these years in his ignorance—the pain, the longing, so many unappeasable things stole over him just as they had when he learned his mother had only recently died, instead of, as he had been told, died when he was born.

"So you see," Decatur had told her, as she now told Todd,

"you see then that I can no more go away, Miss Lytle, than the moon can all upon a sudden rise in the west. He is my son, I am his father, and like the moon I must follow a law that governs the very breath I draw."

"Well, no matter how eloquent he may be, don't you think you have gone a little far by letting him live with you?"

"Live with me?" She was now as thunderstruck as he had been. "I have taught school too long to be accused of such a thing," she muttered, and had she been a good Catholic she would have crossed herself.

"Oh, I have talked till I am black in the face about that, you can be sure," she went on as if in the witness box at last, "but don't you see, Todd, he is right. To come home after all the years and all he has been through, and to see the house where the people were so kind to him as a boy, then to have, on the spur of the moment on his return from the war, opened the big front door and looked up at that long front staircase—which, as he says, as a boy always looked to him like it would never stop until it reached the moon—to start up those stairs and then at the very top of the stairs, with his hand resting for a second, and a second only, on the bannister—to see himself, yes *himself*—coming down those stairs looking straight at him. Decatur knew immediately Chad was his boy. He went back then in his mind to that earlier afternoon, back to the opened door of Mrs. Coultas's room, he heard her again say through the blur of the laudanum, *Why don't you come in since you've come all the way upstairs, Decatur? Close the door behind you, why don't you?*"

"Oh, Bess, for Christ's sake, you should never have listened to that!"

She did not see the expression on her brother's face, or perhaps she would have shut up then.

"You should have made him leave the minute he broached the subject. Wouldn't it be bad enough if he was a white man, but an Indian."

"He has white blood too."

He gave her a look of sour disappointment, almost contempt. "I wonder then," he said at last after a lengthy silence, "where the white blood is kept hidden in his case. If he was any darker, my God, he would be black as a November night."

"But the story, Todd, you must admit is a startling, if terrible thing. Coming back from across, not knowing you had a son, coming back and meeting yourself on that long staircase, in your son. I don't care what people say about him or me, Todd. Decatur can stay for as long as he wants to."

"You sound like you're soft on him," he said, standing up. "And you're in deep besides."

"Let's say," she appeared to ignore the astringency of his words, and she again gave the impression she was by herself, "that I can't resist his story, that's all. Coming back and not knowing you had a son, coming back and meeting yourself in that son. I don't care what happens to me. He must stay. After all, I'm not in it as deep as Decatur or Mrs. Coultas, or Lewis Coultas, once he is back. They're in deep. I'm only on the shore watching them in the deep water."

"And maybe helping them drown!"

She saw that he was finally angry with her, very put out, and rather than say in sharper words all that his disapprobation was bringing to his lips, he left her.

Suddenly all Yellow Brook knew that Chad Coultas was an Indian.

It is difficult to explain this swift and unexpected realization. It began with the boys after school was out, and then it spread to the town and from the town to all the smallest villages of the county.

Was it the fact that Chad had been allowing his hair to grow so that it fell down almost to his shoulders, or, more probably, was it the evening visits of Decatur, who seen side by side with Chad, must have finally revealed to the boys Chad's real origin and character? And then, almost imperceptibly at first, then noticeably, there was an odor now about Chad the boys had perceived, a kind of strong vegetable and animal smell, which they associated with another race than their own.

All at once, at the end of the day's lessons, a knot of boys collected around Coultas as he began his wait for Decatur under the elm tree.

Taking hold of Chad's lapel, the biggest and the fairest of the boys, Richard Woodburn, slapped him.

"Is that Indian in the auto over there your dad, Coultas?" Richard inquired.

Chad shook loose of his antagonist, and raised his fists. At this show of force, all the boys, as if at a signal, began beating him, crying out along with filthy words, "Redskin!" "Indian!"

In a kind of feverish fancy, Chad thought at times that the many fists raised against him were tomahawks coming down upon his face and body.

They beat him until he lay in a mangled heap on the gravel.

It was Decatur himself who was driving off the boys just as Bess Lytle, hearing the uproar, came rushing out of the building.

In a way she was more shocked by the manner Decatur slung the boy over his shoulder than the sight of Chad's bleeding face and mouth. Decatur took him to the car, and almost threw him in the front seat. Then he stopped for a moment to glare back at her and the cowering group of boys.

Bess Lytle, her face unrecognizable in rage, inspired more fear in the group of Chad's assailants than the baleful, unexpected appearance of Decatur, who had been watching as if on cue for such a contingency.

The boys stood in close formation as she addressed them, nearly all of whom were in her class. She told them how despicable and cowardly they were, and then as they thought with relief that this would be all for this evening, she ordered them to march to the principal's office and wait there until she could give him the particulars of their offense.

But she held back the ringleader, Richard Woodburn, and ordered him to come to her classroom by himself.

Richard Woodburn feared Bess Lytle more than he did the principal—perhaps that is why she summoned him. Once he had confessed under her interrogation, she wrote something on a slip of note paper and asked him to hand it to the principal.

Richard looked at the note, the color coming and going in his cheeks.

"He will beat me, Miss Lytle, a hundred times harder than we did Coultas."

"He will beat you even harder if you do not hand my note over to him."

"I know that."

"Why did you gang up on one defenseless boy?"

Richard looked down at the floor boards.

"Because," he said, swallowing thoughtfully, "we should not have an Indian boy in our school."

"Chad is a Coultas. He comes from a very old American family."

Richard shook his head gravely.

"You will deserve all the principal has to give you today," she spoke between her teeth, and dismissed him.

Principal Corwin was known in Yellow Brook among grownups as the "bonecrusher" and by boys as the "ballbuster" owing to his partiality for cruel varieties of corporal punishment. Somehow no parent had ever complained of his beatings. Perhaps because they did not know what to do with their own boys, and so they bowed to the principal's methods for "breaking" them. And the boys, wicked and truant as most of them were, also bowed to this general acceptance of the paddle, the whip, and the hardwood rod.

Today the boys ordered to his office by Miss Lytle saw Principal Corwin select the hardwood rod, almost before they had told him why they had been sent to him.

The principal seemed to the boys an old man, but he was barely thirty, a track and field star and wrestler in his early youth, and today still a practicing athlete in many forms of sport. But his preference was for corporal punishment. They said it kept him in pink physical condition. His waist was so narrow that people sometimes snickered when they saw him only in shirt sleeves until the sight of his forearms and biceps turned the snickering to a kind of awed hush.

All the boys turned a kind of ashen hue once they had confessed to what they had done to Chad.

Principal Corwin had already commanded the boys to stand near the wall, lower their trousers, and bend their heads as far forward as they could when Richard Woodburn entered with Bess Lytle's note in his hand.

Principal Corwin perused the note several times—he had never been a particularly quick reader of the English language.

"You have admitted, Woodburn, to being the ringleader?" The principal spoke in a half-whisper, a peculiar smile ruffling his lower lip.

Richard Woodburn hardly knew what ringleader meant, for he was considerably less trained in English vocabulary than the principal. He was the son of impoverished farmers, and because he was needed on the farm he would soon be forced to leave his schooling behind.

His strange smile coming and going, the principal took the boy's silence for admission, and his chest now rose and fell as he fixed Richard with his gaze. "You'll do for all the rest of the boys." And he motioned the boys facing the wall to retire to the back of the room.

"Take off your pants, Woodburn. Go on, we're all men here."

"And my shirt, too, sir?" Woodburn wondered, for once before the principal had made him strip stark naked.

"I said your pants," the principal barked.

Trembling badly, Richard Woodburn removed his cheap ragged trousers. He did not need to be told to bend over. Principal Corwin raised the thin angry-looking hardwood rod, and Richard gritted his teeth. But to effect even greater pain on the boy, the principal did not immediately cause the rod to fall upon him. One could hear the rod being raised, and while "singing" not land. This happened twice, and one felt the principal might go on raising and not lowering the rod indefinitely without its hitting its target. But then the rod suddenly fell upon the boy's backside, bringing with it easily and noiselessly, it seemed, a smear and rivulet of blood. A second, third, fourth blow fell. Then the principal must have found himself carried away. His breathing might have been heard as far as the road by the school. The rod fell again and again countless times.

It was the group of boys, assisted by the sudden appearance of Miss Lytle, who intervened and all but took the rod out of his convulsive grasp.

Principal Corwin stared at Miss Lytle and the other boys, his face flowing with sweat, his lips covered with a white chalky film, and his eyes a peculiar glaucous color.

"Let this be a lesson to all of you," the principal cried, and his gaze took in Bess Lytle as he spoke. "I'll break every one of you should you be found guilty of misconduct in the future. I'll send you to your graves if need be, but you shall obey me. Do you hear, you shall answer to me!"

Bess Lytle gazed at the principal. She began to tremble with amazement at what she had done. She saw she should have settled the matter herself. She took in the spectacle of her own accomplishment. The boys stood in a little circle watching Richard Woodburn writhing on the floor in pain, his open mouth pressed with an outpouring of his saliva to the wood, his whole lower body exposed for Miss Lytle herself to see, his pain making him reveal his groin stiffening from the torment he had undergone before her astonished, if soon averted, gaze.

"I feel I have been party to a lynching," she all at once muttered, but her words were probably not heeded by the boys or the principal, so occupied were they by the spectacle of Richard Woodburn's blood-stained behind, piteous whining, and almost animal slobbering.

The smell of so much sweat and blood made Bess, retching and groaning, lean against the school wall for support.

Mr. Lewis Coultas was the antipodes, in every way, of Decatur, and although a couple of inches shorter than him (Mr. Coultas was six foot one, in his stocking feet, whereas Decatur was six four), somehow Decatur always looked shorter because of his tendency to slouch and to keep his head lowered as if looking for something on the ground. Moccasin footprints, some wiseacre had quipped.

Lewis Coultas was an incurable speculator with other people's money, and without Eva's knowledge or even suspicion of such a thing, he had been generously borrowing his mother-in-law's (Pauline Stoddard) fortune, which he as quickly lost in questionable real estate deals, finally ruining any future any of them might have. Pauline's financial collapse brought her for a while almost to beggary. Her ancestral home, her farms, her jewels, her other accumulated wealth all went on the block, wiped out as if by a tidal wave. She spent her old age as the manager of her son's pharmaceutical factory, where she supervised virtually unpaid his books and ledgers.

But none of the financial disasters he had engineered bothered Lewis Coultas as much as the galling fact that he had been found physically unfit for military service—he who was practically a stereotype of the rugged white American male. He had gone back to the draft board countless times and insisted he be inducted into the infantry without further ado. Rejected again and again, he had even written a letter to President Wilson, a letter so vehement in its patriotism, and yet in such questionable taste that the communication got no reply for a lengthy while. Then, one day, months later, a penny postcard arrived from the War Department with the laconic message:

Your request has been denied.

What Mr. Coultas's physical defect was, nobody ever knew. Different conjectures were bruited about, however, including one circulated by the wife of the Methodist minister at the Ladies Aid Society to the effect that Lewis Coultas was too *well endowed* to be a soldier. But the fact that he was such an example of strapping manhood made him suffer all the more keenly to be out of uniform.

Indeed many people claimed that Lewis Coultas had ruined his mother-in-law and his wife, stripping them of their fortune, owing to his fury that he had been denied the honor of serving his country. At any rate, shortly after the Armistice when the boys were coming home wearing their medals and being admired for their wounds and injuries, and bands were playing everywhere, Lewis Coultas began making—even more earnestly—the deals which were to level all those who fell under his shadow. Once ruined, the fact came out that he had been worth several millions of dollars up until his fall.

Eva had always believed, and perhaps she was right, that Lewis Coultas did not notice that Chad was unlike him in any way because the two prime disasters of his life, his financial ruin and his failure to win the right to fight for his country, had blurred the rest of his vision, and made him, despite his abundant physical health, a kind of player resigned to sitting out the rest of the game, a man who seldom participated in the life of his family or of the community around him. His absences from Yellow Brook became more frequent, and longer. Finally, he was gone most of the time. Mrs. Coultas once announced at one of her own infrequent attendances at the Missionary Society, "I am as much a widow as if my husband had died fighting for his country."

And so Eva, Melissa, and Chad became accustomed to there being no man in the house, no father at the head of the table.

The peculiar consequence of all this financial cataclysm was that Pauline Stoddard did not hold it against her son-in-law that she had lost everything through his folly. Her second husband, Abner, however, did, and loathed the very sight of the "rangy crook" as he called Lewis C.

"I must see from now on that nothing spoils my second

marriage," Pauline once remarked to her daughter Eva. This statement had brought on a migraine attack for Eva. Eva had always felt from the time she was a small girl that her mother could only devote herself wholeheartedly and completely to her. And in point of fact this had been true until Abner appeared. Pauline's love for her daughter had not so much been diminished by her second marriage—Eva knew better—but her love was shared. Pauline's first husband, and Eva's father, had been nearly twenty years older than his young wife. Only after his death and her courtship by Abner Stoddard had Pauline discovered the nature of real and impassioned love. But Pauline's heart continued to go out to Eva, especially when the new storm clouds began to gather around her grandson Chad.

Even before the "trouble" concerning Chad had come to Mrs. Stoddard's knowledge, Eva had fumed over Pauline's continuing support and affection for Lewis. She even suspected her mother still helped him financially—for who paid for these long trips seemingly to the ends of the earth?

Once when Pauline had referred to Lewis as "young Coultas" Eva had shrieked at her mother, "You *still* act soft on him! On the man who ruined you!"

And Abner Stoddard once used the same phrase in criticizing his wife's partiality toward Lewis.

Then one quiet fall afternoon, Abner Stoddard appeared in the ledger room where his wife patiently labored.

"I have something very serious to speak to you about," Abner told her.

She looked up at him. He was still deeply burned from last summer's sun, for he worked one of his own farms during the good weather, and his hair, despite his years, was only now beginning to go slightly gray.

"Mind you," he spoke warily, "I do not make a habit of repeating gossip."

Pauline was putting beautiful printed labels on the bottles of expensive drugs which were to be dispensed from her son's factory.

"Oh, Abner," she begged him, "can't it wait? I am so rushed just now, can't you see?"

He paled a bit under his tan.

"It cannot wait?" she spoke less plaintively now.

"There's a devilish dirty rumor circulating around town

concerning your daughter." He stopped. Then bending down so that his lips almost touched hers, he asked, "Can anybody hear us, do you suppose?"

Pauline stared at him. "There's certainly nobody listening to what we're saying, Ab." But his own worried face made her add, "We can go up to our own living quarters, I suppose. Yes, perhaps that would be better in case somebody is nearby."

They lived above the pharmaceutical factory now, whereas before Lewis Coultas's misadventures Pauline had been in possession of her own sumptuous twenty-five room home near the river. And yet, Abner thought as they climbed the narrow stairs to their cramped attic quarters, Pauline will go on believing in a crook and a man too cowardly to fight for his country. And he thought of all the glory and the ease they had been deprived of.

"You know I can't abide loose talk, Abner," she told him when they had closed the two doors leading to their private sitting room.

"Just the same, I want you to hear what I have to say, and I want you to be calm. I have to speak."

"Well, then for God's sake tell me what you have to tell me, why don't you!"

"It has to do with Eva and your grandson."

Pauline reached for a cough lozenge and put it on the edge of her tongue.

"To put it bluntly they are saying that Chad is not Lew Coultas's boy."

"They?"

"People all over town. Especially in the saloons. And in the pool parlors."

"Saloons," she spoke contemptuously. "Pool parlors! And then who in creation is his father if it's not Lewis? Have they told you that also?"

He realized that he had entered an area where he was not only a stranger but in some peril himself.

"Pauline, after all, I am only repeating what they say," he raised his voice slightly under her leveling eyes and silence.

"Of course you are!" She spoke with a bitterness he had not known her capable of.

"You see, I've offended you. You're boiling mad at me! All right, I'll say no more."

"You'll tell me now, Ab, or you'll rue the day you began this."

He swallowed hard several times, and did not look at her. Then bracing himself, his mouth parched, he managed to get out, "They say, Pauline, that Chad is the Indian's son."

When her eyes accused him with outrage he had never seen in her before, he almost whispered, "Decatur, you know."

On that she stood up, and then resignedly, as if the name had been a final blow, she sat down heavily.

"All lies. Rotten lies." But her voice seemed to say, "All true."

"But whether lies or not, Pauline, it's spreading like wildfire. You know Yellow Brook."

"Yes, spreading to the saloons and the pool parlors! What credence can be given to anything said there!"

Then when she saw he was licked by his own tale-telling, she delivered the news she had feared to tell him before. "Lew Coultas is coming to see me today. And we will have this thing out!"

"Lew Coultas is coming here?"

"On business."

"Pauline," he began, "look here. If you lend that man any more money, I'll leave you. Do you hear? Leave you!"

"You can rest easy on that score, Ab, I've no more money to lend. No more to be foolish with! Well, then, perhaps I won't see him. I don't know what he wishes to see me about, in any case. . . . But who in particular told you," all at once she thundered at him, "who said to you that my grandson is an Indian?"

"Nobody said exactly that." He was dumbfounded at her sudden tempest of wrath.

Abner saw it working now in her mind, as it had been working in his. Over the years he had never dreamed that Chad was anybody's son but Lewis and Eva's, until he had stepped into one of the pool parlors a few days ago and heard the talk and the laughter and the sneers. And neither, he saw now clearly, had Pauline suspected such a thing. Oh, why had he told her? Why had he repeated saloon talk to the only woman he had ever cared a straw about? He could have bitten off his own tongue.

But at that very moment the suspicion was taking hold of both of them. Suspicion is often more believable than truth, for truth often appears commonplace and unworthy of attention.

Chad was not Lew Coultas's son the rumor blared out as if from some floating megaphone from the street. *Chad Coultas was not a white man's son.*

And Eva, Abner wondered, hanging his head, walking out from his wife's presence without a word or nod from her in leavetaking. Yes, what about this beautiful delicate woman he thought of as his own daughter? How had she come to fall from such a height?

Then came a disturbance which could have flamed into scandal. But this rumor leaked out only gradually, crept along, took some weeks to become known generally, and then was put down as more pool-hall gossip.

But to Bess Lytle the event was as disturbing as if it had been written in letters of fire in the skies of Yellow Brook. More than the wagging tongues which could continue to spread the story, Bess feared her own brother's wrath considerably more. Bess who was usually the one to put the fear of *her* disapprobation in him.

The event was Bess's scandal, Bess's shortcoming and fall.

She thanked providence the "law" had not called on her as a result of this disturbance, and searching about the premises had come upon the number of firearms she kept stashed away—against an emergency.

The occurrence was this. One sleepless night, Bess, feeling feverish, began poring over a battered volume of the letters of Lord Chesterfield. Somehow, in the dead of this night, she found him appallingly selfish and blind to his miserable boy's needs. Then she fancied she heard a door open and close, and from behind the door loud male voices in argument. She wondered if Decatur was talking to himself in his sleep! But then the voices, two distinct ones, were raised in ire, and finally she heard shouts and scuffling and a piece of furniture being overturned.

She went to the closet at the farthest end of the room, her hands trembling badly. She pulled open the door, which was often stuck shut, and got out her father's rifle. (Bess was a good shot, and her father had always praised her marksmanship and cool aim, which galled Todd because their father had never praised the way *he* handled a firearm.)

She went to Decatur's door and listened. There it was, more

scuffling, cries, foul curses, words of such indescribable obscenity she would hear them in her head all the next day and for many days thereafter, words she had perhaps never heard before but which she recognized as the worst one man could exchange with another. Words too low even to be scrawled on the wall of the school house at recess.

She opened his door.

A wrinkled, cankered old man with long white hair was choking Decatur, and Decatur was doing nothing to protect himself from his assailant. At the sound of the door opening, the old man let go of Decatur and faced Bess. As if she were sleepwalking Bess was pointing the muzzle of the long rifle directly at the intruder's head. The old man half-raised his hands, but gave her a look of vicious contempt and murderous loathing.

"Get out of my house, and don't dare ever to return."

Then, to her own surprise, she added, "If you go quietly I will not kill you."

The next thing she recalled, the old man had gone, the rifle was not in her hands, and she was seated in her kitchen, weeping, Decatur close by mumbling comforting words to her. She did not even remember coming down the staircase. He had heated the whiskey and only as she tasted the liquor did she begin to hear what he was saying to her.

"He's my grandad," Decatur said, explaining the identity of the visitor. "Wants me to go back and live with him in the hills till he dies, which he says is soon."

She nodded as she drank sparingly of the hot whiskey.

"Miss Lytle, hear me."

She barely nodded, still shaking.

"I am not an Indian. I mean," he amended this at once when she gave him a kind of wild look of puzzlement, or perhaps contradiction. "I mean, I can't go live in the hills whatever my face says to other people. I can only be me now from this time forward."

"I might have killed him," Bess shuddered at the thought. "God in heaven!"

"I will leave," he told her, "I have compromised you. I'll go."

"You shall not leave!" She spoke with a sort of belligerent outrage.

She wanted him to leave, of course. Then she broke down and wept. She had not cried so many tears since her mother's funeral. Something had broken within her.

Todd was haughty, grand, cold, and at the same time sympathetic when she finally confessed to him everything that had occurred, except for her own weeping. Todd was trying, she saw at once, to be as "understanding" as she always was when his escapades with the town's loose women came to light: escapades that involved bringing them to his house when Bess was away on business, and "cavorting," neighbors reported, for drunken days on end.

Also, she found to her own peculiar disappointment, that he did not order her to make Decatur leave in view of the "coming scandal." No, Todd did not ask Bess to order Decatur out. He made almost no suggestions at all.

"I suppose it was to be expected," he said with infuriating calm, and he stooped down to pick up one of her fallen hairpins from a tiny crevice in the floor near the spinet desk.

"The old man had the most loathsome face of any human being I have set eyes on." She spoke as if she were alone, or still with Decatur the night of the fracas.

Todd turned to look at her on his way out of the room.

"I even believe he had war paint on," she continued. "And Decatur kept saying again and again *I am not an Indian. I won't go back and live in the hills.*"

"Well, maybe he don't think he is," Todd kept his voice very low. "But he'll have to do a lot of convincing to the rest of the world."

Occasionally Eva withdrew a little genuine leather notebook with a mother-of-pearl clasp from a tiny commode in the far end of her bedroom, and she would write down a few broken sentences. She was too nervous now to compose even a short letter, and the little diary, a gift of her grandmother's, and dated so many years before, bore only fugitive jottings, little telegraphic outpourings of anguish and terror.

Today she only had the strength to write: "There is a whirlwind in my brain. I feel all at once I have two husbands."

Close as Eva was to her mother, she still feared her mother's strange occasional meetings with Lewis Coultas.

"Why do you see a man who ruined you, and ruined all of us financially?"

She had said this a thousand times to her mother and penned it countless more in her leather notebook. "The architect of your ruin!" she had screamed once almost in Pauline's open mouth.

And Eva continued to hear the kind of syrupy remark her mother had made more than once: "I will always have a soft spot in my heart for Lewis Coultas."

In times past whenever Eva had mentioned that she wished to divorce Lewis, a look of extreme pain and disapproval came over Pauline's face.

And when, angered by such a proposal, Pauline had inquired, "On what grounds would you divorce him, dear?" the way she said *dear* had made Eva's throat go dry.

"Adultery," Eva had responded, almost choking from the dryness of her throat.

"With whom?" her mother had spoken stonily.

"With scores, perhaps hundreds," Eva had responded.

But that conversation had taken place some time ago. The whirlwind in Eva's mind today was that with Decatur's return, it was not Lewis Coultas who would be charged with adultery.

So that when Eva found out that Lewis was coming home to see Pauline (he had sent the old woman a telegram from Chicago), she was so confused and alarmed over the events of the past days and weeks that she felt Lewis was returning to tell Pauline "everything." That is, that Decatur, and not he, was Chad's father, and that it was not he who must be charged with unfaithfulness, but the hitherto spotless, long-suffering Eva Coultas.

Yet as she thought back over the past fourteen years, she realized that in all this time Lewis had never shown the faintest suspicion of Chad's parentage, and that she herself had not really given it a moment's thought either. She thought of that long blissful afternoon when she had left the door ajar, and the young Indian boy had come to comfort her! She actually did not remember if he had done anything to her at all. Yes, if she were to be burned at the stake she could not honestly say even now, when everything was crashing about her, that she and Decatur had made love that afternoon. It was all the laudanum, it was his extreme youth and beauty, it was her pain over knowing her husband was incessantly unfaithful to her! It was everything and nothing.

Then, as in one of those plays Melissa was always making her mother rehearse with her, one of the main characters appeared as if to tie all the threads of the story together. The main character in this case being Lewis Coultas.

He put down his many valises in the hall, and walked noiselessly up the stairs to Eva's room.

He waited a moment as if to gather up his courage, or perhaps he was thinking of the delicious surprise his return would bring her after so long an absence. He rapped on the door, then heard her sultry "Come in."

When she saw Lewis standing there looking as fresh as if he had stepped out of his bath, she flushed.

"You weren't expecting me, I know." He bent down and kissed her on the mouth, then lowering his head further, he placed his lips on her throat, and touched her breasts.

She could have sworn that the knock on the door would be Decatur's. She had been expecting him, she thought with a kind of rapture as her husband caressed her. Strangely enough Lewis's kisses brought back for the first time with any clarity that blissful afternoon when Decatur had come through the door to her bedroom. All those years she had blotted out the touch of Decatur's long dark hair that smelled like honeysuckle when it is just opening to the air. As Lewis held her to him, her memory expanded further. She recalled Decatur's long eyelashes that had swept her inflamed cheeks, his chin so much smoother, almost satiny, than Lewis Coultas's chin with his unmanageable beard. Yet as Lewis pulled her to him passionately, she could not remember Decatur touching her body that long vanished afternoon. Only later, after he had left in panic, she had found she was lying naked, with only a thin coverlet over her and a musk-like odor coming in faint waves from her legs.

Lewis Coultas's body, though, was very real, and she could feel almost every part of him under his expensive suit. His collar button snapped from the pressure of his embraces, freeing the cloth about his neck, and she looked down to see whether his arms were bare, his muscles so well-defined against her own thin silk dress.

———

She knew that once Lewis had returned, she would have to go to Pauline. She would have to tell her mother that the possibility existed. At least she would have to give Pauline some hint of the predicament she found herself in. But what if, on learning the truth—if it was the truth—what if, by divulging her fear she lost her mother's love and trust! What if, indeed, on learning the "truth," Pauline would transfer all her love and trust to Lewis Coultas, whom she already loved and trusted so unwisely? What if Pauline loved Lewis, and always had?

That was the vertigo and the whirlwind then in her mind.

Lately there had come a thought (like the final realization that comes to the lunatic that he is mad) when she looked into Chad's eyes and touched his lips with her maternal tenderness, she felt she knew beyond the thinnest fragment of a doubt whose son he actually was. There was nothing in the boy's face, his hands, his being that was Lewis's. No trace. Decatur's return, Lewis's return had proved all this to her. Now every time Lewis Coultas opened his mouth or touched his fair silky hair with the comb, the lesson was clear to Eva again, and the pupil, herself, was schooled in its ironclad truth.

And why did Lewis not see it, now that he was back! He always spoke of his Welsh ancestry. That his own people were very dark-complexioned, though he himself was fair as some Norse god. A throwback, Lewis explained his boy's looks. He reminded everybody his great-grandfather had had dark skin and coal black eyes.

Before Eva went to Pauline, though, she would try to persuade Decatur to go away. If he left, the evidence would be lacking to prove them guilty.

But a hunger came over her to be with Decatur, not merely to talk to him, but to taste him again—and it was Lewis's kisses that had stirred up her desire—to touch his forbidden dark lips.

And as she sewed and thought and mapped out her strategy, another scene from that far-off afternoon rushed into her brain. She saw Decatur again in the open door of her bedroom, hardly older than Chad. At her command she watched him close the door and wait obediently, his head slightly bent over. Then he took off his large-brimmed hat and his hair fell over his shoulders. He stepped out of his boots, and his feet were naked—to her surprise and pleasure. They both looked down at his feet as if somehow that nakedness was the meaning of their coming together. Slowly he took off his ragged coat, his blue work shirt, his yellow undershirt. There he stood before her mother-naked, like some large winged bird which had flown out of the trees. She opened her arms to him. She knew beforehand she was doomed. She knew that his kisses meant more to her than shame, safety, life itself. His kisses blotted out from her forever all that had gone before in her life, and she felt now as she relived the vanished afternoon that her own son, born of that day, was also witnessing her love, and somehow sealing it with his consent and approval.

Lewis Coultas would later whisper to himself about his unexpected meeting with Decatur: *I was caught unawares.*

He had almost bumped into Decatur as he was going into the barbershop and Decatur was leaving. It was the first time Lewis had set eyes on the young man since he had gone off for military service, at least fourteen years ago.

"I shook hands with the Indian boy," he would later tell everyone, for that's how Coultas always spoke about Decatur.

He shook hands with Decatur with the haphazard benevolence one bestows on a half-grown horse.

"Did they let you keep your hair long in the army?" Lewis quipped, seeing that all the barber had given him was a very smooth shave, with fewer cuts than he would probably bestow on Coultas.

"Oh," Decatur replied, trying to smile, and blushing under the coppery tinge of his cheeks. "No sir. I have let it grow out since."

"A man should wear his hair the way he pleases," Lewis remarked.

"My grandad doesn't think so," Decatur pointed out. Lewis looked away. He never thought of Decatur as having any relations.

"My grandad," the younger man went on, "don't think my hair is long enough." He laughed shrilly.

The disturbance at Eva's grandmother's funeral all of a sudden came back to him.

"I see," Coultas spoke evasively.

"He says I should come back with him to the . . . hills. But I ain't ever been to the hills, as a matter of fact. My grandpa is like a total stranger to me."

There was a kind of entreaty in what he said, and the mention of the grandfather and the hills made Lewis very nervous. He had nearly forgotten there was an Indian reservation not far from Yellow Brook, though it was very small, hardly more than a compound of very old men and a few "squaws." He had always put on the gas when he drove past it.

"Decatur," Lewis said, coming out of his reverie and taking the younger man by the hand, "you don't look a day older than when you went into the service, do you? Always nice to see you, Decatur. Come by any time, why don't you. One day we must have a talk."

"A talk, yes."

"A chat, informal, you know."

Decatur watched Coultas move through the door of the barbershop.

"So long then," Lewis said, turning round and raising his right hand, palm forward, as if to quiet applause.

But then like a photographer who has hardly paid any attention to what he has shot until he begins to develop the pictures, Lewis was to hold Decatur's image in his brain until that night at the supper table in the company of Eva, Chad and Melissa.

Chad was facing his father at the far end of the long table. Lewis had raised his spoonful of asparagus soup to his lips, but he did not put the spoon in his mouth. Unaccountably he let the green liquid dribble onto his strong square chin, and then caught himself holding an empty utensil in the air.

What had caused him to make a breach in his table manners by dribbling his soup was that he saw facing him at the end of the table not his son Chad but Decatur sitting at the head of the table staring at him. And not tasting his soup either, but it was after all only Chad who sat there like a judge looking into his father's blue eyes.

"Jesus God!" Mr. Coultas cried out, and put down his solid silver spoon with a bang so loud that he cracked the service plate under the soup dish.

"What is it, Lewis?" Eva asked. She wiped her mouth with a

kind of frenzy on the thick white napkin. "Lewis," she repeated when he did not respond, "are you feeling unwell?"

He had stood up. His eyes did not seem to be focused anywhere, they avoided taking in the members of his family.

"I will have to ask you to be excused," he spoke in a voice completely unlike his own.

He walked with a kind of majestic but almost drunken gait out of the room, and they could hear his deliberate but halting steps going up the stairs.

"I'll go up and see what is the matter with your father," Eva said after a long silence.

Chad stared at her with a kind of merciless indifference. As his mother watched him he picked up a piece of white bread and stuffed most of the slice into his mouth.

"I'll be down in a little while, Melissa dear," she turned to her daughter. "Finish your soup course, why don't you, children."

Upstairs in his bedroom, Lewis Coultas was lying down with his high shoes still on, the crook of his thick arm over his eyes.

"Lewis, dear." She sat stiffly in a high chair beside the bed. She had never spoken his name so soothingly, so tenderly.

"Just leave me. It's nothing serious."

"Is it a headache, dear?"

"No, it's not. I never have headaches, remember."

"Can I bring you anything to relieve the pain then?"

He had not removed his arm from over his eyes, and he did not reply.

"He looks exactly like someone I saw in the street today," he mumbled. "Near the barbershop."

He said no more then. Eva waited for what seemed like hours. When she heard him snoring deeply, she rose, stood a while and watched him, then threw a quilt over his legs and went out of the room.

Lewis Coultas was sick for several weeks. He simply stayed in his room, putting on and taking off a multitude of expensive, usually imported, dressing gowns and shaving meticulously, sometimes twice a day. As a result of these ministrations his face resembled a boxer's (actually he had been an amateur boxer in his youth), and he corrected the cuts and abrasions by wearing court plaster over them.

The doctors who attended on him—Eva had called in several specialists, from as far away as Denver, Colorado—were not all agreed on what his illness was. He looked too perfectly healthy for anyone to believe he had ever been sick. But he suffered periodically from a very high fever, which never abated for very long, a fever sometimes so high that one night it was feared he would suffer brain damage if it did not go down.

During his illness Eva waited on him hand and foot, would allow no one else in the sick room, and even slept in a big armchair by his side. He seemed to appreciate her attendance on him, and Eva would have completely reciprocated this renewed love on his part perhaps had it not been for the fact that all during his illness he called her "Pauline." She felt that all her ministrations and nursing of him were unrecognized as hers, and on his recovery, would be unremembered.

Once he was strong enough to come downstairs and take his meals with the family there was never any recurrence of his behavior at the supper table, or of his staring at Chad with that maniacal look.

But a change had come over Lewis Coultas. He seldom looked at anybody straight in the face now, and if he did so for even a split second, he quickly looked away.

"What do you mean, that we need more proof!"

Decatur heard this one sentence very clearly. It came from the kitchen, and the voices were those of Todd and Bess Lytle, arguing. Arguing over him.

Decatur felt his face go hot under the bedclothes. The only time he spent under Miss Lytle's roof was when, like now, he was in bed, under the heavy covers that smelled of camphor. He blushed so furiously that he was certain such a blush would be recognizable even under *his* complexion.

His discomfiture carried him back to another humiliation which had occurred while he was in the army overseas. He had taken off all his clothes in the barracks along with the other enlisted men when one of the soldiers took notice of "something" about his feet, and called the attention of some of the other soldiers. All at once Decatur stood there unclothed, a target for the many staring blue eyes.

"Let's have a look," the soldier who had observed his feet said.

Yes, there was something about his feet!

Soldier after soldier examined Decatur's feet. They were not hostile, or cruel, or even exactly curious. They stared benevolently.

His feet were webbed!

The men studied and stared. Helpless under their scrutiny, fearful they would presently turn their attention from his feet to his complexion, call him Indian or maybe even Nigger, he patiently allowed them to examine him. Each toe, they pointed out to one another, was webbed like that of a duck. And queerly enough the soldiers did not find this peculiarity anything to be ashamed of. Rather they thought it was a mark of something special. They did not laugh at him.

For a long time after the last curiosity-seeker had departed from the barracks, Decatur had sat with his naked feet outstretched, his cheeks burning with shame, as they were now from hearing Todd's voice cry, *"What do you mean, we need more proof?"*

All at once, Decatur leaped out of bed. He was stark naked now as he had been when the soldiers looked at his feet. But the recollection of that past humiliation gave him an "idea" which ran thrilling through his shivering body.

Decatur planned and plotted like a spy or a thief who waits for the right time for a break-in.

Why, what if he was to buy Chad shoes and socks! The idea came while he lay under the camphor-scented quilts at Bess Lytle's. Especially if the shoes and socks were more expensive than Chad was used to.

So he went to the best shop in town, where he was treated with suspicion by a chalk-faced elderly man.

The clerk showed him some socks imported from Scotland.

"But you see, these are too large. I want them for my son!"

"The boy's department is in the basement," the salesman said. He stared with open misgiving at Decatur, then began putting away the men's hosiery he had shown him.

Downstairs he purchased ten pairs of boys' socks, the most expensive they had. As he fished for the money to pay for them, a hundred-dollar gold coin slipped out from his purse onto the glass showcase. The clerk, who was this time a young woman, let out a gasp.

That afternoon Decatur drove Chad to the edge of the fairgrounds which were surrounded everywhere by maples and oak trees, all turning their fall colors. He was surprised and pleased the boy showed no uneasiness with him today in this very isolated region. After all this was the kind of spot which newspapers claim murderers choose, or kidnappers.

"I have got you some new socks, young man," Decatur began.

Chad turned the full glory of his smile on him.

"But my mother makes my socks," he objected faintly.

"That's why I got you these," he lied. "So her hands can rest."

Chad laughed.

"All right," the boy went along with the explanation, and he took the fancily tied package from Decatur.

"But you must try them on for size, you see."

"Oh, but I can do that at home. I'm sure they're the right size if you picked them out."

But he was not able to resist opening the box tied with several ribbons of different colors, and his hand broke through the costly tissue paper and opened the seal, which allowed a glimpse of the first pair of socks.

"No," Decatur said huskily, "you must put the socks on now so that if it is needful . . ."

"Needful?" The boy watched him.

"If they don't fit!" Decatur managed to say. And he was already helping Chad off with his shoes, and then his socks.

Chad's left foot stiffened slightly, then he relaxed in the grip of the brown thick hands with the spatula fingers and discolored nails.

Chad's one foot was already exposed, then completely bare, and Decatur took the shoe and sock off the right one. Both feet were resting in his outstretched massive grasp.

Slowly, Decatur opened up the toes as one would a flower that is not yet ready to show all its petals. Then the gift-giver let out a little funnel of air from his mouth, and a faint but clear whistling sound emerged.

"Yes," the boy sniggered seeing that his friend had noticed

something. "You are looking at it too. Mama says my feet are like a little water fowl's there . . . are you looking at my toes because of that now?"

Decatur had fallen back against the upholstery of the car, and his hands had let go of Chad's feet as one would drop an object when sleep takes over.

"They are a perfect fit, as Mama would say." He heard Chad's voice coming as if from the hills themselves. Then turning to Decatur, he said after a silence, "Your eyes look odd. Do you have a headache? Say, Decatur, are you coming down with something?"

What Chad saw on Decatur's face was perhaps the rushing through the older man's brain of his entire life, his entire life before Chad. Decatur had been defeated and deprived from the beginning of all he needed to have and hold. He had lived suspended by a steel cord, a cord constructed from his own will. He had even breathed through this steel cord which held him to life, that is a life that was nearly death, for he felt he was forbidden to breathe even the air which all those who had surrounded him from birth inspired into their lungs. He had to breathe by courtesy of the steel tube, which was made hollow for him.

He had achieved, accomplished nothing, the realization now came in painful waves over body and soul—*nothing* except by holding on to the steel of the cord and breathing white people's air—until that is, *now!* Until now, having found he had a son. That he saw, would be his only achievement. He would no longer need the steel cord if the boy was his, and he knew he was, knew it as well as he knew his heart was beating. He had known it from the time he had seen Chad at the top of that sickening staircase.

But the boy must be *only* his. He must take him away from that house, away from Eva. He need not take him away from Mr. Coultas because Mr. Coultas had no claim on him.

"Now it's your turn."

He heard these words coming from Chad in a tone as cold and militant as if his captain in his infantry unit were speaking to him.

"Now let's see your feet, why don't you, huh?"

Decatur only lay back against the cowhide of the front seat. He was not only afraid, he experienced a kind of madness rushing over him. And he felt a cowardice he had never permitted himself even to consider when he had seen "action" in France. For the first time in his life he feared he might faint dead away; and why? All because a young boy had asked him, probably playfully, to take off his shoes, and socks *also.*

Then in the panic in which his breathing came, it seemed from the lowest part of his guts, he cursed the day he had ever come back to the town, to the house. And then he cursed his life too, for the way he had been born and brought up, never knowing a mother or father, only his old grandfather on the edge of the woods. No, none of the terrors of his life had ever been the equal of hearing the boy's command *Now it's your turn. Let's see your feet, why don't you?*

Had Chad said to him, *Here is a knife, now go ahead and cut your throat,* how much easier that command would have been for him to obey. For he thought he would be willing to cut his jugular rather than take off his shoes and socks, despite the fact that he had initiated the whole procedure.

How can I? He heard his own voice come from far down in his throat. *I am so much older than you.*

Then the next unbelievable thing was happening. Like a very strong man, perhaps like one of the German prisoners who had escaped one night and tried to kill him in his tent, he felt himself seized by the boy, and all at once his boots and then his socks were almost ripped off him. What had given the boy the strength, the desperate daring? Was it that all his own manhood was leaving him, going off into the boy's hands which looked in the feeble illumination like sudden flares of heat lightning?

Moaning, looking down he saw his own bare feet, brown as the deepest earth, slightly disfigured by all the marching and the wounds of his soldiering, their nails like those of his hands, blackened and discolored.

But the boy, more ruthless than any German prisoner, spread the toes in his fierce grasp, bringing to the light his own birth's secret.

Then somehow not to his surprise Decatur felt the boy's hands flying into his face, as the German prisoner's hands had that time in the night, the white hands of the German prisoner, and now the darker hands of his son flailed against his helpless face, cutting his mouth and smearing the blood as far as his eyes, almost blinding him.

Finally Decatur heard the door of the car opening and the seat beside him vacant, leaving Decatur more dead than the German prisoner of war had left him in his tent in France.

Through the door Chad had left open he felt himself all at once plummeting to the ground. He had fallen hard. He was only half conscious, as he lay with his cut mouth against the decaying maple leaves. It seemed then that his spirit, unequal at last to the pain of his earthly existence, was leaving his body, as had happened when he lay wounded in the Argonne.

When the morning light awakened him, he was bitterly ashamed. But then when had he not been bitterly ashamed! But he was ashamed most of all because it must have seemed to the boy that he had fainted rather than remove his shoes and socks! How could he ask him to be the son, if the father fainted. And he with medals for bravery!

Then he saw to his even greater anguish that his shoes and socks were still removed. And there for anybody to see were his own bare feet, with their webbed and telltale configuration.

"You looked!" Decatur cried as if the boy were still there with him.

"You looked," the Indian repeated as if he wished to mouth the greatest blasphemy he could utter before some stony-faced judge in some trial, perhaps being conducted in hell itself.

Early the next evening Eva heard strange and unaccustomed sounds coming from the second-story bathroom. She felt positive alarm, for both Melissa and Lewis were gone—Melissa had gone to her drama club, Lewis had returned to Chicago, and she supposed Chad was fast asleep in his bedroom.

For several minutes she was too frightened to rise and go upstairs to investigate. Finally she rushed to the bathroom door, and knocked loudly on the thick wood. There was no answer, and the peculiar sounds emanating from within were even more disturbing to her nerves.

She pulled open the door but what she saw deprived her of uttering speech or sound.

Chad lay in the bathtub, the water all around him running with what looked like streams of blood.

She lifted him out of the water, and as she did so he screamed.

His father's oversize straight-razor lay on the floor near the bathtub. He had slashed the flesh between his toes with the razor.

Then she was carrying him to bed, calmly, almost methodically, looking for iodine, bandages, styptic, whatever remedies occurred to her in such an emergency. Neither she nor Chad spoke.

It never occurred to her to call anyone. It was as if what he had done was understood perfectly by mother and son, and mother and son would take all the necessary steps to mend the damage and keep what had happened forever secret between the two of them.

The bleeding soon stopped. Eva and Chad lay back on the bed nestling together exhausted but seemingly happy in what they had accomplished unassisted by anyone else. They felt very close at that moment.

It was almost as if she knew what had caused him to cut himself. And when Chad saw that she was perhaps never going to inquire into the cause of his using the straight razor on himself, he spoke out of the blue.

"I told him I had my own socks, but he wanted to see my bare feet."

"Of course," Eva replied. "That stands to reason."

"And then," Chad went on sleepily, his lips, wreathed in soft smiles, "I took *his* shoes and socks off myself."

She was as quiet as if she had been fast asleep for hours.

"It made him terribly sick when I looked at his feet."

They fell asleep in one another's arms, and only Melissa's return woke them up. She did not even notice the bandages on Chad's feet—for after all that, the wounds turned out to be, if not superficial, not immediately dangerous.

More unnerving than what had happened to Chad was the sight of Decatur waiting in one of his cars every evening in front of the house as the light was failing. But if it was unnerving it was not unexpected.

"Since he doesn't come out of the schoolhouse to meet him," Eva said out loud. "Where else would Chad be but here?"

While she was staring at Decatur in the car, she felt Chad's presence next to her. She saw him stare out at the car.

"Shouldn't you be in bed?" his mother wondered.

Each evening then as the light was failing Eva and Chad would look out the front window and see the car with Decatur.

"It's always a different car, you're right," she murmured.

It might have been the third or fourth evening, when Eva saw that Chad had put on his shoes, and his raincoat and hat.

She did not dare ask him why he was dressed for going out. She did not have the strength to forbid him, or the strength to say goodbye.

She watched him go out to the car, saw the door opening for him, saw him get in, heard the shriek of the engine and the tires, and watched them disappear.

She fell down in front of the window, clutching the bottom sill like a woman who fears she will pitch forward.

"He's taken him for good, see if I am not right as Christ is my witness!"

PART II

THERE IS ALWAYS a strong wind in Yellow Brook about the time of the autumn equinox, but this year, the year of the "kidnapping," the wind waited until November, long after the tornado season had passed. The wind waited until Decatur and Chad had left, one might think. Then it blew for two days and nights without surcease. The town at that time had mostly wooden sidewalks. The gusts and gales fell on them almost studiously, deliberately, maniacally, like a giant that has found a particular morsel he wants to chew. Thousands of small bits and slivers of wood rose like those you see at the Lucifer Match Factory on the far side of the river. The trees, bare of their leaves now for weeks, were stripped also of their bark by the fury of the wind till they too resembled kitchen matches.

Neither Bess nor Eva hardly paid heed to the winds, though at Bess's house, they tore off part of her roof and smashed several of her window panes. The gale also came down her hundred-year-old chimney and cried out like the maniac boys had one time when they had escaped from the local lunatic asylum and tried to find refuge with Miss Lytle.

Bess felt responsible, if not guilty, that Chad had been taken away by Decatur. She felt as accountable for Decatur's actions as if she had been his mother.

"I should have intervened more forcefully," she muttered. "I should have nipped it in its bud before it got out of control."

"How could you be responsible for him kidnapping the boy?" Todd asked her one evening, with indignation.

She turned three-quarters round in her chair and stared at her brother.

"Kidnapping?" she spoke with acute outrage. "How can you call it that!"

"Well, that is what the law will call it," he muttered. "Abduction, taking a minor away without anyone's say-so."

"Even when the one taking him is his father."

"Prove that in court," he scoffed.

She bowed her head like an old woman. They both stopped their wrangling, but it was as if the wind just then took up their quarrel, and its fury shook chimney, foundation and walls with spite and fury.

When the wind had subsided a bit, and Todd had gone off to his own house, Bess sat on without a thought of bed or sleep.

Three fearful recurrent images plagued her now. There had been the appearance of Eva Coultas at her schoolroom a few days ago, her hair in disarray, and her throat nearly bare against the cold. Without so much as a greeting, she murmured, "My boy is gone."

Instead of expressing her own terror, Bess Lytle found herself telling an almost incoherent Mrs. Coultas of how she had known something devastating might occur.

"Something?" Eva mumbled. "What?"

"I saw the old man," Bess Lytle must have looked at that moment as haggard and wild as the mother.

"What old man?"

"His grandfather, Decatur's grandfather."

Eva sighed. She was not listening but Bess went on. "He looked, Mrs. Coultas, like these illustrations of the Erlking. Riding out in the gales and snowshowers, with breakneck speed, his head bare, his white hair and beard flying in the wind, and keeping the whip high above his head, lashing away, not at the horses, but at the wind, I guess. He looked like the storm itself."

Eva had not heard a word, she saw.

But Bess's own mind went back to the third part of the "vision" which tormented her. . . .

Just a day before Decatur had stolen Chad, she had come home unexpectedly early from school. She was about to pass Decatur's door, which he had left open. He sat facing her. He had nothing on at all. He was looking at his feet, and holding the left one firmly in his two hands. Then Decatur had looked up into her astonished face. He slowly allowed his foot to slip out of his grasp and come down to rest on the carpet.

Even for that day and age Bess Lytle was innocent. She had

never seen a grown man naked before. She had stared at him as if his body revealed to her an explanation of everything which she had never understood. And Decatur, having been discovered, merely allowed himself at that moment to be seen.

Then the sound of Eva's voice brought Bess out of her reverie.

"They disappeared without a trace. I don't know what to say or do. Don't know even any more what to think."

Bess sat down now beside Eva in one of the pupil's seats, and took her hand in hers.

Having uttered as if in a thousand voices *My boy is gone* to the winds, to Bess Lytle, to the house and its staircase that had ruined her and would presently ruin everybody who had ever known her, Eva got ready to go to her mother. Stern and immovable as Pauline was, she was the only person probably in all the world who had ever loved her, cared about her, worried over her endlessly. Eva had often mused that if her mother died Pauline would go on worrying about her only daughter from beyond the grave, and until all consciousness had disappeared from the cosmos itself.

But Eva did not know whether her strength was up to the news which she would have to bring to her mother today. She saw that she would not only have to tell Pauline that her boy had been taken away from her, but that the abductor of the boy was his own father, her lover.

The thought came that when these facts were laid before Pauline, her love for her daughter might finally cease, a love without which Eva did not believe she could support her existence.

Eva walked all the way to the pharmaceutical factory, which was situated on the very edge of town, near the beginning of an untouched woodland beyond which one could see the hills. Standing here, tempted to return home without speaking to her mother, Eva recalled how Lewis had ruined Pauline financially to such an extent that her mother was reduced to being little more than a menial for her brother Judson. And Judson had never forgiven his sister for marrying a man like Lewis Coultas.

Judson always behaved as if Eva had deliberately chosen the man who would bring them all to disaster.

Eva threw herself into her mother's arms without uttering a syllable.

"I knew you were coming," Pauline soothed Eva by stroking her cheek, and then taking off her hat with the soft feathers falling from its side, she kissed Eva's hair in whose gold abundance there was still not one strand of gray.

"Judson has been scolding me for giving you too many bottles of the elixir," Pauline said, pretending to rebuke Eva for coming today for more medicine.

"Mother," Eva began when they had seated themselves in Pauline's sitting room and the door to the room and the hall had both been closed. Eva paused wondering how she could break her "news." She took off her gloves and blew on her hands.

"You're cold through and through, dear girl. Let me fix you something."

"No," Eva almost shouted. "I want you to hear me out," she spoke in a lower but even more ominous manner.

Pauline nodded and waited, and passed her hands over her two rings, one a fine ruby, the other her wedding ring given her by Abner Stoddard.

"I have brought you so much sorrow already, Mother, I have no right to open my mouth again in your presence. Oh, to think of the burdens I have heaped on you, and what have I given you in return?"

"You have given me everything a mother could want of a daughter," Pauline responded in a kind of scolding nettled manner. "What would my life be without you, have you ever asked yourself that? Eva, look at you! You look hardly older than when you were a seventeen-year-old girl. I look at that graduation photo of you a hundred times a day."

"Mother, don't, I beg you. I have brought only sorrow to everyone." She looked out the window facing her to the hills which were already becoming a beaten gold color in the setting sun.

"Do you want to go into my bedroom and rest a while? You look so tired, Eva, dear."

"No, no, rest is out of the question. . . . There is something I have to tell you. You must realize that. Something so dire I think I would rather lie down in front of the old Number 4 railway engine rather than say it to you. . . . But, as always, you are my last refuge."

Pauline's mouth set, and she pushed back a strand of hair.

"Mother, you remember when I was so ill about fifteen years ago?" Eva's voice had become as strong and unhesitating all at once as that of an orator.

Pauline nodded, and the color came and went in her face.

"At that time you may also recall young Decatur was a constant visitor to our home." She looked at the hills again as if they would help her through the rest of her speech.

"I had taken too much of your elixir that day, I suppose." She smiled and looked in her mother's direction. "Mother, hear me out." Eva interrupted a kind of murmuring sound coming from Pauline. "For no matter how painful what I have to say may be, it will be far more painful for all later on if you do not hear me out now. . . . He entered my room, then. Decatur. I suppose he was very appealing then, as now. You say, Mother, I have not changed much. But he has changed very little either, in being handsome and appealing, though so very dark of feature." She stopped.

Her mother smiled strangely at that moment. She did not resemble a woman hearing bad news, but rather someone who is being entertained by a familiar yet also strange story of some distant past, a story not connected with the petty and irksome present.

"Yet in all the ensuing years, you see, I had forgotten he had ever been with me that afternoon. Then of course he returned. You know that. He has come back. Nothing in this life ever goes undetected they say. One slip of the tongue and we hear of it later. One fall and we never walk so securely again. I had always thought—and you must believe—I thought I dreamed he had been with me that day. But of course so often in these fourteen years I have looked at Chad, and seen *him* in his face. . . . But as soon as I saw it I would blot it out again, and nobody else saw Decatur in my boy. And you have told me also we have Indian blood in our ancestry somewhere. . . . But then when Decatur returned, and saw Chad, he must have been as dumbfounded and thunderstruck as I so often was when I gazed at the boy's dark face and hair. But it was *more* in his case than being dumbfounded and thunderstruck. I guess he saw in Chad what was his, he saw in him whatever life had kept back from him hitherto. He lost all feeling of propriety and moderation when he saw Chad. And he blamed me especially. Maybe he blamed God."

Her mother sat on like a stone woman, with only her eyes in a kind of blinking blazing life.

"And so, now, he has taken Chad away from me. They're gone away together."

Pauline moved her head then, and her eyes lost some of their fulguration and brilliance.

"You are very unfortunate, Eva, indeed, and yet you are blessed." Pauline spoke almost drowsily.

"Blessed, mother?" She recoiled from the word. "How blessed?" she asked in a deep, muffled voice.

"Because Lewis Coultas could never have given you a son who has inspired such love. You are loved twice, once for yourself, once for your boy."

Eva stared uncomprehending, but her terror of her mother had vanished.

"But what am I to do, Mother, since you find blessing in all this."

"Did I say 'blessing'?" The old woman smiled faintly. She brought her hands down again and again on the heavy armrests of the chair. "When you are as old as I, Eva, you will know that there is almost nothing we can do about the great things except sweep out our houses and wash out our clothes. All the great things are governed by forces over which we have not the slightest control or influence."

"And what are my tasks then in all this?"

"Do nothing, say nothing."

"And when Lewis returns again, for of course he has gone off once more—am I to go on pretending that Chad is his son?"

"I suppose we will have to report to the sheriff that Chad is missing," the old woman said finally. "And the sheriff will do nothing. To protect ourselves, we will have to report Chad gone, by and by."

For just a moment the thought crossed Eva's mind that Pauline was mad.

Her mother then rose and went to a small cabinet and drew out a tiny bottle of something.

"Be very sparing of this, dearest," Pauline advised her.

Eva looked at the small bottle as if it might contain the consolation for all her woes.

"And it is needful, Mother, to tell the sheriff?"

"As a precaution." Pauline's final words echoed dully in her brain as she went toward her home in the deepening twilight. *By and by.*

The true story of womankind is never told, Eva reflected as she wended her way back to her home. Occasionally she would stop and take a few drops of the elixir.

"Pauline still takes the part of Lewis Coultas," she said out loud, looking back at the hills. "Pauline favors men," she went on with her soliloquy. "She thinks poorly of her own sex. Men are princes in her mind, poor mother, and women mere sojourners in the land."

She was also nonplussed at Pauline's calm acceptance of her "mistake" of so long ago. She wondered if Pauline had not known it all along. And then, finally, her mother did not seem too worried at the fact that Decatur had taken Chad away.

"She always takes the man's side," Eva complained, and stopped to lean against a large fir tree.

"If *I* had ruined you financially, Mother," she spoke aloud again now, "as Lewis Coultas ruined you, I wonder if you would love me as much as you love him!"

All at once she felt anger rising against her mother because Pauline had not felt that Chad's going with Decatur was a kidnapping. She wanted her mother, somehow, to cry out in wild hysteria.

Her mother had accepted her sin, Chad's being the son of a man of mixed blood, and finally the boy's being taken away by that father—she accepted it all with perfect equanimity.

Then if all this were so, why even call the sheriff *by and by.*

Eva felt then that she was entirely alone, entirely unprotected from her sin and her loss of her boy, whom at the moment she loved dearer than life.

Coming into her own front parlor at last, after her walk and her visit, Eva drank some more of the precious elixir.

She moaned softly at that moment for she realized Pauline did not believe that Decatur had actually kidnapped Chad. Her mother had used the word "outing."

"They will come back, I suppose," she went on talking to herself. "Decatur and Chad, with not even a guilty look on their faces, and will laugh at all the anguish they have caused me."

Her anger now moved away from Pauline to the ever-absent Lewis. He had never been her husband, the thought now came to her. She had never been married to him except for the meaningless wedding ceremony and its cheap parchment license. No, he had never been hers. He was like a very slightly older brother or a younger uncle who scarcely knew what a wife was. He was always gone. *I see women and financial speculation,* a gypsy had once told her only a few weeks after her marriage. *You are married to a gambler, my dear.* Eva's session with the gypsy had taken place at a church bazaar which was trying to raise money to rebuild the rectory. In addition to the gypsy fortune teller, there had also been that night a sword-swallower and fire-eater, a strong man, and an acrobat who leaped across the top of the small buildings on Main Street without a safety net underneath. *Your handsome young husband will get worse before he ever gets better,* the gypsy's words came back to her now. *Much worse. But, pay close attention now to what I see. Your real husband is a swarthy-complexioned man. Younger even than you. He will cause you intolerable grief, but he will also give you the only joy you have ever known.*

The face of the gypsy woman was all at once as vivid as if she had entered the room and repeated those words which Eva had forgotten almost as soon as the woman had spoken them.

She was brought out of her reverie by the hired girl calling out to her that the sheriff and a deputy were waiting to see her.

Eva heard her own voice of welcome coming out like that of a ventriloquist as she greeted the old sheriff, Jared Haynes, and his even more aged deputy, Ed Wingate.

Motioning to them to sit near her, Eva heard their questions concerning Chad's "disappearance," she even heard Decatur's name mentioned, and saw that the deputy was writing down in a small book whatever fell from her lips.

Eva's attention was still almost entirely absorbed by what the gypsy had told her that evening at the bazaar, and her mind was riveted as if she was watching a picture show while in the presence of the two lawmen. Her mind unaccountably went back from the gypsy to her wedding night nearly eighteen years past. The sight of Lewis Coultas naked had not frightened her, as he stood there near the bed removing the last articles of his clothing, his grass-green garters and his black hose. They have said, she recalled, that very ugly husbands sometimes drive any thought of love away from their brides. But the fact in her case was that Lewis was too handsome, too hairless of body, like some statue in a world-famous museum. His physical perfection froze any passion she felt for him at the very moment their union was to be consummated. In his arms that night she was as cold as the brook in mid-December. What made her grief even more pronounced was that he did not appear to notice her coldness any more than he would have observed the terror and pain of the deer he shot on one of his many hunting expeditions. She was his wife and was meant to be taken. After they had consummated the act, she lay back, stoical, grim, but not pouting as she was accustomed to doing when crossed in her wishes. She said in the iciest, most devastating tone, "You have very beautiful arms for such a strong man." But he was already snoring away and did not hear her. From then on she was indifferent, if not actively hostile, to him in every way.

Her attention was now brought back to the presence of the two lawmen, who were asking her if she had gotten in touch with her husband.

She started, then she responded that she was waiting to hear from Mr. Coultas and would of course give him the news.

She saw that the sheriff was becoming increasingly uneasy with her behavior, and then his face relaxed a bit as he decided she was too worried over her boy's disappearance to be able to speak sensibly.

But Eva was doing all she could to prevent herself from crying out the name of her "real" husband and explaining the source of her actual anguish and worry.

She was also rehearsing in her own mind how she would tell Lewis Coultas the whole truth as she had tried, and failed, to tell Pauline. First she would say, as she had told her mother and now the sheriff, *My son has been taken away from me.* And then having told him of the fact she would go to the crux of the matter and say, *Am I to blame, Lewis, because you were too handsome and fetching on our wedding might? You destroyed my love then because you were too good-looking. Your arms, despite their sinews, looked covered with talcum powder. So that, Lewis, when the Indian boy, some four, five years after our wedding, came to me, I saw he was the true magnet drawing me to love. There was no talcum powder on his arms—they were like burnt earth around bonfires, or Rubens's madder. His hair did not smell of shampoo but of wild birds' plumage, his nails were discolored and broken unlike yours which always look like they came from the hotel manicurist. His breath did not give off the odor of Sen-sens but the hides of buffalo.*

"Mother, what is it?"

Melissa stood before Eva, her hands clasped in front of her like a soprano in the church choir.

Eva looked about her. The sheriff and the deputy were gone. She had no idea what time it was.

"I don't think the sheriff and his deputy were too satisfied with my replies." Eva began . . . . "They seemed to bore holes in me," she went on, stung perhaps by her daughter's peculiar look of wonder and suspicion. "I felt I was in the witness box."

What Eva wanted to say, but could not quite bring out was, *They saw through me—saw through everything I said.*

Then as Melissa went on looking at her, Eva got out the words: "I think, darling, you must know the truth about all of it, but I cannot tell you more at this moment. I hope your love for me will survive it all, as I fear Pauline's love for me has died."

"Mother, dearest, I would love you if you were charged with murder!"

She rose on saying this and knelt down and brought her mother's face to hers.

"The sheriff wants me to explain it all," Eva said, dry-eyed now and calm, "when I cannot explain it to myself. All that I know is what everybody knows, Decatur has simply taken Chad away. They want me to give it a name, kidnapping, abduction. All I can tell them is what they already know: *he has gone away with Decatur.*"

Melissa held her mother to her.

"The one they should ask, Melissa, is Bess Lytle. Yes, you heard me right. She is in love with Decatur. From the very beginning!" Eva's voice rose now, and Melissa released her hands from holding her mother.

"You can't mean that, dearest," Melissa finally spoke with caution.

"Oh, well, have it your way," Eva said. She accepted her daughter's admonition for caution then. "What I meant perhaps is that Bess loves all her pupils. And after all, he was one of them, though fourteen years have gone by."

"I am sure Decatur will soon be bringing Chad back," Melissa spoke now as if she were the head of the household. She stood some distance now from her mother. "It isn't as if Chad went away with a stranger. For they have been taking drives now for weeks together! And besides, think how long we have known Decatur. At least you have, Mother."

Eva stared eloquently at her daughter, and then looked away.

So the grueling day and evening came to an end.

Whether he knew it or not, Decatur had been practicing the abduction of Chad for some weeks, rehearsing it, one might say, in broad daylight, before the eyes of his schoolteacher, before the other pupils, before the town itself, and the great clock on top of the court house. Everybody had witnessed the rehearsal, as they might have wandered in for the try-outs for an Eisteddfod, or Christmas pageant. For, remember, every day at three-thirty school let out, and Decatur sat at the steering wheel of one of his many cars—a Mercer raceabout, say, or a Ford Tudor or even a Chadwick—waiting for the same boy.

"I am waiting for my son," he might have said had the sheriff asked him what he was doing parked in front of the schoolhouse every weekday.

"Your son?" the sheriff might have inquired. "Who is that?"

"Chad Coultas," the Indian would then answer.

There was no such conversation of course. The law was unacquainted as yet with the Indian's waiting at the schoolhouse preparatory to driving home the fourteen-year-old boy. The law, like the town, was sleepy.

Of the ten murders committed in Yellow Brook during the last five years, only one had been solved, and the suspect died in his jail cell before going to trial. He was a Mexican boy suspected of killing his benefactor, who had operated a horseradish factory.

So Decatur had had plenty of practice. Had he planned to murder Chad Coultas he could not have practiced so well. The boy did not really take to him, Decatur believed, but he did take to the cars, to the rides, to the occasional candy he gave him. And finally, Chad took to the very delicate, almost imperceptible touch Decatur bestowed on the crown of his head or on his shoulder blade as he was leaving the car. In the end Chad had spent more time with the Indian than with Mr. Lewis Coultas.

"Why do you pick me up?" the boy had blurted out one day when it had begun to rain hard, and the Indian had not started the motor, while wiping the windshield clear.

"What?" Decatur gulped, and then choked until Chad began to slap him on the back to keep him from strangling.

Recovering from his choking, Decatur responded, "Oh, well, you know."

He started the motor, and they drove to the outskirts of town in all the downpour. Then the rain stopped and the sun came out.

"There should be a rainbow, shouldn't there?" Chad opened the window and stared out. "But there ain't one."

Decatur sat at the steering wheel plunged in thought.

"I will drive you home now."

Chad smiled at him when they reached the house. It was exactly as when the sun had emerged at the edge of town from the black clouds. What did it matter, there was no rainbow?

"Chad," Decatur said to him as the boy moved to get out of the car.

"Well, what now?"

"I will wait for you tomorrow."

"Tomorrow's Saturday."

"Want to go for a drive anyhow?"

"When?"

"Two o'clock?"

Chad nodded, almost smiled. Still, the Indian could tell, the boy did not quite like him, or the rendezvous, meetings, drives. Yet it was better for Chad than nothing. And it was something he was too weak to refuse. Better than playing checkers with Pauline, or having to shoot his basketball alone in the driveway of the vacant carriage house.

Chad watched Decatur drive away. He felt something just then, but didn't know what it was. He touched his own long lank straight hair, and then rushed up the steps of the house.

But the day after his feet began to heal, and he saw Decatur waiting, that was the real rendezvous.

Decatur did not speak when the boy got in the car, but he took hold for a moment of Chad's left kneecap as if to assure himself it was a flesh-and-blood Chad who had got in the car.

Chad did not care where Decatur was taking him this time. He was as indifferent to the Indian, as he always called him in his own mind, as he was to his mother, his sister or his "real" father, Lewis Coultas.

Decatur gave off a smell today like some kind of animal hide. It was not unpleasant, but it was strong. And Decatur thought again of how Chad had cut his feet—but what good had it done—for here he had of his own free will begun the drives again with this stranger.

The only thing Chad thought of was he was cold.

"You're shivering," Decatur said, finally taking notice of his discomfort. "All right, wait." He stopped the car, and turned to get something in the ample back seat.

Chad got so cold he could barely turn around. Decatur held in his hands a buffalo robe. He put it around the boy's legs, and then, having tucked the robe lightly about him, he gazed at his charge.

"We'll spend the night at my grandpa's," Decatur told him after they had driven for a few minutes in silence.

Chad never questioned Decatur as to why they were leaving town, going down back roads, speeding. It was already deep night, and getting colder by the minute even with the buffalo robe around him.

Though he did not particularly like being with Decatur—he thought he was sure of that—he was not sorry to be leaving his home. He wanted to forget Eva, and Eva's having discovered him in the bathtub with his feet bleeding and cut. This was better, speeding away with Decatur.

But from time to time he would stir under the robe, wondering what was happening to him, for this was no drive, no outing—they were going far!

After hours of driving down back roads, with their endless turnings and detours, they came to a clearing, the kind made by lightning hitting the forest and the resulting destruction of many trees. Beyond the clearing were high old pines, pumpkin ash trees, thick groves of frozen shrubs, dying milkweeds and the skeletons of goldenrod and joe pye weed.

"We have to walk the rest of the way," Decatur told him.

The boy refused to budge. Decatur opened the door, and then when Chad did not offer to move, he lifted him up and began carrying him. After a while Chad indicated he would prefer to walk, though he was obviously half asleep.

They walked through the forest and the night for what seemed miles until a gloomy house appeared. There was a dim kerosene light in one of the back rooms.

Decatur did not knock, but he wiped his feet again and again, carefully, and Chad followed suit.

They went inside.

The "terrible" old man Bess Lytle had been having nightmares about sat on a weathered davenport facing them, his white abundant hair more disorderly than ever, his ink-black eyes moving in a kind of rage amid their enormous whites. His face was much darker than Decatur's, and there was very little resemblance between the two men except for the way their deep black pupils would flash from moment to moment.

"Always dropping out of the sky, aren't you. That was always your way, always," the old man sneered. "Whose brat have you got there?" he glowered at Chad, who opened his mouth in astonishment, perhaps disbelief.

"No brat," Decatur mumbled, and put his hand lightly on Chad's shoulder.

The old man was cutting some tobacco leaves which he had dried. Occasionally he would lift a piece of tobacco to his lips and taste it.

"I curse the day I ever set eyes on you," his grandfather continued to speak between putting pieces of the tobacco in his mouth. "You brought me bad luck. You'll bring that brat worse luck!" He waved his knife he had been cutting the tobacco with. "Who have you stolen him from?" the old man raised his voice, and his eyes moved unaccountably all about the room.

Decatur remained silent. The muscles in his jaw moved as if little rivulets were passing under his skin there.

"I've seen that snot face somewhere," the old man went on with his harangue. He rubbed his forehead with the hand holding the knife dangerously close to his skin. "Know I've seen him. Ah!" he cried, his face lightening a bit. "He's Pauline's grandson. He's a Coultas," the old man continued accusingly. "You'd better watch your step with him if you know what's good for you."

"We're on an outing," Decatur recited now as if Bess Lytle were prompting him in his lesson. "The boy likes to take drives."

His grandfather let loose of the tobacco leaves and the knife, and settled back even more deeply into the weather-beaten davenport. He kept looking from Decatur back to Chad, and then he gave a long, baleful steady stare nowhere in particular.

"I didn't think you could ever have fathered a dog, Decatur," his grandfather spoke almost inaudibly.

Decatur's face flushed violently, and Chad noticed for the first time a rather long and jagged scar against his temple, a scar that did not blend in with the beet red color coming from under his coppery complexion.

"You should apologize for that remark," Decatur said, and stepped up closer to his grandfather.

"Apologize to you?" the old man pretended outrage, and then laughed in a way that put his two guests on edge. "Apologize to a whelp like you? Why didn't you die in the trenches like a real man? Did you hide during the battles?"

Decatur seemed to be weaving, almost waltzing before the old man, like a tree that is topheavy and about to crash.

"You are a half-breed cur, a disgrace to your own race and the white man's," the old man pointed his finger at him. Then the grandfather called Decatur a name which Chad had never heard before, but whose sound alone sickened the boy.

Whatever the word meant, it drove Decatur to a pitch of fury, and deliberately raising his hand he struck the old man across the mouth. He was about to hit him again when Chad seized Decatur's fist.

"Let him hit me again if he wants to," the old man addressed Chad. "Half-breeds ain't men. He wasn't even good enough to get killed across the ocean! Not fit for cannon fodder!"

Chad observed that as the old man went on cursing and ranting his mouth was filling with blood from where Decatur had struck him.

"Be glad I didn't finish you." Decatur pronounced these words as he pulled the boy toward him, and they hurried out the door of the house.

Outside it was raining lightly, and Chad fancied as they got into the car and Decatur was arranging the buffalo robe about his feet, that the light in the house went out. But then he saw another light go on in the third story, brighter and of a yellow cast.

Decatur all at once was talking a blue streak. "Up until a few years ago," he told Chad, "up until then my grandfather—if he is my grandfather, who knows?—was very young-looking. He used to grin when men thought he was only forty or forty-five. Then something happened to him. It was a letter someone sent him maybe. It was probably only the third or fourth letter he ever received through the U.S. mail. All at once his hair which had been raven black turned white as a snowdrift. His hands lost their nails, and his eyes blazed at you in the rage you see in them now."

Decatur stopped speaking all at once, and swallowed spasmodically.

"He used to keep me in the cellar tied with chicken wire," he went on. He did not notice that Chad had closed his eyes tightly. "But I learned to get out of the chicken wire just like Houdini, and then to fool the old devil I would put myself back in the wire at night so he wouldn't know I had escaped. . . . That was when I walked all the way to school—to Bess Lytle."

Chad's eyes came open, and he half turned to look at Decatur.

"Did he beat you when you was tied with the wire?" the boy wondered.

Decatur turned to gaze at him, almost forgetting to keep his hand on the wheel. "What do you want to know for?" Decatur wondered.

Chad had closed his eyes again. He also tried to shut his ears against all the whirlwind of the words coming from his companion.

"But you struck him and he is an old man," Chad suddenly interrupted him.

"I might have known you would take his part!" Decatur spoke with fierce bitterness. He seized a plug of tobacco and bit off a piece.

And while biting and chewing the black tobacco Chad heard a string of words so vile and intense he fancied he was seeing

Indians brandishing long knives around some mountain bonfire. The curses went on for what seemed minutes.

Lewis Coultas's written excuse for not being able to see his mother-in-law (due to a "pressing engagement" in Chicago) arrived shortly after Eva had left Pauline's. The excuse, in the shape of a telegram, had been delayed unaccountably by many days from its origin.

Pauline's seeming coolness at what Eva had divulged to her came from stunned disbelief, perhaps, or from the fact that it was hard for Eva's mother to think badly of her loved ones.

But the pitiless revelations which Eva had made to her mother that blustery fall afternoon gave her a sleepless night that her own medicinal remedies were powerless to assuage. A kind of iron gong seemed to sound in the dead of night keeping the old woman sleepless, and then just as she was about to fall into slumber she would hear the cries of the chimney swifts. It seemed to her they screeched: *Your grandson has Indian blood.*

For the first time since it had occurred she was carried back to her mother's funeral and the appearance there of an old Indian man who had insulted everybody at the ceremony. He had shrieked out at her, "Your own mother is one of us," it seemed to her he had said, "and you are likewise. Look at your face in a still pool of water and see if I am not right."

It was then, in the dead of night, she had risen and called the sheriff.

She thanked fortune she would not have to talk with Lewis Coultas. She did not know what it was he had wished to confer with her about so urgently. He must know she had no more money to bestow upon him.

"My grandson has been abducted!" she recalled her own dry pronouncement to the sheriff.

Then they had crossed the state line, Decatur and Chad.

Decatur slammed on the brakes as the car passed beyond the boundary marked by flashing red and yellow flares.

"What's wrong with you?" Chad had sat bolt upright in the seat and was staring at his "abductor."

Decatur barely heard him. He was talking, but not to Chad. He said, "I never understood cause and effect, that is one of my troubles. Why, for example, should just pressing a trigger cause the target, when that target is a man, to cease being a man with a name and a home and become blood-soaked rags without speech or movement? And what, now, crossing one white line and then crossing still another, makes a man more liable to punishment than he was before he crossed them?"

"What lines are you talking about?" Chad wondered.

"Cause and effect, I told you. My trouble is I don't understand the universe. I never think about God. But I often think I do not understand the universe . . . . Well, wake up!" He cried in sudden fury. He slapped Chad.

"I have committed a crime for you, do you hear, but I wonder if you are worth it."

"You must have known what I was worth when you took me," the boy shouted back, oblivious perhaps he had been slapped. "So why start to complain and whimper and whine about me now like all the rest of them do back in Yellow Brook."

Decatur slapped him again.

"Good," Chad exulted in the blow.

"Now you listen to me," Decatur began. "Never, never in all my twenty-eight years in this hell world have I whimpered or whined. Get it straight. Your mother has done that sufficiently for the rest of the human race."

Decatur turned a look of such frenzy and choler on the boy that Chad's head lowered and bent forward as if struck from behind.

"You aren't worth kidnapping!"

Decatur had stopped the car.

"Kidnapping," the boy murmured, but did not dare look at Decatur.

"That is what I have done to you in the eyes of the law. Crossing state lines with a minor. Abducting."

"But we're only out riding," the boy spoke almost piteously.

Decatur studied him wrathfully.

"No, you're not worth it," he began again. "I have made a bad, bad mistake. You belong with Eva and Melissa. Your dad, they say, never bothers to come home to see you, let alone claim you."

"Why is crossing the line *it?*" The boy's voice had a pitch of terror.

"It?" Decatur took the wheel again and began driving slowly in no particular direction. He laughed almost like his old grandfather. "And when we are arrested," he went on mumbling and shaking his head, "when they find us, we will lie like everybody else we know lies. I will tell the police, *'Why officer we were only out riding, and got lost. The boy's mother knows we were joy-riding, and besides he is my son.'* " Decatur laughed again the queer laugh. " *'By stealth officer. By hidden stealth unknown even to the mother, and certainly to the boy's putative father.'* "

"You talk like a crazy man."

"So," Decatur continued, " *'so officer, you see we are innocent though we have by sheer coincidence crossed the state line.'* "

Chad covered his face with his hands.

"I will take you back to your mother," Decatur told the boy. "Once I've had a decent night's sleep somewhere. I'll put a tag on you like they put on Christmas presents they don't want: Returned owing to an undetected flaw at time of purchase."

"Maybe the law won't believe an Indian," Chad snapped. "And you'll go to jail anyhow."

"I will tell you something."

Decatur was talking to Chad after they had stopped at one of the houses he claimed he owned even though it was situated across the state line near a clump of pine trees. When Chad looked around suspiciously Decatur told him he owned the place lock, stock and barrel. There were only two chairs in the front room and in the adjoining room a king-sized bed already made up. Several floor lamps were placed in the front room as if on display.

"If you will give me your undivided attention," Decatur went on, using a phrase habitual to Bess Lytle. He moved his right hand over his face as if his hand would prompt him.

"I know this," Decatur began haltingly again. "I know, Chad, you are mine. My flesh and blood. That is what I have been looking for all this time. Women—I have loved them, yes, but they were not my own flesh and blood, you see. Now it has happened, what I never dreamed possible. When I came back to Yellow Brook I did not know I would find this fulfillment."

Chad turned away angrily from him, but the Indian took him by the hand this time gently and made the boy face him.

"I returned to where I had begun. Your house, the long staircase, that room. And your mother. You see I cannot believe it happened the way it did. But I know it happened when I see you. I see her in you also, but there is more of me in you, much more. Why would I have taken this risk, don't you see, if it wasn't because you are all I ever will have, whether you want me or not. Don't you see that? I know you do not care for me now, you are fighting me, maybe you will always fight me like I fought my grandfather."

"You struck an old man."

Decatur shrugged. "Without a son, what is a man? He could have thousands of women, would that quiet his heart? You don't know—you are a boy. But if a man has his own flesh and blood, he has reached a height that no matter how far he falls later he will always say, pointing upwards, *I got that far, I reached that pinnacle.* You're my *up there.* I know you are mine. I know all this better than I know the sound of my own blood coursing through my body. You can't *not* be mine. Let Lewis Coultas come with the law, let him take you from me, let them shoot me maybe, and bury me under some river-bottom—you will still, walking above me on the earth, be mine, your breath and the way your blood courses through your own body will be coming from me."

"I am afraid I don't understand, Decatur," the boy almost wailed.

"Did I say I expected you to? Not at all. I expect nothing from you. I know you don't love me. I have been far from you too long. Anyway, sons hate their fathers."

"They hate their fathers, you said?"

"Yes, hate them, that's correct." Some drops of perspiration fell from his brow to his lips. "Hate me then, Chad, but admit I am your dad."

"No."

"You can't not admit it. Look at me. Look at our two arms together." He took the boy's right arm roughly in his hand and rolled up the sleeve. Then he held both their naked right arms together.

"Do you see that color," Decatur spoke out of breath. "That is not the color of Lewis Coultas's right arm."

Chad pulled away from him. He wandered over to the high window, and looked out into the black night.

Standing almost as far from the boy as when he had waited for him at the schoolhouse in his car, Decatur said, "I am your dad."

"My dad," Chad repeated desperately, vertiginously. "If you are him," he began, wheeling about and facing Decatur. "If you are my father, I think it will kill me!"

"No, no, Chad," Decatur said. He walked over and took both his hands in his.

"See here, you think you will die now, but you won't. . . . And one day, one day you will love me. I know that is true. Don't scoff. You will love me, and that day may not be as far off as we think."

He almost whispered these last words, and then walking like a drunk man, he went over to one of the brand new chairs, sat down, and plunged his face into his outstretched hands.

"I will never love you," Chad said. "Never. If I live a thousand years, nailed to a cross, even, and I can only come down from that cross if I say I love you, I will say, no, keep me nailed to the wood, for I will never love this man. . . . I will never love you, Decatur."

Decatur kept his head buried in his hands, and a soft almost inaudible moan came from deep within him.

"I hate you. I despise you," Chad said.

Decatur stood up, and looked in at the bed in the next room.

"We'll go to sleep now before it gets any later." He waved his arm in the direction of the bed.

Chad stared at him in a wild kind of unbelief.

"We have a lot of running to do tomorrow before they catch up with us. From the posse, you understand, or whoever they are that are coming after us. So you get into bed, and I will follow."

What occurred thereafter was never very clear to Chad. Later, a good deal later, when he was in the presence of the deputy sheriff and his father—by his father now I mean Lewis Coultas—when he was back in Yellow Brook and was being interrogated in the big dark wood of the jury room, what had occurred was even less clear to him.

Chad had described later to Melissa (the police had finally taken him home and his sister was waiting for him in the front parlor) how they had been "arrested." Before dawn Decatur had gotten up and gone out to bathe in the river. Chad was still sleeping, but he had been given so much coffee the night before his sleep was not deep. He had heard something. At first he thought Decatur was still in bed beside him, for there was that smell in the bedclothes that he came now to associate with his companion, the smell of rain on leather. Chad went out on the back porch and saw the sun rising.

But as he told Melissa, he could not remember whether he had seen Decatur coming out of the river dripping from his swim or whether he had first seen the police holding him all naked as he was, and putting the handcuffs on him.

As the officers were leading Decatur away, it was then that Chad had run up to him and, surprising probably himself as well as the police and Decatur (certainly Decatur), he had thrown his arms around the Indian and held onto him for dear life.

"Don't worry," one of the policemen said to Chad, "we won't let him get away."

Chad kicked the officer, and the officer roughly shook the boy in return. "Don't lay a hand on him." It was Decatur speaking, but his voice sounded as distant as the other shore of the river.

"Did you come with him willingly?"

Chad had looked around from where he was seated in a big kitchen chair facing the law officer. Decatur, he realized, was not present.

"Yes," the boy had spoken softly. "I think willingly. We go for drives in his different cars."

But what Chad had almost been about to say and then stopped dead was *I have never seen a grown man all undressed before. I never seen my own dad, I mean I never seen Lewis Coultas without no clothes on.*

And like Bess Lytle, his teacher, before him, what haunted him was the remembrance of the very dark, bare and glistening body of the Indian in all his exposed nakedness.

The law-men surrendered Chad to his sister.

She held him to her and kissed him around the eyes, though he was dry-eyed now and quiet.

Lewis Coultas, who had come back from Chicago a few hours before, stepped into the room briefly and took Chad's hand. Melissa pointed out later that Mr. Coultas looked like Prince Albert with his high collar and careful grooming.

But it was clear Lewis Coultas did not know what to do about the disgrace. He barely said boo to the boy, but finally managed to get out, "We will have a good talk later, Chad."

"It was your Uncle Judson who sent out the search party," Melissa told Chad once Lewis Coultas had left the room.

"Isn't he your Uncle Judson also?" Chad said, pressing his head against Melissa's breast.

"Oh of course, of course. You know, dear, I had forgotten Uncle Judson has only one eye. The other one is made of glass."

"I once walked into his private office," Chad recalled, "and he had taken out his eye. He gave me a funny look, and he even smiled a little. Then he put back the glass one in all that empty red socket where his real eye had been."

"Oh, Chad, stop it, for pity's sake."

She kissed his hair nervously.

"So he crossed the line then with you," Melissa began her own interrogation.

Chad nodded apathetically, nestling against her more comfortably still.

"He didn't make you come with him, Chad?"

"Oh, no."

"And he didn't harm you or use force?"

"Nothing like that. I did tell him though that I despised him." Chad spoke with a kind of odd longing in his sleepy voice.

Melissa took his right hand in hers.

"When they handcuffed him and led him away, it made me sick to my stomach."

"Your feelings, then, came to the fore?" she said rather primly.

"Oh, Melissa, what do you mean by that?" He extricated himself from her embrace.

"I mean, Chad, that you care more for Decatur than you do for Lewis Coultas."

He stood up and faced her. "I despise Decatur! I have told him that I despise him!"

"Say that same sentence again, then, as if you mean it!" She waited, and smiled.

"I don't know what you are talking about."

She laughed almost boisterously, certainly maliciously.

"I believe you have the closest connection of any two people I have ever known," she said finally. "Deny it if you can."

"Mama and Papa aren't close, Melissa?" He spoke almost like a small boy.

"What an absurd question! Do you think they are? There's nothing they have in common at all except they both wear their wedding rings still. Perhaps they've grown too fast on their fingers to be removed!"

"So you accuse me of being closer to an Indian than anybody else!"

"He is your father!"

Chad drew back from her as if she had thrown a heavy object against his breast. He colored violently.

Melissa was studying Clad closely though pretending not to fix her gaze on him at all. Her eyes flitted away and then returned to his features. What disappointed her to the point of anguish was that the Chad she loved was changing. He was becoming a young man. Already there were traces of down, the coming of a beard across his upper lip and over his satin cheeks. His voice was getting huskier also, and he breathed heavily. She mourned the passing of his childhood when they had been so close. In fact, she could not bear it.

"What on earth did you find to talk about, you two?" Melissa tried to take on her cool sophisticated manner.

He fidgeted with the pearl buttons on his jacket sleeve.

"Oh, I disremember, Meliss."

The tremolo of her laughter echoed around the room.

"All right," he snapped. "He said," and he stopped to swallow several times, "he said just what you got through saying to me!"

"And what did I say, Chad?" she spoke now like one of the characters in the plays she was always rehearsing.

He turned a dark red and waited. "He said," he spoke like a boy in catechism class, "he told me that he was my father."

He gave her a look of desperate entreaty unlike anything she had ever seen on his face before.

"And how does he know who he is the father of?" she murmured.

When he stared at her with an earnestness that discomposed her, she went on in a nervous, jittery manner unlike her, "I mean, how does he get to be so sure?"

Like a boy talking in his sleep, Chad replied, "He looks at me all the time when we're together, and then after he's looked to his heart's content, he will usually say under his breath *'Jesus, yes it's so.'* "

Melissa puffed away on another of Eva's English cigarettes.

"Melissa," he began. "Will he be sent to prison do you suppose?"

She blew out one cloud of smoke after another, and picked from her teeth small particles of the tobacco.

"My angel, I have no idea. None whatsoever." She put down her smoke and began arranging her beads. She tossed them as if they were a bunch of flowers, behind her back, then seized the beads and brought them back properly around her neck.

"He was a soldier, and decorated," he said aimlessly.

"He loves you," Melissa said, and her words sounded like a curse instead of a statement. She continued acting as if rehearsing for a play. "Don't you see he didn't care what price he paid if he could have you with him for a while?"

She pulled him toward her by the shoulder.

"Waiting for you by the schoolhouse every evening for all that time, frightening old Bess Lytle."

She lit another cigarette though she had not finished several others lying crushed and crumpled like caterpillars on mulberry leaves.

"You are lucky, Chad, to have someone who loves you like that. Nobody ever loved me. Not enough to abduct me anyhow. Do you hear me? You are lucky. No one has ever wanted me. Mama claims to love me, but she doesn't. Papa doesn't seem to know how I got here, and he always looks at me surprised to see I have stayed on uninvited. So, see how lucky you are!"

"Stop it, Melissa." He dried his eyes on his jacket sleeve.

"I wish we would never grow up. I do fear it so!"

"But aren't you going to be a movie star one day?"

"Oh, I suppose so." She stamped out the new cigarette. "But you will look back on being kidnapped as the best time of your life, see if I am not right! I almost like Decatur for it, horrible as he is, always stooping over like he had come out of his wigwam."

"Is he quite horrible?" the boy mumbled almost inaudibly, but she heard him.

She laughed shrilly, even hysterically. "You see, Chad, you are *learning* to care for him. "It will take time, of course," she pursued it with bitter insolence, "But you will never find anybody else who loves you enough to risk jail for you."

"Anything but that. Anything, I say! I will never consent to it!"

Everybody could hear Eva's outcries as she quarreled with Lewis Coultas early in the morning. There was a general slamming of doors, and the perfunctory sound of weeping. Then one heard Lewis's heavy tread on the worn carpeting of the staircase as he went down into the dining room.

Melissa quickly opened the door to Chad's room, "Mama wants to talk to you right away. Where's your bathrobe, dearest?"

Chad painfully opened his eyes, badly swollen, and stared crossly at her.

"Why, it's hardly day," he protested.

"Day or not, they've had one of their terrible rows," she began. "How you could have slept through it is a marvel." She sat down on the edge of his bed. Her hand toyed with his hair hanging over his eyes. She kissed him on the neck, then more slowly on his lips.

"You must go to her right away, dear. She's in a dangerous mood."

Chad was tightening the cord to his maroon dressing gown, when Eva appeared and almost dragged him after her into her room.

She sat down and began holding pieces of cotton soaked in camphor to her nose and eyes.

"Pay careful heed now, Chad," she began. "Your father has agreed to a dreadful thing without my knowledge . . . . Sit over there, precious, and try for once to pay attention. Where are your house slippers? You can't sit here barefooted in this cold. Here," she cried, and threw him a wool comforter. "Put that around your poor feet while I tell you what this is all about.

She blew her nose and then pressed the camphorized cotton pieces again to her nostrils.

"You are going to have to talk with the sheriff," she said as if by his doing so she would never see him again, and he would perhaps be going to his death.

Chad went very pale, and pulled on the frogs of his pajamas.

"What am I to tell the sheriff, Mother?"

She looked blankly at him.

"Ah, that is just what I told your father. You expect a child to know what to say to those hard-bitten old harum-scarums at the court house! Why I wouldn't trust one of them around the corner. And to let a son of mine—"

She stopped. She kept looking at his feet, and then groaning, looked away again.

"My dear boy, you'll have to go, or they'll come and make me let you go! Do you understand? That's all there is to it."

She looked exactly like Melissa then in one of her strongest dramatic roles. She rose and walked unsteadily over to where Chad sat with closed eyes. She pressed him heavily against her breast.

"Don't keep your eyes closed, darling, or you'll break Mother's heart."

He looked at her then, and they held one another close.

"You mustn't be afraid," she whispered to him in a voice too shaken by emotion to be comforting.

As she held him to her her eye was on a heavily-stoppered small bottle. She would look away from the bottle and hold him to her, and then her eye moved again to the bottle. She picked up a solid silver spoon and poured a bit from the mysterious bottle into the gleaming center of the silver.

"Drink this off, precious. It will give you strength."

She plunged the spoon into his mouth. He choked on its almost suffocating strength, and she handed him a tumbler of very cold water, which he drank with the relief of a man who had not tasted a drop of liquid for days.

A thing occurred at that moment which Eva at first believed was caused by her having taken a teaspoon too much of the powerful elixir, but which later, on reflection, she decided was owing to some law of her own destiny.

The huge pier mirror facing her all at once gave every evidence of being seriously cracked, and from this aperture she saw come streaming out a kind of flame which, as it entered the room, settled on Chad's head so that he appeared to be wearing a chaplet of fiery feathers.

"Don't, whatever you do, touch your head!" Eva admonished him. But as she spoke he nonetheless made a motion to raise his hand to his head. She caught him to her and felt the flames enter her own body, but she experienced no heat or pain from the fire. At the same moment she could have sworn she was hearing the voice of the gypsy who had told her fortune so many years before. Yes, fire and gypsy were more real at that moment than her own boy caught in her desperate embrace.

"What is it now, Mother?" Chad's impatient voice aroused her from her reverie, her plunge into that other kind of world. She would, she realized, never be able to explain it.

Then, almost pushing Chad away from her, she stared at him. His head was entirely free now from the fiery chaplet, but his face had gone the color of deepest copper.

"What am I to tell them, did you say, dearest mother?" He spoke into her own distraction.

"Tell them, Chad?" She looked about the room, and her eyes fell upon the mirror. Ancient as it was, she saw it was without any crack or fissure whatsoever.

"Tell me, Mother, then!"

"Oh, well, tell them as little as you can, Chad, dear heart. Answer them if possible with just a yes or no to their confounded questions. Or better still, dearest, just tell them you don't remember. Yes, that's the best way. Do you hear? Just tell them what you told me, darling, that you . . . and he . . . always went riding together. After all, he is like your older brother, a friend of the family, a steady caller at your house through the years."

"The years, Mother?"

"Tell them he is close as family, then."

She saw with some trepidation that the medicine was working very fast now on her boy, as witness his face growing ever more deeply colored.

"Close like my father?" He gave out an almost heart-scalding sigh.

She pulled him again toward her and kissed him frantically.

"Go, darling. Lewis is waiting for you downstairs, don't you know!"

She kissed him now across his eyes.

"Tell them nothing!" She gasped out after him.

Eva heard her son's footsteps leaving the room, for her eyes were now fixed helplessly on the mirror. All at once she rushed out after Chad. Then again the strange thing took possession of her. She could have sworn she saw as he went down the many steps of the staircase the chaplet of fire about his hair, a sort of ominous halo. Chad stopped on the stairs and, looking back at her, smiled faintly. As he did so the flame disappeared from his hair, and then, throwing a kiss to her, her son disappeared out of sight.

But the echo of the gypsy's contralto lingered, and the vision of the red flame about his head. She stood in front of the massive mirror, touching its cold surface, staring into its fathomless glass.

Lewis Coultas was waiting for Chad in his Willys-Knight auto. They drove off with such precipitation one would have thought they had been fired upon. They raced through the slumbering streets, and then came to an abrupt halt.

"But that's the jail!" Chad cried looking at the building before which the car had halted. He turned to gaze at his father accusingly. "I don't want to go in!"

"But you're not going into the jail, Chad, you're going to the judge's chambers." His father spoke for the first time in Chad's memory with a certain tender concern.

"I don't want to go!"

Lewis waited, loosening one of the top buttons of his Mackintosh.

"Tell me I don't have to!" the boy implored him.

By way of answer Lewis Coultas took the boy's hand in his.

"See here, it's only for a few simple questions," he encouraged him, "and then we'll go for a spin. Won't you like that? You like riding."

Chad struggled with the hot tears in his eyes, but then they fell heavily to his chin and cheeks, and from there to his knitted new tie, and to the vest Pauline had hand-sewn for him.

"After all, you don't know anything to tell them—much." Lewis Coultas touched Chad in the same way Decatur had, on his shoulder blade.

Then the boy felt the strange medicine he had taken from the solid silver spoon clouding his eyes, making his tongue heavy.

Then there they were in what to Chad looked like an ark of a room, the ceiling giving the impression they extended on up into the sky itself, a sky overcast and black but limitless, and down from which God himself must be looking.

An old man with deeply-furrowed cheeks, with a heavy belt at the side of which a gun was resting, was already addressing him while Lewis Coultas sat nearby occasionally touching Chad's sleeve.

The old man was effusively kind to Lewis Coultas, the boy observed. He reminded Mr. Coultas of how they had met at the racetrack some years ago, and that they had also spoken to a broker they both knew about some investments long ago.

But whether it was the red liquid he had taken from the silver spoon, or some other cause, Chad suddenly had difficulty in believing he was sitting in the courthouse being asked questions. He felt as if he was only imagining the terrifying ordeal, and that soon he would wake up in the protection and company of Decatur as they traveled lickety-split through the prairies and past swollen rivers.

Then Chad thought the old lawman said "*Little man*" rather abruptly. Lewis Coultas was tugging at his sleeve.

"He's not used to being up so early," came Lewis's explanation of his boy's behavior.

The gutteral laugh of the sheriff came to Chad now, as well as the question, "Did he use force, Chad?"

"Who, sir?"

"Why, the man who took you away," the lawman began now the examination, and he no longer bothered to look in the direction of Lewis Coultas. He was bearing down hard now on Chad.

"He is a member of the family," Chad echoed his mother's instructions.

The old man nodded encouragingly, and shuffled some papers on the table in front of him.

"But you see, sir, he is a good deal more," Chad spoke as if sipping the red liquid from the spoon.

There was a great, ascending silence. Chad's words, he felt, were going up in a dizzying vertical rise, direct through the ceiling, through the dome, on perhaps to the Almighty, or to a choir of angels, who were all listening to him, waiting patiently for him to speak at last, warning him that anything less than the absolute truth now would not be countenanced.

"He is my father," Chad said, and then repeated this sentence several times.

"Now my boy you must explain, you must be clear. Take your time, but tell us what it is you mean."

As if from a considerable distance, perhaps from the Willys-Knight auto, Chad could also hear Lewis Coultas urging him to think before he spoke, but still he must tell the truth.

Chad looked up at the dizzying height of the dome of the ceiling.

"I have been aware for some time," the boy began, and both Lewis and the sheriff were giving him nods of encouragement. "I say, it was proved beyond the peradventure of a doubt," (some of the old lawman's phraseology came into the boy's mouth), "it was all made clear, the truth, you see, when we compared our two feet. We had taken off our shoes and socks, understand. Or I had, and he had, I guess, later."

Chad kept his eyes on the ceiling, which seemed to become lighter and brighter as he spoke.

"It was clear to me that we both had webbed toes. I can take my shoes and socks off here if you wish to see . . . ."

The sheriff had risen and was saying something to Lewis Coultas but still he allowed the boy to go on speaking.

"Continue," the sheriff said when the boy stopped.

"But you see, sir, you do not need to examine our feet if you want the truth. You have only to look at him, and then me, to see we are both . . . webbed and Indians. We speak the same language, I do believe. I fought him off at first, but . . . ."

"Tell us how you fought him!" The old man had sprung from his seat as he often did at the trials of men accused of murder.

"You have only to look at my hair, and then his, and see that . . . ."

Lewis Coultas had also sprung up from his seat now and was raising his voice, as if he was the defense attorney in this trial.

"Can't you see, for pity's sake, the boy is not well!"

"Be seated until I have finished, Mr. Coultas," the sheriff admonished him. He had risen as he spoke and loomed over both Lewis Coultas and Chad, and then having, as perhaps he intended, reduced them to silence, if not submission, he sat down heavily, all two hundred and seventy-five pounds, in his chair which squawked and gave under his weight. The sound of the wood giving, like the cry of a woman in pain, perhaps the sound of Justice herself as she listened alongside the sheriff to a young man of good family brazenly perjure himself, repeating again and again what seemed to the old lawman a kind of blasphemy, certainly shameless prevarication and bold-faced deceit unknown to him in all his forty some years as an upholder of public decency and order.

"I am sure," Chad continued. "Sure as I can feel my own pulse," he touched the veins in his wrist, "that he is my father. That is why I believe I despised him so and struck him across the mouth as he struck his grandfather. I denied him, but the other part of me, sir, the boy he took away, went willingly, let himself be claimed by him. I had never been claimed before by anybody, never had a father before, and when I saw him looking at me as we both faced the mirror in the big hotel—"

"Stop!" the sheriff cried. "Right there. Not one more word, I tell you!"

But the sheriff was too late. Chad was going ahead just as Decatur had gone ahead driving with him beside him, always onward as they plunged together into the prairie, heading perhaps for canyons and defiles and mountains still to come.

"I knew even if I came back to Yellow Brook I would only be coming back to it now as a stranger because I had become his son."

"What mirror are you talking about, Chad?" Lewis Coultas spoke in unaccountable irrelevance and his tongue was as sleepy and thick as that of the boy he was addressing, though Eva had not given him any of the red liquid from the silver spoon. "The mirror you looked at one another in?"

"This child is desperately sick, or desperately wicked—whichever!" the sheriff had risen again, but he looked like a man who is slowly retreating from the room under the muzzles of guns pointed in his direction.

He had flung open the door of the witness room as one

would open a door on curs that had wandered yelping into one's sanctuary. He pointed with his arm extended for Lewis Coultas and his boy to go out.

Picking up his new hat, and taking Chad by the hand, Lewis Coultas walked out of the room.

"I will see you, sir," the sheriff spoke to Lewis Coultas in icy indignation, "when I have the occasion, if the occasion should ever rise."

Had he struck Lewis Coultas with a rawhide whip the younger man could not have gone out from that room more gladly. And though he carried his great height like a king, as usual, he felt at that moment that he crept, slouched, and bent under the humiliation and shame of what had occurred.

Eva had barely gotten dressed when she heard the front door flung open with such force that the hinges themselves gave out a kind of scream as if they were being wrenched from the wood. Then the voice of Lewis Coultas rang through all the lower recesses of the house and rose like smoke and flames to where she sat immobile.

Lewis half-dragged, half-carried Chad up all the stairs, and all but threw the boy into his bedroom, and was attempting to lock the door on him when Eva appeared.

"What on earth are you doing?"

"I am locking up your son to prevent him from being sent to jail!"

"You look and act like a maniac," she expostulated, and seized the key to Chad's room and pulled it out of his hand. "You shall not lock a child of mine in his room!" she spoke between her teeth.

"A child of yours! What have you been filling your *child*'s mind with, will you tell me," he began now in earnest. "What in God's name have you said to him that he should so disgrace all of us by the speech he has just spouted to that clown of a sheriff!"

Eva folded her hands and gave him a reproving look, which unaccountably calmed him.

"I suggest we go downstairs to the back parlor and not inform the entire community of what you are shouting about."

She preceded him downstairs holding the key to Chad's room

so stiffly in her right hand that one would almost think it was a light showing them the way.

Inside the quiet back parlor, she closed the door as peremptorily as he had closed Chad's door on him.

"Shouting and hallooing like that," she scoffed.

"You should shout and halloo also if you had been witness to what I have had to be witness to!"

Lewis Coultas had sat, or rather collapsed into the best chair in the room. Eva remained standing. She put the key away in her dress pocket, and straightened the brooch on her breast.

"Tell me then what has occurred," she spoke in a voice which brought to her mind Bess Lytle's manner of speaking to delinquent boys.

"He has denied before the sheriff that I am even his father," Lewis commenced, his eyes flashing through the pallor of his face. His strong handsome hands trembled, and he then held them together to prevent their shaking.

Eva's face would have shocked him had he been looking in her direction. She also went white under her expensive rouge and lipstick, and then a kind of pink tinge came over her cheeks, which vanished quickly as an even more pronounced pallor overtook her features.

She had never heard her husband so wrought up or so eloquent. She fancied Daniel Webster might have sounded so. But being so distraught herself, for a while she was only aware of his emotion, and not the context of what he said. Only gradually did she begin to hear *what* he said.

"Can you imagine what he told the sheriff? Can you begin to take all he said into account? Sitting there bold-faced as a practiced outlaw swearing almost upon oath in as saucy tones as he can muster that there was no kidnapping, no abduction, that all he did was go willingly with his friend, the Indian."

"Decatur." The word fell from her mouth, but was unheard in the tempest pouring out from her husband.

"And that this damned Indian," he went on, "is in truth his own, his real father! He pronounced all this in my presence and in the hearing of the sheriff!"

Her head had lowered slowly like someone falling into a deep sudden doze.

"Are you listening to me?" he roared and approached her with such energy she held her hands to her face protectively.

He paused at the sight of her haggard, distorted features.

"Listening to you!" She raised her face and stared at him with a fury he had never seen on any woman's face before, or indeed on any man's.

"Listening!" She began again. "You have pierced my ear-drums so that I will be deaf as a stone from now on with your roaring and bellowing! Who would not have listened? The very house is about to fall down about our ears from listening to you!"

"And what do you make then of all I have told you, my fine lady?"

She looked about the room like one who has all at once lost the thread of the discourse.

"What do I make of it, Lewis," she spoke very softly. "Why, this. You have frightened the poor boy until he has gone babbling, that's what I make of it. Taking a mere child and having him grilled and inquisitioned by a merciless hardened old reprobate of a lawman! I am ashamed of your manhood for letting your own boy suffer such treatment. No real father would have permitted it!"

He repeated her last sentence with a kind of murderous lull in his voice.

"And now I have a question to put to you, since you have always found yourself so superior to all other mortals, especially your despised, always-in-the-wrong husband!"

"You will lower your voice, Lewis, or I will leave the room."

"Ah, my voice," he now began to whisper and his whisper was somehow louder to her ears at that moment than trumpets. "I can even write the question I want you to answer on a piece of paper, and I will see to it that even the pen makes no sound as it writes!"

She had stood up.

"You may use your normal voice, Lewis. I only ask that you do not scream."

He stood a few inches now from her, his throat working convulsively, and he swallowed wildly like a man who has come near to drowning.

"Who is the father, then, of this young devil?"

"How dare you put such a question to me in my own house?"

"*Your* own house?"

"Yes, mine! For this house belongs to me and my mother,

who has paid all your debts since the ink was dry on our wedding certificate. You don't think for one monent, do you, that you are the one who has kept a roof over our heads all these years, or has provided us with food and raiment, do you? You have given me and my family nothing but debts and excuses. You have no moral right to ask me any question! *'Who is the father of my boy?'* Only a blackguard would think such a question, let alone utter it!"

"I am not going to be put down by your histrionics."

She held her hands now to her ears, and as she did so, the key to Chad's room fell from her pocket to the floor. He picked it up and threw it on the long table which occupied the center of the room.

"Only today," he now spoke in a choked gasp, almost as if she had left the room and he was muttering alone, "just an hour or less ago as the boy was being, according to you, third-degreed, in that hideous court or witness room or whatever it is, I noticed that there was nothing in the boy's face, or hair, or lips or eyes that had any vestige or faintest resemblance to me . . . I have listened to Pauline for years as she spoke of your family secret, that far back in your ancestry you have Indian blood . . . . But what I saw on that boy's face was nothing distant, or far away, or long ago . . . ."

Eva had let her arms drop to her sides, but Lewis stood now directly facing her, and he took both her arms in his hands, and held them.

"Whatever this boy's long-ago ancestry may have bestowed on him, it could never make his face shine like copper as it did when the sheriff and I heard him out. The face that shone out at us as he spoke today and uttered one defiant insult after another at me, at the law, at God maybe, that face is nearly pure-blooded Indian. There is not a drop of my blood in his! You must know it, you must have always known it, for you are with him all the time. You must know whose son he is!"

"I am too ill to hear you out," she groaned, and wrenched her hands free of his grasp.

He seized her by the sleeve of her right arm, and drew her back to him. Then as she struggled against him he suddenly let go of her, and slapped her cold-bloodedly several times across her face.

"You know who his father is, and you shall pronounce his name here and now!"

"I will pronounce nothing, I will tell you nothing, Lewis Coultas, for you are not the support and mainstay of this house. All that I have, and the crumbling walls of this mansion itself, are gifts from my family, whom you have ruined catastrophically. You have no moral right to ask me which way the wind blows! If you think your boy is an Indian, then think it, and go back to your western vagabonding."

He struck her now full in the face, but she only smiled at him as if he had conceded her a victory she was always hoping he would bestow on her.

Smiling under his blows she went on. "The countless women, adventuresses, harlots who make up your retinue must miss you! Not one living soul missed you here when you were gone, and you are gone for the most part of the year, and every year. You are not missed because all you contribute to the sustenance and maintainance of this house is the sighs of relief we breathe when you are away from it. I owe you no explanation for anything."

"You slept with an Indian," he told her then, putting his mouth almost directly against her mouth. "I see it in every line of your face, every blink of your eye. And I see Decatur in every line and blinking movement of his black eyes in the face of that infernal brat."

PART III

ALL CHAD COULD REMEMBER LATER on was Lewis Coultas patiently helping him get dressed in his Sunday best. Lewis must have pulled him right out from the bedclothes in the cold and damp, helped him into his long underwear, and knee-high socks, and put on the long trousers and stiff jacket he hardly ever wore now that Eva had quit sending him to church and Sunday school.

"Where are we going, Papa?" Chad asked between yawns as Lewis walked him through snow-covered streets.

"We're going to take a train ride," Coultas replied. He was bemused that the boy did not offer any objection to leaving with him, though of course he was still half asleep. Perhaps, Lewis decided, that was how the Indian had taken him away. It was that easy.

"We will have a really fine train ride, Chad, and we will have breakfast in the Pullman car, hear."

Chad nodded, and held Lewis's hand.

All at once Coultas stopped and looked down at the boy from his considerable height. "You can still go back if you want to."

"Back?"

"Home," Lewis told him. "You can go back. But I thought, you see, breakfast on the train would be nice. And in Chicago, I am going to buy you a new suit of clothes. The one you have on don't fit anymore."

Chad nodded and began walking with Lewis toward the depot.

In the Pullman car, Chad observed Lewis Coultas putting on the dog (it was Eva's description of him, but Chad had never seen him do it before): tipping the black porters, and letting them take off his outer coat, brush it, and his jacket underneath, and then straighten his high collar. They did a little of the same to Chad, but he pulled bashfully away.

It was still very dark outside the train.

One of the porters now brought Lewis and Chad each a cup of steaming coffee.

"He's too young for it," Lewis quipped. "But he says he's big enough to drink some," Lewis chuckled. "Yes, young man, you need a new suit, no question about it," Lewis spoke for the benefit of the porters who were looking down at Chad. "We'll try to forget everything back home, won't we, Chad? We'll turn over a new leaf, you and I, and start from scratch. You'll see, Chad. I'm going to make up for everything I haven't done up to now."

Chad found himself nodding. He was so filled with sleep that even the strong black coffee had almost no effect on him. From the windows of the fast train he saw the first slender threads of dawn. It made him shudder, and then all at once snowflakes began lashing against the window panes, and blotted out the sunrise. It became virtual night again.

Then they were in the splendid, gleaming dining car, with the stiff white linen napkins spread over their knees, drinking more of the strong coffee and dining on steak and fried potatoes, eggs with great golden centers, sprinkled with little red dots of something, and all the gooseberry preserves they wanted.

"What will they say when they look in my bed?" Chad asked Lewis Coultas.

"I am your father, Chad, and I can take you where I will. Do you understand that?"

Chad gazed mournfully at Lewis Coultas, but then seeing the splendor of the repast, and the honeyed smiles of the porters, what could he do but nod assent.

"I am wiping out the past with a sponge," Lewis muttered almost too low to be overheard. "You and I are beginning all over again."

Melissa wakened her mother about twenty minutes to noon to give her the news of Chad's second disappearance. She stood a long time silent by her mother's bedstead, saying nothing. At last she said after noting a movement of Eva's left hand, "Mother, dear, are you awake?"

Eva removed the cotton pads soaked in witch hazel from her eyes, and lifted her head up and nodded.

"Mother, Chad has disappeared."

Eva rose and put her feet in her carpet slippers.

"And where is his father? Where is Lewis?"

"Gone likewise, mother."

"How very queer. I dreamed last night that Lewis had taken Chad away on an ocean steamer." She held her right hand to her throat for a long time. Then she began putting on a pair of brand new silk stockings. She went to her dressing table and looked at herself. Then she buried her face in her hands, after which, pulling herself up straight in front of the mirror, she daubed some vanishing cream about her cheeks.

"You also have a visitor waiting downstairs."

Eva exchanged a look of meaningless ferocity with Melissa.

"Well, who is it, Melissa, who is waiting to see me? Don't tell me I am due at the courthouse too!"

"It's only Miss Lytle, darling. But she's in great agitation over something. She's left her schoolroom just to see you."

"Then she must bear even more horrible tidings. I wonder if I have the strength!"

She combed out her hair, and then began brushing it with savage thoroughness. A short desperate sob escaped from Eva, almost resembling the sound of Chad's toy pistol going off.

"God in heaven, Melissa. And are you sure the roof of the house has not blown away also, and that the parlor is not on fire?" Then she added, "Bess Lytle waiting downstairs to see me before my day's begun!" She abruptly turned to face her daughter, and cried out, "Where can he have taken that boy?"

Eva more or less repeated her litany of words on greeting Bess Lytle, and to her own surprise threw herself into the schoolteacher's arms.

"Thank God you've come, Bess," Eva spoke perhaps sincerely. "As Melissa has told you, Chad is gone." She looked about as much as to say, *Of course we shall never see him again.*

Bess arranged herself in one of the straight-back chairs. She thought over again the speech she had already rehearsed for Eva, but the words would not come.

"I'm here, Eva, to ask you a kind of favor."

"Ask away, my dear, you know I'll grant it," Mrs. Coultas spoke emptily. "You've already conferred many favors on me and my boy. And you've done me much good by leaving your class to come here today. I am in your debt."

"You may not be so grateful to me, my dear, when you hear what it is I want to ask of you."

"You surely know by now, Bess, you have my implicit trust." Still, the mother stirred uneasily as to what was coming.

"A kind of scandal has burst, Eva. You must be aware of it."

"I am only aware that at this moment my boy has been taken away from me."

"Of course," the schoolteacher spoke consolingly. "But the scandal is of course related to Chad directly. They say, everywhere, Eva, that Chad is your boy by Decatur!"

"They?"

"Your boy told the sheriff as much during the hearing."

"They call that a hearing when the poor child was taken out of bed in the middle of night and subjected to a third-degree cross-examination!"

Bess clasped and unclasped her worn leather pocketbook, and then at last laid it on the thick carpet by the chair she sat in.

"The favor I want to ask of you, Eva, is that you will come with me now to Judge Hebbel's chambers, and let him know the whole truth."

"Chambers?" She stared at Bess in the manner of one who hears an indecent proposal.

"Yes, the judge's chambers," Bess spoke with strained caution, almost trepidation now, for she did not want to lose Eva, did not want to jeopardize the favor she so much required.

"And what am I to be charged with, will you tell me?"

"Eva, you are charged with nothing and you know it. But you can tell the judge the truth about all that is setting this town aflame."

"The truth, Bess. Good God, I am afraid I have never known the truth about anything. And am I to be asked to testify about truth when my own boy has been stolen from me by that cheap scoundrel who ruined me and mine! What truth do you want me to testify to?" She stood up, then catching herself, she muttered a kind of apology, and sat down.

"You cannot be indifferent to the fact that Decatur is being held in jail among common criminals. On a charge which I do not believe he is guilty of. Eva, listen to me. I am your friend, I bear you only good will, you and your boy and Melissa. Do hear me out. You cannot wish for Decatur to be charged with something he is innocent of."

"And what is it he is innocent of then?" Eva spoke now like one of Bess's chastised pupils.

"Kidnapping your boy," the schoolteacher said. "He is charged with a serious crime. Will you allow that?"

There was a queer silence in which all sound in the town seemed to have been suspended.

"Judge Hebbel," Bess went on with her plea, "can release Decatur unconditionally if you will only tell him the truth."

"The truth," she gazed wrathfully now at Bess. "I have told you I do not know the truth."

"Eva, we are not at the opera house now watching some play. You must tell Judge Hebbel everything, and then he cannot hold Decatur, cannot bring him to trial—or maybe send him to his death!"

On this, Eva put down her glass of fruit juice and nodded vigorously. Bess saw that she had got through at last.

"You must save Decatur," the schoolteacher went on, "and the only way you can do that—please forgive me now for what I am going to say. You must tell the judge that Decatur is the father of your boy, and that he did not, therefore, kidnap Chad, he had no evil intent."

"That they went riding together," Eva almost babbled now. "Every afternoon, riding. And in different cars."

"Are you going to be all right, Mrs. Coultas?"

Stung perhaps by the teacher's use of her surname, Eva cried, "Mrs. Coultas, I am afraid, is always all right. It is a great pity, however, she did not die years ago."

Bess came over to the chair Eva was seated in, and knelt down by her, and touched briefly her silk stockings.

"You do not want Decatur to come to such an end!"

Eva was dry-eyed, stone-like, and if not calm, in a kind of state close to paralysis. But she finally said, "No, I don't want him to come to harm."

"Then will you come with me now to Judge Hebbel. He is waiting for us."

"Oh, Bess Lytle," Eva spoke at last and touched the schoolteacher's face with her right hand laden with many rings. "You who are so immaculate and pure, who have always followed the voice of duty. Think what you are asking me, though I am sure you do not really know what it is you are asking. To tell the truth!"

"But you will save him, Eva. Save Decatur. I know you want that! You say I am immaculate. You are mistaken. I know you love him. And I know it because of what I too feel for him."

Eva pressed her finger against Bess's lips.

"You don't need to say more. I am at your disposal. I have been through so much these past days, telling Judge Hebbel what I know will hardly add much to my anguish and my shame. Shall we go?"

But it was Bess who was weeping now, and holding Eva to her small hard bosom. Rising at last from their close embrace, Eva called out to the next room, "Melissa, darling, get mother's hat and heavy outer coat from the cloak room if you will! Bess and I are going to the courthouse now."

They walked through the heavy wet flakes of snow which gathered about their hats, Eva's veil, and which transformed them into hoary old women. Their feet sank into some of the small drifts, but they proceeded walking with the deliberateness and calm of women strolling in June sunshine.

"Be glad you were never married, Bess," Eva was saying. "You must in fact be a very happy girl. You have your work, and you have your children who are your pupils by day, and then you have the companionship and love of your brother Todd for your evenings and your days of rest."

"But, my dear friend," Bess expostulated, "you have two fine children, and you have, after all, Lewis Coultas, your husband, and you have a mother and brother!"

"Oh, I know I must sound ungrateful and thankless, Bess. Perhaps I am. But from my first day of marriage," (she nearly said wedding night), "I have known nothing but disappointment and pain. Oh, Bess, Bess, what am I to tell Judge Hebbel?"

"Tell him," Bess replied with unswerving directness, "that you don't want Decatur to be unjustly imprisoned for a crime he has not committed."

Eva fluttered her veil and shook the snowflakes out from it.

She studied Bess through the storm, and tried to frame the words that would not offend or distance Bess from herself.

"You are so protective of him, aren't you?"

"I taught him," Bess replied with a kind of grim satisfaction. "He was my pupil. I was in a sense . . . like his mother."

Sweetheart, Eva thought to herself, *secret sweetheart.* But instead of saying this she said, "Everybody is disappointed in me when all's said and done, Bess. Everybody."

"Nonsense," Bess replied, and taking a handkerchief she wiped the snow from her lips and face.

They had reached the courthouse, about whose front portals the snow had gathered as if to force open and then invade the building. The clock from the tower of the courthouse was striking the hour, but Eva did not count the times it struck, though it seemed to strike a hundred.

They were ushered into the judge's chamber by the bailiff, a shriveled lank man who was chewing something in a mouth which had only three or four teeth, and whose left hand trembled badly as he opened the heavy brass-plated door leading to the chamber.

"They would not . . . execute him?" Eva whispered to Bess, in a last plea for assistance before her ordeal.

"Ladies! Dearest ladies!"

It was Judge Hebbel's bass voice ringing out as if all the courts in the world were coming into session. He took both women by the hand and pressed those hands warmly. He bowed until his pince-nez almost slipped from his immense aquiline nose.

Judge Hebbel should have retired from the bench many years before, but there were few, if any, legal minds in Yellow Brook, and he had been urged by the mayor and the prominent citizens to stay on "in perpetuity" if necessary.

"How kind, indeed noble, of you two splendid ladies to come out on such a day." The judge thanked them, and pointed with one hand to the snow beating upon the high windows. He motioned the two women into comfortable chairs about a long kind of table which resembled Eva's dining room set when all the leaves were put in for a banquet.

Eva studied the judge's violently colored eyebrows which met over the bridge of his nose. It was obvious to her that he dyed his eyebrows, but curiously enough allowed the hair of his head to go alabaster white. He apparently had no eyelashes. His mouth resembled a half-healed sore. A stenographer, a woman of sixty, now entered, and opened her shorthand pad.

"Miss Lucy Ebersole," the judge indicated the stenographer, who forced a grin, and seated herself as far away from the conferring parties as possible.

Judge Hebbel placed his two index fingers over the bridge of his nose, hiding for the moment where his eyebrows met, an action which suggested a quick prayer to the Almighty.

"A strange and unheard-of occurrence, this spiriting away of your boy," the old jurist began. "Chad, isn't the young one called?"

"That is his Christian name, judge, indeed." Eva looked briefly to Bess.

"Be at ease, my dear," the judge addressed Eva. Then, grinning painfully he inquired under his breath, "How is Pauline?"

"Not well, your honor."

"I am grieved to hear that." He waited as if for his grief to release its grasp on him. "Pauline," he now addressed Bess Lytle, "is a woman without equal in this county or indeed this state. She survives sorrow and disgrace like twenty Rocks of Gibraltar." He shook his head mournfully, and then smiled.

"I wish I had half my mother's strength and resourcefulness," Eva spoke, now, interrupting the judge. "Without her, your honor, I would have foundered long ago."

"No, my dear, no!" Judge Hebbel raised his voice. "I cannot allow you to speak ill of yourself. Not in my court!" He laughed heartily and then placed both his index fingers over his mouth. This was the signal which those who knew his courtroom procedure recognized at once as meaning the business at hand had begun in earnest.

"I believe, my dear Eva," the judge now almost whispered, "you have something to say in defense of our dusky friend Decatur. At least my respected acquaintance Miss Bess Lytle, here, has so informed me."

"She does indeed, Judge Hebbel," Bess spoke up when there was no immediate response from Chad's mother.

"Let her speak in her own good time," the judge addressed a mild reproof to Bess. "We have all the time in the world in my courtroom . . . Eva, my dear, what say you?"

"He must be given his freedom, your honor."

The stenographer's pen raced with the words.

"Nobly said, indeed!" Judge Hebbel cried with an edge in his voice. "But *why?*" the old man then almost thundered at her.

"Why?" Eva spoke now in the supercilious tone with which she addressed her husband and her hired girl. "Judge Hebbel," Eva began, and she half rose from her seat but at a kind of grimace from the jurist she sat down again firmly in her chair.

"My dear friend," Eva went on almost blithely. "Would any court in our free land penalize a man who went riding with his own flesh and blood? Please answer me, your honor, if I am not presuming on your dignity and authority."

"Presuming, my dear lady. Not at all, not at all. . . . But, my dear, let me remind you, the questions are to be mine," here he laughed with wiley admonition, "and the answers *yours.*"

"Then, my dear Judge Hebbel, let a mother speak what is in her heart. . . ." Eva gave a final look at Bess, like a woman who will now throw herself from a parapet. "Many years ago, your honor, both he whom you call the dusky young man, Decatur, and I . . . we fell, as some might put it, by the wayside."

There was a kind of drumming sound heard then. It was the judge's one index finger this time beating a kind of tattoo on the long banquet-size table.

"I, at least, fell by the wayside, your honor," Eva was oblivious to the judge's obbligato. "I had been grievously ill. My brother, the surgeon, had prescribed what turned out to be a rather strong narcotic. I took it frequently for the dreadful migraines which have afflicted me ever since my wedd—my marriage, your honor. Young Decatur, then a mere boy, came to bring me necessities from time to time. . . . The door to my home, indeed the door to my sleeping room was ajar on this particular day. . . . He came in, and the pain that day was most pronounced."

She saw by looking sideways that Judge Hebbel's eyes were closed, and a kind of sickly smile played about his faded pink lips.

"He comforted me that day, your honor, for the many sorrows which I found life had bestowed on me. A faithless husband for one thing, the ruin of my mother's life and the destroyer of her inherited wealth. My own nights were sleepless over the shame and humiliation which my husband had rained down on my mother and brother . . . . We fell, together, Judge Hebbel, Decatur and I. And from our fall, came Chad Coultas, who is our son."

She rose then without interference from the jurist.

"You have therefore only one duty, your honor," her whisper came out. "Let him go."

Judge Hebbel stirred as if from some deep slumber he heard the fire engines scream and the firemen beating down the thick mahogany doors of his court with their axes.

Bess was holding Eva in her arms, and the stenographer had rushed out to bring back water and whiskey.

When quiet had returned to the room Judge Hebbel was heard speaking at first unintelligibly, or at least almost inaudibly, and then in what appeared to be instructions to the jury, though this was not of course a trial, but a mere informal conference, as the judge later explained to Bess Lytle.

"My dear lady," the judge was addressing the ceiling rather than Eva, "I admire—I cannot tell you how much—your frankness and your nobility, your taking such a risk in letting what you have feared would be a stern, if fair, auditor, be present at your confession."

"You *will* free him, then, Judge Hebbel?"

He struck his fist now on the table in displeasure at this interruption, but at the same time he smiled quickly, and went on. "You have shown great courage, and let me add, wonderful womanliness in unbosoming yourself today. Your secret, if secret it is, my dear lady, rests perfectly safe with me. You are in the hands of one who is as benevolent, although a dispenser always of justice, as your own beloved mother Pauline. You have uttered your story therefore as if to a tomb, and I am that tomb into which your secret has fallen, to lie there forever undisturbed."

The judge had risen, and with a kind of lightning look bid them rise also.

"And you will save him, judge, then? For all he has done is gone driving with his own flesh and blood!"

The judge took Eva's hands in his and kissed them. He also, after his embrace of Mrs. Coultas, received the hands of Bess

Lytle in his, and then gave both women a kind of exalted benediction.

Raising his hand again as if to invoke silence or secrecy, he flung open the heavy doors of his chamber, and vanished into the enormous corridor beyond lined with spittoons and heavy flags and banners and countless oil paintings of heroes, naked savages, and benevolent white-wigged clergymen.

If the train with Lewis Coultas had been dazzling, the palatial hotel Coultas took the boy to afterwards was in many ways even more splendid, though of course no scenery raced past from its great windows.

So, then, this was the world where Lewis Coultas had his real life, Chad thought somewhat sadly, not at all in Yellow Brook with its board sidewalks and ruined opera house, and the turreted mansion where he lived with his miserable mother and Melissa.

As Chad stood gaping at the glistening jewel-like lobby with stylish men and women walking stiffly past him, Lewis called to him, and he followed, stumbling slightly after his father into a mammoth sitting room. They were preceded by bellhops who were dressed like generals, a housekeeper who summoned in turn two maids in white starched aprons and tall hats, and who brought in huge silver pots of tea, silver dollar sandwiches, and sherbets. Lewis greeted each and every one of the attendants like friends of long-standing.

All at once Chad noticed that Coultas was wearing white gloves. He had certainly not had them on during the ride in the Pullman cars. Perhaps white gloves, he decided, were required for all this ceremony now taking place around him, in a residence every bit as majestic as some old castle inhabited by a king.

The attendants had barely bowed out when two somewhat young women, who resembled the principal singers in the *Victor Book of the Opera,* appeared. They both wore long necklaces and drooping earrings and had on unusually high heels. The two ladies greeted Lewis effusively, holding him to their bosoms for what seemed to Chad an eternity, and after kissing him on the mouth, and even his ears, they turned their attention to the boy himself.

"But you never told us you had a son!" the younger of the two women exclaimed. She had hair of such an extremely light color that it almost appeared white.

"This is Minnie," Lewis introduced the lady now to Chad. "She is a very special friend who you too will grow to love. And not to slight this other beauty," Lewis turned to Minnie's companion, "meet Cora, Chad, Minnie's sister."

Both ladies now centered their attention on Chad, bending down slightly (they were unusually tall for ladies, especially owing to such high heels), they gave him even more kisses than they had showered Lewis Coultas with.

"What a darling child, Lewis, though bashful as a little quail!" Cora now turned her attention again to Lewis. Cora, who was older than Minnie by perhaps two or three years, had raven-black hair, and her eyes were of a strange green color which in a certain light looked almost black.

"You'd be bashful, too, Cora," Minnie contradicted her sister, "if you came all the way from Yellow Brook." She kissed Chad industriously again.

The strong and conflicting perfumes coming from each of the ladies made Chad somewhat unsteady on his feet.

"Your dad has painted this old town red more times than a crowned head of state," Minnie began talking to Chad in earnest, never leaving off holding him by the hand. "What he'll do, however, with you in tow this time is anybody's guess. But Cora and I will see you are properly chaperoned, rest easy on that score."

Before another word had been said, another group of bellhops arrived at the suite—the doors to the rooms were evidently allowed to remain wide open—and six huge bouquets of flowers of all kinds and hues, were brought in.

"Minnie wanted your rooms to have a springtime-fresh touch, Lewis!" Cora cried, and she held Coultas to her as tenaciously as ever Eva had held Chad during times of family crisis.

Lewis, as if drained from so many hugs and kisses, sat down on a brand new davenport, and sighed happily, shaking his head as if in disbelief at all the glory he saw before him, the ladies, his boy, and enough flowers to stock a greenhouse. Chad noticed for the first time that Lewis Coultas was wearing a sumptuous gold watch chain which moved rhythmically as his athlete's chest rose and fell. He had to admit at that moment that

Lewis looked indeed incredibly handsome—perhaps the ardent glances and embraces of the two rouged and perfumed ladies had brought this perception home to the boy.

"We've come to the city to buy my boy some new clothes," Lewis smiled as he noticed the admiring glances Minnie and Cora were bestowing on Chad.

"If you're going to that old haberdasher of yours," Minnie began, "I must step in and forbid you. I know a tailor who will be perfect for your young man. He may be more expensive than your old haberdasher, but he is a tailor who could make clothes out of moonbeams," Minnie finished. Then holding up a hand as she saw Lewis about to say something contradictory, she called out, "I'll hear no more about it, Lewis. Cora and I will accompany you and Chad to the tailor's!"

"A man is not always the best judge of clothes, Lewis," Cora seconded Minnie's plan. "And we have our days and evenings free and at your disposal!"

"So you are Lewis Coultas's son," Minnie had sat down now next to Chad and was for the first time studying his features carefully.

"Well," Chad began hesitantly, "according to some persons—"

"That will do now, Chad," his father said firmly but benevolently.

"But let the little chap finish," Cora now chimed in. "Lewis, don't be such a stern daddy."

"Oh, he can say anything he pleases," Lewis pouted a little, and then Minnie leaped up and went over to him and again covered him with kisses.

"He must resemble his Mama more than he does you, Lewis," Minnie finally observed. "Though he does have one blue eye that is a bit like yours. Do you resemble your Mama, darling?" Minnie inquired of Chad.

"If you know anything about children or heredity," Lewis Coultas began with icy authority, "you'd know that children often do not resemble their immediate parents, but take after their forebears."

"Dear hearts all," Cora now raised her voice. "If this is the beginning of an altercation, let me put an end to it. We are all here for another of our galas, and I for one will not allow any note of discord to arise. As for Chad's appearance, Lewis, I see you in every line of his handsome face, and certainly in the two dimples in each of his cheeks."

Lewis flushed deeply, and his lips twisted in a bittersweet smile. He gave a bow of thank you to Cora.

Talk then settled down to topics which did not touch on anyone's deep feelings, and often indeed one heard only the sound of the teacups being lowered, or a silver spoon crushing a lump of sugar.

After what seemed like endless hours of quaffing tea and exchanging kisses in the great imperial suite, the party of Mr. Lewis Coultas finally all got up, arranged their clothing, and leaving the doors to the rooms still gaping wide open, they got into a car as huge as the hearse which was used in important funerals back in Yellow Brook, and drove directly to the tailor Minnie and Cora had in mind.

They had to walk under an awning of green that gave the impression of extending several miles, and then they entered a long almost vacant front room with gloomy wood paneling. Two gentlemen dressed in silk suits like the elders of the church Chad attended came out at once and shook hands with Lewis, and bowed stiffly but amicably to Minnie and Cora.

"The young man here," Lewis began, addressing the tailors and at the same time removing Chad's hat and touching him briefly on his brow, "is in need of a suit. However," Lewis added, "as the boy lives in the country, we have in mind something durable, if you catch my drift."

"Now see here, Lewis," Minnie interrupted, and bowed to the younger of the tailors. "I have to beg your pardon perhaps but country wear is not for this young man. He needs something for the unexpected occasion. I am sure no matter where he lives there are those special occasions."

"There are outings in the different cars," Chad began, but a look from Coultas silenced him.

"There you are!" Minnie agreed with the boy. "He needs a suit for driving with friends!" As she said this she could not resist giving the boy a quick kiss, which brought a look of icy dismay from both the tailors.

After several hours of deliberation which taxed the tailors almost beyond endurance, four suits were decided upon, and Lewis Coultas gave them the address to which the clothing should be forwarded.

"But will the name Yellow Brook be sufficient on the packages?" the older tailor wondered.

Mr. Coultas chided the tailor on seeming to question the correctness of the address, and reminded him he himself had bought clothes from the present establishment and that the records would show they had reached Yellow Brook without incident.

Upon straightening out the address and the destination, Mr. Coultas drew from a wallet almost the size of a small tablecloth some bills of impressive denomination and handed each of the tailors more or less a fistful.

Then with a sound similar to that of a departing flock of great water birds, the company of Coultas, his son, Minnie and Cora departed, and were heard driving off with fanfare in the rented car.

The tailors, dropping their measuring tape and pencils and their record book, allowed themselves to slip into the rich leather of a single ottoman in the rear of their establishment.

The elder of the tailors, after sighing deeply several times, exclaimed, "Thank fortune none of our regular clientele were present to witness such a menagerie!"

Dinner was held that evening in a private dining room which was surrounded on all sides by marble columns and Italian chandeliers. Although Chad was put in the place of honor at the large round table at which all were seated, it was clear that Minnie and Cora were the real guests of honor. Liquor being forbidden at the period of this story, the ladies nonetheless helped themselves openly to a peculiar frothy-looking liquid which was kept in silver buckets under the table.

"You will be the best-dressed young chap in Yellow Brook," Cora kept repeating after every glass of the liquid. She would shake Chad gently each time she made her remark about his new suits for he was by now having trouble keeping his eyes open. He had been on his feet since three o'clock in the morning, and if he were asked by Bess Lytle this very moment whether it was dawn, night, or next week, he would have been unable to give her a satisfactory reply and would have been marked zero.

"Oh, I'll take Chad upstairs myself, ladies," Lewis finally said at the close of the meal when all were toying with a baked Alaska and French brandy.

"Don't be long though," Minnie beseeched her host as Lewis and Chad gave the ladies a very good evening and withdrew from the private dining room.

Lewis would not let him go to sleep just yet. Chad never remembered his dad being so attentive and taken up with him.

"You made a big *big* hit with the ladies, yes siree, you did," he told the boy. "You heartbreaker, you!" He punched him in the ribs. "Chad, listen to me. You do take after me, say what they will."

Then he kissed the boy rapturously, and bade him go to sleep.

Awakening all at once with a start, Chad was unable to tell whether it was morning or still some long stretch of the evening. From outside he could hear boat whistles, and the passing of cars, and an occasional police siren. There were still prevalent the smells of perfume and the frothy drink which had been kept under the round table in the dining room, but there was no sign of Coultas. He noticed, however, that the door leading to his room was partly ajar.

He put his bare feet down on the thick yellow carpet, and almost crept over to the half-open door. He hesitated but then drew it open, only to see that it led to another unoccupied room with a door also partly ajar. With great caution, like a person opening a combination safe, he pulled this door wide open.

Before him in a king-sized bed lay sprawled out Lewis Coultas, surrounded on both sides by the two ladies. They were all stark naked. He had never seen a woman naked before, and he had never seen Coultas stripped down to his bare skin. It was a sight as overwhelming as when his uncle had taken out his glass eye, exposing the terrible red of the socket.

Much later, very much later, he would perhaps understand why the ladies Cora and Minnie thought Lewis such a "dashing" wonderful paragon of manhood. But to Chad gaping at the large somewhat red breasts of the women, their huge wreaths of pubic hair, and the fiercely stiff penis of his father, all immersed in a kind of militant slumber which also resembled the piled-up bodies of corpses, caused the boy to begin walking swiftly backwards, as if were he to turn his back on such a sight of flesh he might somehow bring himself to even greater misfortune.

Back in his own spacious room, he gagged for a long time, but nothing would come up. He went to the toilet bowl and urinated copiously, indeed endlessly, all the time looking at his own penis, and then pulling up his pajamas stared at the rather sparse velvet covering of pubic hair only now beginning to appear at his groin.

Then he began dressing very carefully, and combed his hair with the comb Melissa had once given him on his birthday. He left the door to his room ajar as he had seen the other doors in this manner, though he had no intention of returning to his room. Instead of using the elevator he walked all ten flights down to the lobby. The descent cleared his head a little.

In the lobby—which did not look as splendid or so golden as it had the evening before, but a kind of gray tinsel color—he saw nobody in evidence except for two young men who sat behind the guest register, and they were as dead to the world in slumber as Lewis Coultas and his two lady loves.

Chad decided on the spot he would walk home. He had forgotten how far away from Yellow Brook he was, probably owing to the fact that it had been so pleasant with Lewis Coultas in the Pullman acting like a great kingpin whose fists coined money at will, for each time Chad had lifted up his eyes Lewis was giving a silver dollar to some porter or attendant.

But even if in his dazed state he had remembered how far Chicago was from his home in Yellow Brook, he would have walked to the ends of the earth in order to get away from Lewis Coultas. The horror of seeing him stripped naked between the two women had made him acutely ill. He also now recalled his mother's hints uttered during her various illnesses about the "terrible" life of her husband.

But having seen Lewis Coultas as he *really was,* Chad all at once felt a great burden being lifted from him, for Lewis Coultas, he now saw, could of course never be his father. The spectacle of him between the two women proved that.

And yet, he pondered, how could Decatur be his father either?

He was so overwhelmed by both these contingencies that in the middle of the street where only a few cars were slowly moving about and some horses and wagons were hugging the curb, he let out all at once a great cry of humiliation and pain. A few passersby on their way to work or coming from a night's revel, stopped and stared at him biliously, then went on their way.

As the day tried to dawn over all the smoke-ridden city, Chad realized he was leaving the world of Lewis Coultas behind him, and was going in the general direction of the sun itself, which must lead to home. Yes, once he was safe back in the mansion in Yellow Brook perhaps neither Lewis Coultas or Decatur would ever trouble him again, for after all, he hardly ever set eyes on Coultas, and Decatur had come into his life as from out of a dream. And like those dreams which recur again and again, Decatur always appeared the same, and again like in dreams, said almost nothing that one could remember.

Trying to keep his progress always due east, he finally came to a road gorged with vehicles of all kinds, including many horse-drawn drays. He stood on the curb, and held his right hand protectively over his eyes, though no strong light troubled his vision.

All at once from out of all that hullabaloo around him, Chad heard a rough male voice shout, "And when did you drop out of the sky?"

Chad stared at a young man wearing a tall silk hat who was busy snapping his fingers in the boy's face. "You! I'm talking to you! What are you doin' here starin' like you were paying the earth your first visit?"

When there was no response from Lewis Coultas's son, the owner of the silk hat pulled Chad by his velvet lapel, and then cried out boisterously, "So you are alive after all. You see I was beginnin' to think you was one of my own waxwork figures I have stashed away in my jitney over there." He pointed to a kind of truck which could have easily seated a whole Pullman car of diners. "Mr. Elmo Lejeune, at your service," he identified himself, and broke into a series of hoarse and even choking guffaws.

"But you're black as a mulberry, ain't you." He touched Chad's cheeks as if some of the dusky color might rub off on his hands. "Why, you must be the last of the ten little Injuns then, ain't you?" Again came the throttled sound of his laughter.

At this Chad began to sob a little.

"Don't tell me you're a crybaby in the bargain." He took off his high silk hat, and as he did so, his own very curly red hair fell in an undulating mass about his cheeks, which were the color of strawberries and cream.

"Now, I'll tell you what," Mr. Elmo Lejeune began as he slammed back on his head his silk hat, and studiously considered Chad. Occasionally he would open and then close his mouth as if he had not quite taken in all of the boy before him, and then he was finally able to bring out: "Damn it, mate, I can't just leave you here, all by your lonesome now can I? So if you won't be puttin' up any objection, I'll take you along with me, provided you actually know where you're goin' to. And if you do know where you're headed for, maybe I can drop you off there on my way to Toronto, Canada. If, that is, you do know where you're from and where you're off to!"

Chad nodded almost imperceptibly, but the man in the tall silk hat saw that brief nod, for he saw everything within eyeshot.

They hurried together across the dangerous, throbbing street, and came up short to the jitney itself. This vehicle was gaudily painted, and reminded Chad of the wagons which paraded through the streets of Yellow Brook at circus time.

Before Mr. Elmo Lejeune opened the ample door of his bus, he made a little introductory address to prepare, he said, the young man for the "spectacle within."

"I don't want to open this majestic door to the panorama inside without a little preamble, for if I know a scared boy when I see him, that scared boy is you. You said, by the way, your name is what? Aha, *Chad* it will be, and pleased to meet you indeed. Now as I am a student of human nature, being in the entertainment business, I observe you have got a very susceptible disposition and you go off the deep end at the drop of a hat," here he doffed his own hat and grinned, "which is why I've no doubt somebody has left you all by yourself on the curbside in a big bustling city street. You was too susceptible for them to handle, eh? Now, therefore, Chad, when I open this door and you peek within, don't bawl or cry out, for what you'll see ain't dead people, but life-sized dolls. Wax! Every last one of them, and every one of them is mine!"

With this Mr. Lejeune flung open the door with such panache that Chad felt the big crimson curtain of the Opera House in Yellow Brook was going up before his eyes.

Peering within the vehicle Chad saw seated each in his or her own individual throne, a complete entourage of kings and queens, heroes and giants, angels and devils, and Jesus and his Disciples.

"Meet the cast, Chad!" Mr. Lejeune took his silk hat off again and bowed to all the assemblage within. It seemed to Chad at that moment that the wax figures moved slightly, at least their eyes did, and on some of their faces queer little smiles played about their very red lips.

Seated beside Mr. Lejeune at the wheel of the jitney Chad observed the older man made no effort to start the motor, and appeared plunged in thought.

"I'm afraid you still haven't told me, my dear young man, where it is in fact you are on your way to," Elmo Lejeune spoke with the gracious delicacy one would expect of the owner of a whole car full of crowned heads.

"Yellow Brook, I'll be hanged!" the waxworks man cried on hearing the name of the place to which Chad was headed. "Why that's almost directly enroute to where I'm bound for in Canada. Why, Yellow Brook's near the Blanchard River, ain't it?

Chad nodded appreciatively. Still, Mr. Lejeune made no effort to get under way with all his cargo, but showed he was thinking very carefully, and probably his careful thinking had to do with his passenger.

"You're mighty dressed up for an Injun boy ain't you?" he observed. "Those duds you have on are pretty special. And pearl buttons on your little jacket!"

"Pauline sewed those on," he informed Elmo Lejeune, and he looked admiringly at the buttons. "Pauline is my mother's mother, but she likes to be called by her Christian name."

"And your family, along with Pauline, are waiting for you at Yellow Brook?"

Chad smiled faintly, and then began haltingly to try to tell Mr. Lejeune how he had come to be in Chicago, and before that how he had gone driving with Decatur who claimed to be his father, and before that he described the visits he received from the Indian at Bess Lytle's, but at last becoming lost in such a confusing tangle of events, he came to a halt, and looked into Mr. Lejeune's eyes as if he needed a prompter.

Mr. Lejeune however raised his right hand like a referee announcing victory (or perhaps defeat) and drew from his breast pocket a large stick of licorice.

"Have a little sweet, Chad," he told the boy, and he started the motor. Before they knew it, they were soon leaving the great smoky city behind them, and only the sound of Chad eating the candy was audible for a lengthy while.

"I'll have you in Yellow Brook in under twenty hours or I am not Elmo Lejeune the theatrical impresario of the Canadian Rockies!" He laughed at his own designation for himself. "Yes, sirreee," he went on, "I've heard a lot of tall tales and fanciful cock-and-bulls, but, by jiminy your story beats 'em all hollow. But if you say you're goin' to Yellow Brook, I won't argue with you, and I'll take you to the very door of your mansion where you say your Mama and Melissa are expecting you."

Every so often, when there was a lapse in the conversation, Chad felt Mr. Lejeune wiping his mouth with a handkerchief free of the black licorice stains.

"You're such a handsome chap," his friend would explain, "that dark as your complexion is, I don't like to see any needless stain on your lips."

There was a faint perfume clinging to the handkerchief with which Mr. Lejeune wiped his mouth free of the licorice which reminded him of the smell emanating from Minnie and Cora in the great hotel back in Chicago.

"A penny for your thoughts, Chad," Mr. Lejeune would say every so often, and Chad would give a real start for actually he was wondering if perhaps the sheriff would not consider the ride he was now taking with the theatrical impresario another example of kidnapping and abduction. He was too bashful to share this suspicion with Mr. Lejeune.

Every so often they would stop at some little town with wooden sidewalks, and Mr. Lejeune saw to it that Chad ate a hearty meal because of the all-night drive ahead of them. But Chad noticed that Elmo ate almost nothing. He would simply keep looking at Chad and every so often heave a great sigh.

"What is it, Mr. Lejeune?" the boy finally got the courage to ask.

"When I see you, I wish I had got married and had a son," he confided. "Did anybody ever tell you how handsome you are, Chad?"

"No," he mumbled, coloring violently under his coppery complexion.

"I found that being a theatrical impresario, you see, sort of interfered with the matrimonial estate . . . . All my wives left me." He sighed again. "So here I am, getting on to being thirty-five years old, and all I have to show for my life is a jitney full of wax figures!" He laughed in spite of himself, and Chad joined in.

Mr. Lejeune then went up to the cash register where candy was on display, and he purchased a whole bag full of caramels, nougats, and butterscotch, and handed them to the boy.

They drove now with a good deal more speed than before, owing to the fact that they met fewer and fewer cars, and as the light began to fail, they appeared to be the only vehicle on the road.

As the night progressed, or, as Elmo joked, about the Middle Watch (he had been a sailor he said in the Royal Navy), the theatrical impresario said it would be better if they got a couple hours of sleep now, so that he could finish the next stretch of driving refreshed.

Elmo brought out from among the assemblage of wax figures—all of whom now looked sunk in slumber—a couple of blankets and wrapped Chad and himself snugly under these, and then said very gently, and a bit sadly, "Good night, my dear friend, and I hope the angels dry your tears."

As he was drifting off to sleep Chad felt Elmo's lips gently touch his left ear, and then move even more gently to his forehead and from his forehead they brushed faintly his lips. He kissed the boy so briefly and even more gently than Melissa ever had. His lips also had a kind of syrupy taste which made Chad feel he was again sipping from Eva's solid silver spoon some of the medicine she had administered to him.

Presently, he heard Elmo Lejeune snoring deeply, and saw his head thrown back against the cushions. He did not feel sleepy himself, and staring through the windows of the jitney he caught a glimpse outside of a spectacular sight: all the stars and a planet or two were in glorious and perfectly clear and dazzling array, and appeared so close to earth at that moment that Chad held his breath. Orion, his belt shining like diamonds, and Castor and Pollux all appeared to beckon him to come outside and enjoy their spectacle free of the roof and confinement of the jitney.

Chad found himself wandering through the forest nearby, still looking upwards at the sea of heavenly bodies which now seemed even closer to earth. Then without any warning, the aurora borealis streaked across the horizon, and to add to his astonishment he saw two falling stars descend one after the other.

Before he knew it he had wandered deep into the forest, and then all at once while still looking above, he came upon a narrow winding road which somehow looked familiar to him.

Turning about where he thought he had left the jitney, he saw that he had wandered a great distance from his friend Mr. Lejeune and had been so taken up with his star-gazing he realized he did not know now in which direction his friend the impresario was waiting for him.

Again he stared at the lonely road which seemed so familiar.

Then in that hushed silence of starlight and pine forest he heard the sound of horses' hooves, the creak of wagon wheels, and the snap of a whip. He found himself standing in the direct path of the oncoming horse and wagon, but as if he had again just tasted the red medicine from Eva's silver spoon, he felt powerless to move.

Brandishing a great long whip above his white head, the driver of the wagon came to an abrupt stop within a few inches of the boy standing in his way. Waving his whip again and shouting a stream of oaths and filthy names, the driver leaped from the wagon perhaps with the intention of killing the party who had stopped his progress.

Both Chad and the driver all at once let out cries which brought odd echoes from the slumbering forest.

"You're him all right," the raucous hate-ridden voice reached Chad, who began stepping backwards as he recognized the driver as Decatur's grandfather.

Chad only rubbed his eyes, as the old man took hold of him and shook him roughly, his spittle flying onto the boy's face.

"Where is *he,* you filthy little bugger?" the old man threatened, and raised the whip again. "Have you killed and left him for the crows, as he deserves!"

To Chad's bewildered *"Who?"*, spoken more like a moan than

a word, the old man cried out through his spraying spit, "Who but your own dad who sired you on that white woman! Where have you left him this time, and what are you doin' here in the dead of night dressed like some little sugarplum prince?"

"Ah," the boy tried to recollect, "I left him with some ladies," he explained, then realizing that it was not after all Decatur he was talking about, but Lewis Coultas, he backtracked to say he was mistakenly talking about someone else.

"Like your dad, a born liar," the old man cried, and he brought the whip down on the boy's shoulder. "Get in that wagon and no more of your lip if you don't want more of this bullhide brought down on your deceitful puss."

Seeing no way of escape, Chad jumped into the front seat of the wagon which was covered with a worn buffalo hide.

They drove for some time in silence until the old man remarked, "A blue eye and a black one don't look right in a face, now, does it?" He mumbled something else. "We'll have to do something about it." There was a strong smell of liquor coming from the old man.

Chad unconsciously touched his blue eye, and the old man laughed and reaching down helped himself to a swallow from a dusty bottle.

"We're goin' by stages today," the old man explained, "And what a co-in-cee-dence, ain't it, running' into a brat like you in this no man's land. . . . And you say you left him in bed with some women."

"No, sir, I misspoke."

"Here comes the lies now, just like him. Misspoke what, my precious jackass?"

"The man I left there with the women was not him."

"Not your own flesh and blood dad?"

"It was my dad Lewis Coultas who was . . . in bed with the ladies."

"*Was* your dad, hear him! I told you and he told you, didn't he, that you have only one dad, and that's him, the full-blooded descendant of full-blooded Ojibwa chiefs."

The old man roared and mumbled and even screamed on and on. Chad looked apprehensively about him, then kept his eyes glued to the road to see how and where he might jump.

"We'll take care of that blue eye, don't you never fear," the old man went on, drinking freely from the whiskey. "We'll make it black as the other. No great-grandson of mine can have one eye that is blue, or I'll know the reason why. Didn't Decatur tell you 'twouldn't do, to have a blue eye alongside of the black one?"

"No, sir, he didn't mind the blue eye."

"Didn't mind the blue eye! That was all he talked about with me. He cursed your blue eye, said it must be made black like the other, like his eyes. He was not pleased coming from so far off to find his son don't have two eyes that matched."

Chad's accumulative sense of terror now froze him to the seat. To jump now, he opined, would be too dangerous, and the old maniac might run after him even if he succeeded in jumping.

" 'Twill only take a minute to take out the blue eye, and 'twill be done for once and all, and Decatur will be satisfied then you are his boy."

Despite his terror Chad began to feel drowsy, perhaps owing to the sound of the horses' hooves, or possibly because he had had so little sleep for the past few days and was totally exhausted from all he had seen and heard since Yellow Brook.

They finally arrived at a large wooden frame house on the outskirts of some town that Chad had never set eyes on before.

"What are you starin' at like a crazed buzzard?" the old man growled, and he took him by the scruff of the neck with his powerful iron grip, and pulled him out of the wagon and into the front room of the house, whose door had been left ajar.

"So you couldn't wait, could you, to be with your own great-grandad, could you? Was walkin' on the edge of the world to find him. God in heaven, you are ugly with one blue eye, and one black. Out it must come!"

Chad surveyed the room carefully, and noticed that the old man had put the bullwhip he had threatened him with earlier in a corner nearer to Chad than to himself.

"Now you want that eye removed, do you not, so that at least you'll have only one proper black eye to look at people with, and admit the easier that you are an Indian yourself, though mixed with rotten white blood."

Seeing the old man was so deep in his cups that he was not focusing his eyes now properly in any direction, Chad moved closer to the bullwhip.

Then as if coming out of his drunken state and acting cold

sober, the old man drew out a knife as if from thin air and advanced toward the astonished boy.

"This will see an end to blue eyes!"

But as he lunged at his great-grandson he slipped and fell and the knife slid almost to Chad's left foot. Chad picked up the knife and at the same time seized hold of the bullwhip.

The old man leaped to his feet but saw the boy facing him with the two weapons, knife and whip. He wiped his stained mouth with his filthy sleeve.

"Put that knife and whip down, do you hear, or I'll put out both your eyes, do you mind me? You better obey me now or by Christ, I'll put you where the dogs won't piss on you!" In desperation Chad struck the old man now full in the face with the bullwhip. The great-grandfather fell heavily to his knees, and there was a sound as of bones breaking. In his increasing panic Chad struck his assailant again and again. The sight of blood rushing out in streams from the old man drove Chad to still greater exercise of the whip. He beat Decatur's grandfather now with random blows, all over his hands and chest, and then backing toward the door, holding the whip and the knife against any further aggression, he slammed the door shut, and leaped into the wagon. Though he barely knew how to manage a horse, he soon found himself driving off at dizzying speed toward the east as he saw the first feeble light of day.

Large garish-colored posters suddenly went up everywhere in Yellow Brook announcing the forthcoming appearance of the Great Magician Thurkell with a cast of fifty, and a wild animal act of tigers from India, jaguars from Nepal, sword-swallowers, fire-eaters, and of course the unparalleled feats of magic of Thurkell the Great himself, direct from his triumphs in Budapest, Paris, London, and Tokyo. Thurkell's appearance in Yellow Brook was, however, not completely overpowering and sensational as one might think, for he came to the town rather frequently, and his engagement at the Opera House (where Sarah Bernhardt and Houdini had also appeared) drew crowds from twenty counties and the three states adjoining Yellow Brook.

"It will do you good, my dear, to see Thurkell and his menagerie," Pauline spoke coaxingly to her daughter in the front parlor. But Eva barely heard her mother. "Besides," the old woman went on, removing her pince-nez and staring at her daughter's pallor, "I have already asked Bess if she will accompany us, and she has of course agreed."

Eva smiled in spite of herself.

"Mother, dearest, I believe it is you who want to see the Great Thurkell!"

Pauline bowed her head and flushed.

"Of course I will go with you, Mother . . . I doubt, though, I can enjoy it with my dear Chad gone." She gave out a dry short sob, and took out her handkerchief.

"But, darling, if, as we think, he is with Lewis! What have we to fear?"

"You always have something to say in favor of Lewis, Mother, when I'd think you'd be the last person on earth to forgive him for the predicament he has brought all of us to! How can you even think, let alone say, that my boy would be safe with such a hardened reprobate!"

Eva now wept uncontrollably and insisted against anything her mother could say to the contrary that Chad had been kidnapped and abducted by Lewis Coultas.

As evening began to settle down, however, calm was restored and Eva went upstairs to dress for the Opera House. After some hesitation, she decided to put on one of her most elaborate and sumptuous evening dresses, and she thought over her mother's sensible promise that the Opera House, with its vestige of past grandeur, and the personage of the handsome, raffish Thurkell, might take her mind off the anguish and sorrow which had afflicted her for so many days and nights.

She spent so much time putting on and off her different necklaces, earrings and brooches, that Pauline finally had to come up and insist she stop delaying.

Pauline had rented a car large enough to seat ten people. They had the driver stop for Bess, and then they all drove off in a rather convivial mood to the Opera House.

The head usher himself took the ladies in charge, and brought them to the finest and choicest seats in the house. Their rather regal entrance brought a great deal of whispering, sounds of disapproval, and rude laughter from the upper balconies, and even from the quality downstairs. But Bess's fierce glance of rebuke at the whisperers and guffawers caused most of the disturbance to die down, or at least be less audible. But everybody in the Opera House had their eyes on Eva. Her story was at the height of its scandal and disgrace.

A man in evening dress with a monocle came out from behind the gold and purple curtain and after raising both his hands for silence, told the audience that there would be a slight delay. He looked at his pocket watch, and then said regretfully, "It is now half past eight, but we should be getting underway in a mere ten minutes more, kind ladies and courteous gentlemen."

There were first boos, and then a meaningless burst of applause.

Although the doors to the auditorium of the Opera House had been closed by the ushers, shortly after the speech of apology, words of protest and anger were heard from behind the closed doors and a kind of scuffle ensued. The house lights had dimmed during the disturbance, but presently the door to the auditorium was flung open, and a man walked in and went down the main aisle, pushing back both the ushers who tried to detain him.

As the man walked majestically down the thick carpet of the aisle, a "spot" light from the top balcony centered its light on him and catching him like a bullet in its target, there was revealed for every eye the face and figure of Decatur himself, dressed in a brand new suit and silk cravat. He carried a Borsalino hat over his breast.

If the outcry at Eva's presence had been contemptuous and deriding, the sound of the audience at the sight of Decatur was a kind of grumble of awe and a moan of uneasiness.

His mouth opened and his flashing teeth gave such an appearance of fierceness that quiet descended on the spectators, and the quiet was succeeded then by the first notes coming from the orchestra.

Decatur strode on and took a seat not far from where Eva and her mother and Bess were seated. He turned sideways and gave them a faint bow.

"So he is free!" These words escaped from Bess, but they seemed to come from Eva, who having looked at Decatur once, did not dare gaze in his direction again.

The whole house was now engulfed in darkness, and as the music swelled up, Eva grasped her smelling bottle and held it to her nostrils. But Bess, taking Eva's hand in hers, whispered,

"So you see, my dear, our appeal to Judge Hebbel was not all in vain."

Once the curtain had gone up, the audience was treated to one splendid dizzying display after another of magic and the miraculous, the savage and the dangerous. A beautiful woman was cut in two by Thurkell himself, and then rose from her severed body more perfect than before, a savage jaguar and leopard leaped through hoops of flame, and a young man was beheaded (the use of mirrors, Bess reassured Eva). And then in an "entr'acte," the Great Thurkell himself in a demonstration of his mental telepathy told volunteering members of the audience what they had in their bank accounts, what they had eaten for supper, how many children they possessed, where and when they were born and so on.

"But there is an unusual presence here tonight, ladies and gentlemen," Thurkell raised his bass voice until one thought it could be heard far beyond the roof of the Opera House, certainly beyond the courthouse and the frozen waters of the river.

An attendant then handed Thurkell a cape of flaming red, with satin gold lining, and a kind of walking stick encrusted with diamonds in the shapes of hyacinths surrounded by emeralds and rubies, and holding this instrument like a wand, he asked in a choked voice if there was any young man in the audience who was fearless and intrepid enough to willingly risk his life tonight.

A heavy rather resentful silence fell over the entire house.

Pretending choler and irritation, Thurkell whipped his great cloak about him, and flourishing his wand, stepped to the edge of the footlights. He peered out into the inky assemblage of heads and hats, and then, as if exasperated beyond endurance, he stretched out his right hand so that his cape appeared to move out toward all his auditors as if he were enveloping every person seated there with its immense folds. Then breathing out his impatience and displeasure, he cried:

"I know you are there, for Thurkell knows all hidden thoughts, all deep-seated secrets!"

Moving his head as if to penetrate into nature's most hidden mysteries, the magician then exclaimed with wild relief:

"There I see the man I have been in search of! Stand up, I command you, young man, rise!"

It was Decatur, who thus addressed, now rose, then, hesitating only a moment, with a quick glance at Eva, walked out into the aisle and on toward the stage.

Even his bitterest enemies admitted later he looked resplendent, though he had never appeared so dark-complexioned as the golden light of the Opera House set off his hair, grown rather long and falling almost to braids, and his almond-shaped eyes flashed with fierce expressiveness.

"Come up the steps to the stage, my dear friend, please do not hold back, for I have been expecting you. Your soul is a mirror and has betrayed its depths to me, but those secrets I will never reveal to any but the Divine Master himself, and only if he demands I divulge them! Yes, you are the one who has been selected for the ordeal to come!"

Decatur appeared almost to take flight and soar noiselessly and swiftly up the steps to the great stage from which John McCormack had once poured out his soul.

Thurkell embraced Decatur and for a moment entirely wrapped the younger man in his cape's folds. Then Thurkell kissed Decatur on his brow, eliciting a kind of groan of uncertainty and dislike from the audience.

"You will now see, ladies and gentlemen, one of the most dangerous and unforgettable phenomena in the history of prestidigitation and magic, a feat known from before the Babylonians, and passed on to me by the magicians of ancient Egypt!"

Thurkell then bowed almost to the floor again and again.

"And now my young friend," Thurkell addressed Decatur, "you will remove your coat and your shirt so that all those who are watching us out there will know that we conceal nothing!"

Decatur hesitated only a brief moment, and then quickly removed his new jacket, cravat, shirt and finally, after a questioning look at Thurkell, his violet undershirt.

Half-naked he looked very much like the portraits of the Indians in the courthouse gallery leading to Judge Hebbel's private chamber.

A murmur half of approval, half of outrage rose slowly and sleepily from the opera house, and ascended like thick smoke to the building's roof.

What followed was never clear to any of the spectators that night. As Thurkell raised his wand upward, Decatur seemed to rise to the very roof of the Opera House, but he rose in a circle or cubicle of flames. His entire form was outlined by chaplets of blue and yellow fire, his hair became a diadem of conflagration, and from his mouth sprang like serpents countless coiling shoots of fire and smoke. He appeared to rise and float over the entire assemblage of rapt and breathless onlookers.

Then what sounded like a cannon-burst split the air, and before anyone could utter a word, Decatur was restored to himself. His shirt and jacket were again on, and people wondered indeed if he had ever removed his clothing, or that he had ever for that matter like a phoenix turned to flame and ashes, and thence back to flesh and blood.

Despite themselves, the witnesses to this extravaganza emitted a unanimous cry of approval, and from every side came shouts of "Decatur!"

Judge Hebbel stood up from his cordoned-off seat in the front row and bowed endlessly, as if the entire evening were owing to his auspices and patronage.

A cry from Pauline, however, added a discordant note. "Bring water!" she was imploring. Eva lay fainting in her arms.

Decatur had already reached her side, and pressing a flask of something to her lips, he knelt down beside her. When she opened her eyes, and briefly touched him on his cheek, a great rumbling kind of groan rose from the audience, like the sound of explosives under water, and then in front of all those eyes Decatur bent down and kissed Mrs. Coultas again and again on the mouth.

Dawn came at last to the great city on the lake, even though it was barely visible in the windows of the mammoth hotel suite where Cora, Minnie and Lewis Coultas slumbered on in rapt and naked embrace. While they slept the lake had been on one of its rampages, and had sunk several cargo boats and drowned all their crew.

Rising at last, Lewis, after tripping over one of the girl's high heels and extricating one of Minnie's stray hairpins from his own luxuriant hair, put on his favorite bathrobe, a deep blue garment with designs of pea-fowl on it, (a wedding gift from Pauline which he refused to discard), and crossed the two rooms to the bathroom adjoining Chad's sleeping quarters.

Lewis observed that Chad had wrapped himself in blanket

after blanket so that the boy's head was not even visible. Lewis whistled, but the covers did not move.

At home Lewis often shaved in front of the boy while catching up on all the news he had missed during one of his frequent absences from home. Today he did not depart from this ceremony, and as he lathered his face and sharpened and honed his razor, he told Chad what a big hit he had made with the ladies.

"A word of caution here, though, Chad," Lewis said, stepping into the room and addressing the huge pile of comforters on the bed. "Don't tell your mother that ladies were present, do you get it? A little secret between you and your dad, kid?" Lewis gave forth a restrained laugh, which as it died away took on a worried tone. "Chad," his father called, barbering his cheeks with majestic professional strokes. "Oh, I say, Chad!"

Lewis put down his razor and went over to the bed. He shook the boy gently. But instead of the feel of flesh, Lewis's fingers only sank into the down of the comforters. He threw off all the bedclothes then and discovered nothing under them. This time he whistled as loudly as any of the retinue of the Great Thurkell. He swore. He threw all of the pillows and comforters on the carpet, and made such an outcry that Minnie hurried into the room.

"What on earth is the matter?" she began, but Lewis merely pointed to the empty bed. Minnie took this rather too calmly for Lewis's patience, and he snapped at her as a result.

As they faced one another in their exasperation and wonder, Lewis gave out with, "My son seems to have a faculty for being kidnapped!"

"Kidnapped!" Minnie cried in the tone of surprise a lady of high social station might employ. "What are you talking about, sweetheart?"

"Sweetheart is wondering how he will explain the boy's disappearance to his wife and mother-in-law, that's what sweetheart is talking about!"

Minnie folded her arms and stared at him unsympathetically.

"Look here," he shouted, "I have to go to the police station."

"Now you look here, Lewis Coultas," Minnie broke in. "How do you know your boy is not at this very moment in the lobby or the dining room having breakfast. Good heavens, Lewis, I've never seen you so beside yourself. And all over a young boy!"

Lewis's face burned at this last remark. "Only a young boy," he repeated her phrase nastily.

"I apologize, my dear, if I seem indifferent to his absence. I do apologize," she spoke worriedly at the sight of rage on his face. "I'm touched to see you are so concerned about young Chad. After all, if you are his father—"

"What in hell do you mean by that?" All of Mr. Coultas's anger came out in that interrogation and Minnie fell back a few steps in genuine alarm.

"Don't scream at me, Lewis. You are too much in my debt if you care to recall, to shout at me . . . I said what everyone must observe, that's all. That boy does not look like your son. He doesn't look like your boy for at least two generations back. I can speak my mind if I want to without having my head chopped by you."

He began throwing on his clothes, until he was dressed for the street.

"I'll see you, then, once I've talked to the police," Lewis said as he walked out of the room. He gave her a brusque little kiss.

"See here, Lewis," Minnie expostulated after him. "I know a fine private detective who can find Chad for you. The police will do nothing, you mark my words."

"We'll see about that," Lewis fairly roared at her, and went out.

Minnie and Cora were in the more palatial of the five principal dining rooms when Lewis Coultas sauntered in, a toothpick in his right jaw, and more wrinkles in his forehead than the ladies had ever observed before.

"That boy has disappeared into thin air!" Lewis slumped down into a chair at the table with the ladies. "What do you think his mother will say?" he moaned. "As I said, he was already kidnapped last month."

"Will you please, Lewis, stop talking nonsense. Kidnapped! How do you think such language will sound if we are overheard," Minnie began again in the same vein of her first talk with Lewis upstairs. "I suppose Cora and I will be considered accomplices to his disappearance. That's about the way things are shaping up! Cora, darling, don't you get the drift?"

"What was the name of that private detective of yours, Minnie," Lewis wanted to know.

"Now you're talking sense," Minnie congratulated him, and raising a tumbler of apricot juice, she toasted Lewis. "I've already, for your information, alerted Mr. Wilbur Harkey," she gave the name of the private eye.

"Wilbur Harkey," Lewis repeated the name. "By Christ, let me tell you, I'm ready to go see the Witch of Endor to find out where that damned little scamp has gone to now. . . . I suppose the little bastard went home to Yellow Brook."

"Is your wife as dark-complexioned as your boy?" Cora wondered suddenly while finishing the last of her beefsteak.

Lewis turned a sickly pale.

"I beg your pardon," Cora apologized and quit chewing.

Lewis's eye rested just then on a big diamond ring on Cora's little finger, and Cora under this scrutiny put her hand in her lap.

"My wife is blond as the sun," Lewis spoke with the same nasty glint in his eye he had had in the suite upstairs.

Minnie spoke a few conciliating words, and Cora and Lewis relaxed a little, and raised their fruit juice glasses in a halfhearted toast.

"Lewis, darling," Minnie began then, "you mustn't be surprised at Wilbur Harkey's age now." She began industriously putting on her lipstick and loosening the veil on her hat.

"Is he a youngster?" Lewis asked almost savagely.

Minnie put away her lip rouge.

"Wilbur Harkey is not a spring rooster, would you say, Cora, darling?" Minnie replied, winking at her sister.

Cora was still flustered at Lewis's ill-temper and for his having looked at the diamond ring on her finger with such an accusing expression. She was about to explain away his suspicion by telling him she had inherited the ring from her aunt Idabelle, but then the signal was given by Minnie for them to depart to the offices of Mr. Wilbur Harkey.

Lewis Coultas was almost as shocked to set eyes on Mr. Wilbur Harkey, private detective, as he had been when he looked under the bedclothes and saw there was no Chad.

Wilbur Harkey gave every appearance of being not a spring rooster, but a man well over ninety.

The girls, Cora and Minnie, furthermore, remembered him

from a time when he was still dyeing his hair a kind of raven purple, so that now on seeing him after some lapse of time, they at first barely recognized him owing to the fact he was wearing his huge mop of hair in its natural white color, and it was uncombed, flying in all directions. His massive jaw was filled with gold, and the network of wrinkles which had greatly multiplied since their past acquaintanceship gave him the appearance, in Lewis Coultas's eyes at least, of a man gone over by the headhunters.

But the spirits of the party of Mr. Lewis Coultas were raised considerably when they were ushered by Mr. Harkey into a sumptuously elegant suite where room for one hundred persons could easily have been found, and the finest French champagne was being served in Venetian glasses by attendants in tuxedos.

"You see, ladies dear," Mr. Harkey began, "I knew you were coming, and I knew what fare you would expect!" He laughed boisterously, almost hysterically, and his laughter ended in a great fit of coughing which resembled the barking of an ill-tempered watchdog.

They all drank now with pained and polite expressions on their countenances, but as the champagne was superb, they found themselves shortly in a better temper all around, and Lewis, as was his peculiar habit, put on his white gloves, which brought a silent look either of disapproval or rebuke from the aged and trembling Wilbur Harkey.

Mr. Harkey wiped his faded blue lips with a thick velvet cloth, and then with almost as much ostentation as the Great Thurkell, produced from his breast pocket an oversized gold fountain pen, dipped it in a mammoth inkwell, and then pulled out from his desk drawer a tiny volume resembling an address book used by titled ladies.

Exchanging somewhat annoyed glances with Minnie and Cora, however, he put down the small book, and began, "You are looking, if I am not mistaken, Cora and Minnie, at my wedding finger which now bears *two* wedding rings instead of the customary one. I see the surprise especially in Minnie's brown eyes, but also in your hazel wide-open ones, Cora. Ah, well, allow me to expatiate. You perhaps did not notice the mourning band I bear across my chest," here he opened his jacket slightly to show an expensive piece of midnight-black silk. "My adored spouse Gabrielle passed away one year ago today, but her place has been more than adequately filled by Emma Lou, who was, as you will recall, my secretary, until our recent wedding. Emma will bear me company as I go down the shady lane of my life. Nonetheless, model wife and secretary as my second wife is, I could not bear to give up the wedding band from my first marriage, and so with Emma's tolerant and gracious compliance I now bear two rings," here he flashed his withered wedding finger for all to see, "on the self-same digit!"

Then letting out a great and even frothy "harrumph" Mr. Harkey got down to business.

"I must have, sir," he addressed Lewis Coultas, "the particulars. But we will begin of course with the more paramount facts first, though as you will see, and as perhaps our ladies may have told you, it is the *particulars* I am most famous for, and which, to tell the truth, has made my name what it is today."

Without warning however, at the end of his preamble, Mr. Harkey let out so enormous a belch that both Minnie and Cora blushed under their rouge and Lady Esther face powder.

Again the champagne came to everybody's assistance, and ignoring Mr. Harkey's breach of etiquette, everyone drank plentifully again, smiled and nodded.

"What particulars do you require?" Lewis Coultas's voice now interrupted the sounds of drinking and approbation. As he spoke Lewis inserted his finger in his high stiff collar, loosening it just a slight degree.

The champagne had made Chad's father with his ash blond hair and sky-blue eyes look particularly handsome just then, at least the two ladies thought so, and there crossed both Minnie and Cora's minds with a kind of horror the memory of the dusky, burnished, fiercely-Indian countenance of the disappeared Chad—though of course he did have, after all, one very blue eye like his Dad's.

"I am told, sir," the old detective began, "that you are missing a son." He said this with an edge to his voice that perhaps such a fact was doubtful.

"Ah, that," Lewis said in the manner of a man who is reminded of some trivial and certainly unimportant detail.

All three, Minnie, Cora and Harkey, stared at him doubtfully, and Minnie wondered if the champagne had put him off balance.

Then rousing himself under the fierce scrutiny he was receiving, Lewis managed to say, "Yes, sir, my boy, about fourteen, disappeared from my hotel suite. I believe it was last night sometime, wouldn't you agree, Minnie and Cora?"

"And the name of the hotel?" Mr. Harkey cried, preventing any rejoinder from the ladies. He was writing carefully in his small notebook.

"The majestic hotel facing the lake, of course," Lewis contested.

Mr. Harkey hesitated a moment on this particular, and then murmured with gentle conciliation. "To be sure." Raising his voice now to courtroom volume, the old man inquired, "He is your only son?"

"Thank God, he is, sir," Lewis replied. Then swept along by all the confusion and consternation of the past days, he went on. "My boy was kidnapped a few short weeks ago by an Indian friend of our family."

"East Indian or North American?" Mr. Harkey wondered, placing his gold pen against his front teeth.

Lewis, rapt in his own tangled recollections, managed to reply: "The man, the Indian, name of Decatur, claimed he was the boy's father, and took him for spins around the country in his fancy cars. Waited every evening at the boy's school, so the two could go motoring. And so on!"

Mr. Harkey looked at his gold pen reproachfully, shook it, put it down, then raised it again, and stared long and hard first at Lewis, then even more accusingly and censoriously at Minnie and Cora.

"Who occupied the hotel suite, sir, from which the boy vanished?" Mr. Harkey wondered icily.

Lewis touched his high collar again, and gave it a hard yank before saying, "I would have thought that was clear, sir, since the boy was traveling with me. It was my hotel suite of course!"

"And you occupied this suite only with the boy, Mr. Lewis Coultas?"

Mr. Harkey waited with the gold pen raised almost in the manner of a band conductor. Lewis gazed wonderingly at Minnie and Cora whose eyes, however, were fixed on the floor.

"For your information, sir, I must tell you, that these two ladies also graciously agreed to share the hotel suite with my boy Chad and me."

"Capital! Capital indeed!" Mr. Harkey rejoiced unaccountably, and put both pen and notebook down. "See here, my dear Coultas, I am glad to be able to tell you that this is not a difficult case at all! Not by a long shot! It reminds me, nonetheless in some of its particulars," and he leaned heavily on the word, "of the rather notorious Aurelia Fairbanks Meadows case, which I solved in under twenty-four hours. Seems, back some years, that Aurelia's grandmother, who was worth forty million dollars, had disappeared unaccountably from a fashionable horticultural show in a fashionable suburb. As the old lady had not made her will, Aurelia was in a state bordering on collapse, indeed paralysis. . . . I found the old woman myself asleep under a big rubber plant. She had decided to take a nap, had overslept, the horticultural gardens closed their doors on her, locking her in, and it was I who found her still sleeping peacefully under the rubber plant. . . . She died, however, several days later, and left all her money to an anti-vivisection society, bestowing not one red penny on Aurelia Fairbanks Meadows." Mr. Harkey then removed a large blue bandana handkerchief from his breast pocket and blew on it loudly.

Mr. Coultas had been attempting for some time to break in on Wilbur Harkey's anecdotal digression without success, and now fearing the old detective might go off on another narrative, he stood up and said brazenly, "I am afraid I must disagree with you, sir!"

"I beg your pardon," the detective spoke with an air of icy contradiction. He held the bandana over his mouth now like a cowboy.

"This is certainly far from an easy case, if I may disagree with you, Mr. Harkey! This case has ramifications. . . . Look here," he appealed now not only to Mr. Harkey but to his lady companions, "I am in very bad odor with my wife Eva and her family, sir. Especially Pauline, my mother-in-law. To put it bluntly, as I know you would wish me to do, Mr. Harkey, I have mishandled her—my wife's family's—fortune in speculative deals which did not, damn it all, bear fruit. If her only son is not found, our Chad, Mr. Harkey, I am facing more than total financial ruin. I am facing prison!"

"Ah, to be sure," the old detective spoke with lofty indifference. "Shall we return to the particulars, however. . . . Now as to your boy's appearance. This is most crucial. Have you by any remote chance, a photo of the young chap?"

"I do indeed, Mr. Harkey," Lewis almost bounded up, and he drew out a Florentine billfold, and from it, after many delays, took out a small photo. "Although this was taken a year or so ago, two to be exact, it is him to a 'T'."

As Mr. Coultas was attempting to put his Florentine billfold back into his pocket, however, a number of gold coins of obviously great value fell from the wallet to the floor, plus what appeared to be several uncut diamonds.

At that moment Mr. Harkey gave the impression of a man who has been physically attacked. He waved his bandana helplessly, stared into the middle of it suspiciously, and then closed his eyes like a preacher in prayer. He was persuaded perhaps to open his eyes by Minnie who was pushing the photo of the disappeared boy into his outstretched palm, and saying something to the old detective too low for Lewis to hear.

"Aha," Harkey exclaimed, staring at the photo. "Must have been taken with a very fine lens to show such detail. . . . But, what have I in hand?" He glanced around at the company with outraged suspicion. "What photo did you say this is, Mr. Coultas, will you tell me?"

"My son, the disappeared boy, sir."

"But this is a photo of an Indian child!" Mr. Harkey retorted accusingly. He waited for an explanation, then hearing none, he spoke in his favorite stage whisper, "Why, he must be a full-blooded Indian. Good-looking of course, but all the same—"

He almost flung the photo in the direction of Mr. Coultas, who picked it up from the table which separated him from the detective.

"You see, Mr. Harkey, the truth is there is distant Indian blood somewhere in his mother's ancestry." Mr. Coultas waited for this bit of information to break some of the tension now rife in the room.

"But I beg to differ with you, my dear Mr. Coultas," the detective spoke now, if not wrathfully, with the sternness of a judge of the highest tribunal. "This very dark young man, charming of course as he must be to members of his own race, does not resemble you in any faintest detail, or I am a blind man!"

Both Minnie and Cora fell back against the upholstery of the chairs they were sitting in as if the verdict of guilty had now been brought in.

"He has, nonetheless, sir," Mr. Coultas went on doggedly, "one blue eye, which the photo does not bring out."

"Ah," Mr. Harkey sighed in a sudden conciliatory way, and asked to see the photo again, which Coultas immediately handed to him.

"Would it be the left eye?"

"No, sir, it happens to be the right one. That's it," he nodded as Mr. Harkey tapped with his pen on the photo.

"The right eye of course!" Mr. Harkey cried, and Minnie and Cora sat erect again on their chairs. "Why this makes my task then all the easier, Mr. Coultas," the detective spoke much more encouragingly. "You should have immediately told me of these particulars when our interview began. As I told you, then, and as Minnie should have informed you from the first, I stand by particulars. And the particulars in this case is the right blue eye! No question about it!"

Mr. Lewis Coultas and the ladies now rose. Mr. Harkey proceeded to kiss both Minnie and Cora on the mouth, and pressed Cora's hand in her fox fur muff vigorously, and then as a final send-off gave Lewis a resounding thwack on his broad back.

"One last word still," Mr. Harkey said to his guests at the door of his suite. "My fee is four thousand dollars."

Lewis bent forward slightly at hearing the figure, but catching sight of Minnie and Cora's eyes upon him, he straightened up to a convincing military posture and muttered with a forced smile on his countenance, "To be sure, sir, to be sure."

When Chad awoke, he was holding fast the reins, and the horse, a sorrel mare, was ambling ahead steadily. But instead of traversing any broad smooth road, Chad saw the horse was taking him on a narrow and winding one. All at once from amongst the many little hills surrounding the road, the sun burst forth in all its glory, wrenching from Chad a sob of delight, for he knew he was at any rate progressing east, though where he was he had not the faintest notion. He shivered with the early morning cold, and flipping the reins, he urged the horse to go faster.

As they were passing a large field of corn shocks, Chad noticed in the center of the field a huge scarcecrow standing in the midst of the shocks, but unlike most scarecrows he had seen this one was garbed in a rather sumptuous mantle and on top of his head there rested a real diadem. Chad tied the horse to a telephone pole, and climbed the barbed wire fence with some difficulty, and then stared his fill at the scarecrow which looked down on him benevolently but sadly. Chad almost fancied that one of the scarecrow's eyes blinked at him, and then he noted that one eye at least was made of glass, while the other was socketless and empty.

"Poor old fellow," Chad mumbled. Then looking around, he saw that almost everywhere someone had put up signs of varying colors and sizes, but all bore the same legend:

ABANDONED ACRES.

WHOEVER ENTERS HERE DOES SO AT HIS OWN EXTREME PERIL!

"I can't let that good mantle and crown stand here in an abandoned field," Chad told himself, and he quickly removed the garment from the scarecrow and then helped himself also to the crown. It was impossible to believe that either crown or mantle had been placed on the body of the scarecrow for very long for they looked, at least to Chad, brand new.

Though he had no looking glass to see himself in, he felt that he must look extraordinary once he had put on both the mantle and the crown, and even the mare lowered and raised her head when she saw him coming back to the wagon in his new apparel, and she neighed again and again at seeing the change in her driver.

"So up and away," he urged the beast, and they ambled on in the direction of the rising sun, Chad looking down constantly to admire the rich stuff of the mantle and occasionally touching the rather elaborate diadem, and completely forgetful that he was driving a horse and wagon without having been taught to do so.

About an hour later, the horse pricked up her ears and nearly came to a full stop. Chad listened intently, and then distantly he caught the sound of a kind of wailing and groaning, even a sort of snoring, and these sounds were punctuated by the clash of cymbals, and the beat of more than a few drums. Urging the horse forward, despite his apprehension, he began to hear, the nearer he got to the first sounds, a chorus of human voices giving forth a kind of wild and uncadenced hymn singing.

As the wagon began to ascend a steep hill, Chad saw at the very top of the incline a rather spacious building resembling a barn which carried on its roof the cross of Christ. A crowd of at least a hundred persons all dressed in nightgowns and carrying banners was approaching the horse and its driver. At this very moment, the sun rested on Chad so brightly that he could barely see an inch ahead of him. Chad could hear the footsteps, nonetheless, coming directly up to the wagon.

"He has fulfilled the prophecy!" a tall bony man in a purple robe cried, who Chad would later discover was called Brother Phineas.

Chad was now barely able to see. The man in the robe had come to within a few inches of the wagon, and he moved a small cross held in his right hand.

"Wake up, chosen one," the man addressed Chad directly.

"Bronze as the earth, just like the prophecy foretold," the man known as Brother Phineas now addressed a handful of persons likewise dressed in robes, who thronged about the wagon.

"Come down, anointed one, come down," Phineas admonished Chad, who at last relinquished the reins and jumped to the ground. Turning his back to the blazing sun, he faced the crowd of robed men and women.

"We have been waiting for you, wonderful youth, for countless ages!" the same Phineas now went on. He had a shock of straw-colored hair, wide green eyes, and a thin very red pair of lips. His entire face was so covered with freckles he resembled a light-skinned Negro.

"Our waiting is at last at its end," Phineas spoke to the other robed figures. "Brothers, behold the messenger!"

The robed men and women began embracing and kissing Chad.

"Where is your scepter?" the freckled man inquired.

Chad's eyes fell on the bullwhip lying on the floor of the wagon. He picked it up cautiously and held it up for the freckle-faced man's inspection.

Later—perhaps months, even years later—Chad realized that there was nothing he could have done at the time to disabuse the men about his true identity. For one thing he was much too tired to set them right, and besides every time he tried to raise his voice by way of explanation, they drowned him out with their chanting and hymn singing, calling him the voyager from beyond the realm, long-expected, and he who arrived at the very split second of the prophecy. The only possible drawback to his being the "true messenger from the other realm" was that his scepter looked too much like a common rawhide, but this discrepancy was ignored when one took in his dark, almost black complexion save for the one blue eye, and it was his complexion more than anything else which bespoke him as the authentic herald.

Brother Phineas and his assistant dean named Brother Silvester now led the procession, both men taking Chad carefully by the arm like arresting officers with a prisoner. The chanting and hymn singing continued so loudly that Chad several times broke loose from his preceptors to put his fingers in his ears, but Brother Phineas rebuked him so severely that Chad allowed his arms to be taken hold of again, and they proceeded up the steep hill to the church.

After countless huzzahs and the clash of cymbals and the beating of drums, Chad and the two deacons now entered the old barn remodeled into a church. Upon entering the door through which cows, sheep, and horses once had made their way Chad caught sight of a dining room which even dwarfed the palatial salon of the hotel on the lake in Chicago. A banquet was already in progress, but as Chad and the deacons entered, all the diners stood up stiffly, and each placed his right hand over his heart and they all pronounced some words in unison.

Chad was ushered to the head of the table on a seat raised higher than the other diners by a towering dais. Once he was helped to sit down, all the diners raised their glasses to him, and again he heard some words which were totally unintelligible to him.

"What is in the goblet?" Chad managed to raise his voice loud enough to be heard this time.

"The ceremonial wine of course," Brother Phineas seemed shocked by his ignorance. 'You certainly have that in your realm," he added with careless ill humor.

Chad's attention strayed now to another mammoth open door in the side of the building beyond which he could see smoke rising from the carcass of an entire ox which was being roasted by two young men wearing only towels about their middles. Chad felt he would be much more comfortable assisting them in roasting the ox than sitting at the head of a table of people who were drinking goblet after goblet of wine.

Chided and urged on by Brother Phineas, the boy began tasting the liquor in the goblet which seemed to him both sweet and corrosive at the same time, and caused him first to sneeze violently and then to cough for a considerable while.

After hours of eating and drinking, a white-haired man wearing goggles leant over him. It was Brother Averil, a retired deacon who still led the congregation in prayer when he was up to it.

"What is the text of your sermon today, Brother?" Averil now questioned Chad.

The fierceness of the old man's countenance caused Chad to babble, but when the retired minister put iron pressure on his arm, Chad in panic recalled a stray sentence or two from his Sunday school class, and after repeated urging and nagging on the part of the old man, the boy got out:

"A horse is a
vain thing for
safety."

"And what book of the Bible is that from, my dear young Master?" the old man wanted to know.

"From the Psalms of David of course," Chad was able to reply.

"And you say that is your text today?"

Chad nodded, and began chewing on the tough half-cooked barbecue of ox, and then, sighing, he took a swallow from his sixth goblet of wine.

The next thing Chad recalled was that he was standing behind the pulpit which came almost to his mouth, staring down at a huge Bible, and then confusedly peering out at an enormous multitude of faces looking anxiously at him.

He then heard Brother Averil announce the text of the sermon with quavering voice: " 'A horse is a vain thing for safety, the Psalms.' "

Vigorous and prolonged applause greeted the citing of the text just as Chad's head fell with a bang against the great gold Bible open before him.

Lifting his head against the blow he had received falling against the pulpit, Chad realized perhaps for the first time that all those anxious faces out there were waiting for him to say something! He who could barely say ten words in succession in Bess Lytle's remedial English class.

There was a stony silence of many minutes, and then the rising tide of coughs, throat-clearings, and mutterings, followed by an angry and rising murmur of impatience and at last anger.

Stepping a little to the side of the pulpit, Chad raised his right hand, and there was an incipient burst of applause.

He began, "My flesh and blood father, on the first occasion of kidnapping me, once quoted to me a saying from Shakespeare:

'Mislike me not for my complexion'."

A strong tempest of applause vibrated through the roomy barn-church.

Encouraged by this show of support, Chad continued.

"My father who kidnapped me first is 100 percent Ojibwa, that's a redskin of course, but my next, and real father, that is the one whose name I bear, told Minnie and Cora, his lady companions in the big hotel on the lake, that he'd got to the place where he didn't give a tinker's damn if I was his flesh-and-blood son or not because the one thing a man has to have if he is a man is a son, and it's better in the long run even to be stuck with an Indian boy than nobody at all, and he was therefore settling his bet on me, and if they didn't like it they could both take a plunge in the lake."

People in the audience now began rising and exchanging comments with their neighbors in loud voices, and one elderly woman came clear up to the stage and bent her ear to be able to catch more clearly what the unusual speaker was saying. Brother Averil had risen too—he was seated a few feet from Chad on the platform—but having risen he hardly knew where or how to proceed.

But as the entire concourse of some two hundred people in the audience became more restive and anxious, more bewildered and out of humor, Chad himself was growing more relaxed and at ease telling the story of his life.

"Cora and Minnie were not the kind of women I am used to," he went on, though his voice was almost inaudible by reason of the buzz and hum and shouting coming from the audience who were now all on their feet and beginning to stomp.

"The sight of these ladies without anything on lying next to my dad . . . for even if Decatur is right, and he's not my dad . . . still does Lewis Coultas have the right to sleep with women when he has my mother for his wife? I don't think Bess Lytle herself would have been able to stand what I had to stand, and that is saying a good deal. The day the parents of one of her pupils shot the superintendent of schools to death—that was before I went to school with her—she took that murder in stride, for the sight of blood don't make her turn a hair. But I think she would never have been able to stomach my legal dad Lewis Coultas carrying on with two ladies in a state of nature in one of the most expensive hotels in the world. That is why I am here today, ladies and gentlemen, I could not stand the sight of my legal dad lying stark naked there in the bed with them."

Cries of "Stop him!" "Is there no end to this rigamarole?" "How can the Church tolerate such a travesty?" "He is out of order!" "Arrest that scamp!" and so on resounded through the church.

Chad was weaving now around the pulpit, and finally left its precincts entirely and stood dizzily at the very edge of the stage.

"I have learned, though, ladies and gentlemen, through all of this, one thing, and that is the text I have memorized from Sunday school:

'A horse is no use at all except to
escape with—hits the nail on the head!'

"For if my great-grandfather had had his way I would not be here today for he had planned to do away with me to spite his grandson Decatur, or at least remove my one blue eye."

Chad pointed a bit sheepishly now to his eye.

But then there occurred what might be called a mild kind of riot. The pent-up rage and shame of the congregation at having to hear such disconnected, trivial and unintelligible discourse coming from what seemed more and more apparent was a child, caused men and women to begin slapping, then striking, and finally beating one another. Fisticuffs flew as in a mining camp on a Saturday night.

And everywhere cries from the strong and younger men were heard. "This calls for tarring and feathering!"

Men now began running in the direction of where the ox had been roasted, and great containers with the tar already inside were lifted on the same flames which had been used to roast the ox.

Although Chad had left the stage and was wandering about by the huge vats of tar being heated, nobody paid the slightest attention to him.

Four young men now appeared from the cellar of the barn carrying huge sacks full of goose, hen and duck feathers. They carefully opened the bags, and began putting the feathers down on a clean pair of sheets.

"Why don't you go on home on your pony, kid," one of the boys sorting the feathers remarked to him surreptitiously, "This is strictly church business, so get out while you can get!" The boy giving this advice then helped Chad straighten his diadem and tuck up his mantle. "Your pony is right over there," he admonished him.

Walking backward, however, so as not to miss what was going on, Chad saw two of the young men who had been roasting the ox now leading Brother Phineas and Silvester, their hands tied with stout cord behind them, toward the cooking vats of tar.

Brother Phineas especially was extremely upset, and kept swearing he was innocent, but Silvester spat in the faces of one of his accusers. Without more ado they were then stripped of the remainder of their clothes, and while other men held them securely the tar was spread over their trembling bodies. Phineas was silent on this treatment, but Silvester raised his voice saying that he was being scalded and burnt to death, but his cries were stilled when some of the hot tar was placed directly over his complaining lips.

It took very little time, Chad saw, now seated on his wagon and holding the reins, for the feathers of duck, hen and goose to be applied as generously on the former deacons' bodies as the tar had been.

Everybody surrounding the malefactors, however, gasped either in admiration or perhaps unbelief when they saw the two men who had once been pillars of the church suddenly transformed into huge ostrich-like birds, waving their arms now transformed incongruously into flopping wings.

Some of the congregation then catching sight of Chad in his wagon shouted, "Imposter! Renegade! Heretic! Sodomite!" and though they made no effort to come after him, Chad raised his whip and his horse began trotting smartly onward, and Chad soon lost sight of the strange spectacle of the tarring and feathering.

A peculiar and ominous change was taking place in Lewis Coultas as he awaited sunset of the next day, much to the disappointment and vexation of Minnie and Cora. He was not the wonderful "playmate" he had been in times past, and although they all three went to bed frequently with one another that day prior to receiving word from Wilbur Harkey as to the whereabouts of Chad, both Minnie and Cora, in private conversation with one another, deplored Lewis's present lack of zeal and loss of his old pep and spunk.

"All over a kid who is not even his!" Cora complained.

"And I think he is actually homesick for that bedridden frump of a wife of his," Minnie chided with distrust.

The girls were also very put out that Lewis had had the gall to place a framed photo of Eva in their sleeping room. Her undoubted beauty (which Cora laid to the photograph's being retouched) irked both women to the breaking point. To solace themselves, Minnie paid one of the more experienced bellhops to bring them all the champagne he safely could, and also a gramophone and some Paul Whiteman records.

The two girls danced together, drank the champagne and would look in occasionally on Lewis who sat glumly by Eva's photo garbed in a brand new dressing gown which he had purchased in one of the spiffy hotel men's shops that morning.

Occasionally Lewis would rise, sip some of the ladies' champagne, and dance a few steps with Minnie, then with Cora, in his bedroom slippers above which were visible imported gleaming gold and red garters.

"Your worries will soon all be over, honey," Cora tried to cheer him. "When sunset comes and old Wilbur Harkey arrives, you'll see. Nothing can happen to that boy of yours, remember!"

Lewis stopped dancing and stared at Cora.

"What are you talking about, you simp!" he shouted. "Everything can happen to a boy like that, and *does.*" He glared at both women with fiery indignation. "Sometimes you both make me sick!"

"Well, see here, Cora and I are not having our finest hour with you either," Minnie shouted back. "Your visit has become more of a wake than a gala, if you ask me."

"Gala be damned," Lewis raised his fist, threatening. "It's sunset, ain't it, and that boy is not here as promised, by Jesus."

"Now, now, children," Cora interposed, "let's not get riled, after all we have been through over the years. Let's keep cool and collected, dear hearts. Steady does it!"

Appeased a little, Lewis went up to each girl in turn and kissed and hugged and pressed their bosoms as only he, after all, knew how. They danced another threesome and were getting to feel more like old times when there was an almost brutal banging at the door to spoil everything. Cora shut off the gramophone, and Lewis quickly slipped on some trousers and a tie while Minnie went cautiously to the door, listened studiously, and then recognizing that familiar breathing, opened the door.

At first, however, she feared she had encountered a perfect stranger, for the countenance before her was not familiar. But when the stranger threw his arms around her and cried, "My dearest love," she recognized the old detective, for what had occurred between sunset and sunset was that Wilbur Harkey had, perhaps inspired by Cora and Minnie, gone back to his old practice of dyeing his hair again a kind of purple black, as well as retouching his rather long eyelashes and thick eyebrows, so that if he looked no younger (Lewis thought he looked one hundred), he was a continent away from resembling the old white-maned detective who had promised results by sundown.

"Sit here, Mr. Harkey," Lewis offered him a place on the ottoman. "And allow me to pour you some champagne, sir."

"Never touch spirits when working on a case," Wilbur Harkey intoned, winking at Cora and Minnie. "Honor bound . . . I will help myself, though, to one of those Havana cigars which I see lying on the stand here."

It was actually Minnie's last cigar (Lewis did not smoke), and she parted with it rather ungenerously. Lewis helped the old detective light up with a common kitchen match, and then all four parties faced one another like persons waiting for the judge's entrance into a packed courtroom.

"We have news of your boy, Mr. Coultas," the detective began after coughing violently and staring at the cigar. He produced another kind of bandana handkerchief, this one of a bright crocus color, and he wiped his entire face very carefully before putting it away.

"Lots of news," the old man finished, and shook his head.

"But where in the blazes is he?" Lewis spoke in choking impatience.

"Now, now," Cora cautioned Coultas. "Let good Mr. Harkey proceed in his own time and fashion."

"Well, damn it, as I said before he walked in, it's sunset, ain't it, and now an hour past it!"

"Mr. Coultas," Wilbur Harkey spoke soothingly, "let me say this is a much thornier case than the Aurelia Fairbanks Meadows affair I told you about during our first professional conference." Mr. Harkey was speaking in a mellifluous tone while working energetically the two wedding rings on his finger.

"Aurelia Meadows be damned to flaming hell and back, sir! You were paid to bring my boy home by sunset, and by Christ, where is he? I ask, you, *where is he?*"

"And where, my good sir, is the four thousand dollars owing me?" Mr. Harkey cried, and patted down his recently dyed hair.

"You shall not have one red cent until the boy is safe and sound in my hands."

"Now, gentlemen, gentlemen, let us not lose our heads," Minnie interposed.

"Indeed, we should all be calm in a situation like this," Cora agreed, and finished her fourth glass of champagne.

"Be that as it may," Mr. Harkey went on, shuffling some papers which he had brought out together with his crocus bandana, "I have had reports, however, of the runaway."

The papers which he was shuffling were apparently telegraph wires, and putting on some spectacles so thick his eyes resembled fish swimming deep under water, Mr. Harkey commenced to read:

"A boy having one blue eye and one black one and of distinct Indian cast of countenance and complexion has beaten an old man, another Indian, nearly to death, but the old man refuses to prefer charges on the grounds he and his assailant are blood kin."

Upon this Mr. Harkey removed his glasses and stared quizzically at Lewis Coultas.

"Second," Harkey went on, slamming the glasses back over his eyes, "he robbed a local shrine of its mantle and diadem and, so garbed, totally disrupted the one hundredth anniversary of the Resurrection Epiphany Pentecostal Church by posing as a Messiah, and delivering an address to the congregation of such foul obscenity and indecency that it resulted in a riot and the tarring and feathering of the principal deacons. . . . This boy is now at large somewhere in the northern wilderness of Michigan."

"Rotgut!" Mr. Coultas cried, and rising seized the telegraphic messages from Mr. Harkey's emaciated fingers. He stared at the documents with loathing and unbelief, and then without any warning whatsoever, tore them all to shreds and flung the pieces in the old man's face.

"There are laws on the books concerning such behavior, let me warn you, Mr. Lewis Coultas. Laws concerning assault and battery!" the detective wailed and looked at the scraps of torn paper and then at Minnie and Cora.

"Yes, Lewis, for God's sake, be careful what you are about," Minnie begged him, and she recalled just then having seen an old scrapbook of his write-ups and of his short but brilliant career as a pugilist.

"Yes, Lewis, for once pay heed to what Minnie is saying. Do not let that temper of yours get the better of you in this situation," Cora added her entreaty.

"Will both you whores keep your traps shut!" Lewis now vociferated as Cora chimed in with her sister.

"Look here, Harkey," Lewis now took the floor, "and quit winking at these dames as you palaver. You were to bring my boy back by sunset, instead of foisting off on me these ridiculous trumped-up accusations masquerading as telegrams. Telegrams which you yourself probably wrote! You are a humbug and a disgrace to your profession and your sex coming in here with hennaed hair like some old madame in a sporting house. By Christ, I won't allow it! I won't have it!"

And without warning he picked up one of the footstools and threw it into the largest of the windows, smashing it almost completely.

Minnie, Cora and Mr. Harkey all held their hands over their heads expected to be attacked; but when no more violence was forthcoming, the two ladies, with a good deal of whispering and muttering and countless expressions of sympathy and effusive apologies, ushered Mr. Harkey out of the suite and into the hall.

Out of Lewis's earshot, Minnie tried to explain the unspeakable behavior of Mr. Lewis Coultas to the old investigator.

"He has taken leave of his senses, Mr. Harkey, all over that child who is not even related to him at all—in the view at least of Cora and me. He seems to be totally infatuated with the little half-breed, and your not being able to produce the boy as scheduled at sunset, has evidently unhinged him. And here Cora and I thought he was the personification of steadiness and dependability. Ah, how wrong one can be in one's estimate of another human being!"

Mr. Harkey gazed at Minnie with icy skepticism written over his flushed face. But as the detective was about to say something, Cora handed him a thousand dollar bill, which the old man examined on both sides before pocketing it without so much as a thank-you.

"Now whatever you do, dearest Wilbur," Minnie admonished him, and kissed him several times on the cheek, on the mouth and then over one of his eyes, "whatever you are tempted to do or say, don't for mercy's sake, go off this case! Do you hear me? We have been through too much together, Wilbur, for you to shirk this task!"

Mr. Harkey thought over her advice, and reluctantly nodded.

"I have never been so abused," the old man complained. "In all my fifty odd years as attorney, private investigator, holder of public office . . . never, never have I been so grossly abused! I should sue him."

Minnie again covered his face with her kisses.

"No, darling Wilbur, pray don't even think of such a thing. Please think back to all our old trouble together. *Hush,* remember, you told me then, is our motto. *Hush* it shall be today and from this time hence. Produce the boy, that's all we are asking of you. Produce him, and then we can let the whole thing go hang!"

"Ah, what would the world be without the ladies," Wilbur Harkey exclaimed and took both Minnie and Cora in his arms. "Such sensible advice, my charming dears. You should have been members of the bar! You would have brought a new note to jurisprudence and the law courts!"

At this moment the elevator finally arrived and the two ladies kissed their hands at the old man as he prepared to leave them. Minnie slipped the elevator man a bill and told him to convey the gentleman to a taxi at once.

Once Wilbur Harkey was gone, Minnie and Cora threw themselves into one another's arms and gave vent to their frustration and general indignation.

Returning to the suite, they found Lewis soaking his head in a chamber pot of ice water. He looked up and grinned at them. They had never seen him look so handsome, with the ice water running down over his exposed chest and the tattoos on his arm. His indisputable male charm stifled any speech of complaint the ladies might have given forth. Minnie rushed over to him, and gave a resounding kiss on his "rugged bosom" as she called it, and Cora followed suit.

"Why can't you forget him?" Cora wheedled.

"Who is *him?*" Lewis simpered, touching her nipples.

"That Indian boy," Minnie muttered, nestling in one of his armpits.

"Yes, and why don't you divorce Eva?" Cora begged him. "We could open a gambling house and make all of us a sizeable fortune."

"Oh, God knows, God only knows," Lewis again became melancholy, but then grinning negligently he allowed the two women assiduously to undress him, and then, mother-naked, he was led to the bedroom.

Wilbur Harkey was so discountenanced over his treatment at the hands of Lewis Coultas, and to a lesser degree by the cooing insincerity of Minnie and Cora, that he cancelled further engagements at his office and returned at once, without informing his wife of his early arrival, to his fifteen-room apartment overlooking the now savagely churning lake.

As he removed his two scarves, ear tabs, his horse blanket of an overcoat, his beaver hat, and his three vests, he thought he heard coming from the front parlor sounds resembling, in his peculiar phrase, *serious osculation,* the wet, repeated kind.

In deathly fear of adultery (as he had always feared it in his first marriage to Gabrielle), Mr. Harkey staunchly cleared his throat persistently and noisily, coughed his usual four or five times, and knocked a door weight or two out of his way before opening the door on the front parlor from which the sounds were issuing.

He found, to his pleased relief, that his chauffeur, Hibbard Grady, was blowing on a cornet, while his wife, Emma Lou, sat in rapture at the tea room table. Two cups of coffee were in evidence, and a small bowl of whipped cream (Emma Lou always took her coffee Viennese style).

Emma, a young brunette of about 19 with heavily penciled eyebrows and an elaborate Cupid's bow mouth, leaped up from her seat at once, but showed no trace of guilt or fear before her husband.

"What a delightful surprise!" Emma cried, and immediately offered her face to Mr. Harkey for his kisses.

Meanwhile Hibbard Grady, having bowed to his employer, was busily wiping his mouth of saliva, for the exertion of playing the cornet had obviously taxed him. But just as he turned to take his leave of Mr. and Mrs. Harkey, the investigator thought he noticed a copious residue of lipstick on the young employee's cheek, but Emma had already closed the door on him before Mr. Harkey could verify his suspicion.

"My only dearest," Emma cried, "you look utterly exhausted!" She cradled her husband tenderly in her arms as she said this. "Why don't you sit here, love of my life, where the strong upper-light won't hurt your very sensitive eyes."

His wife's consoling words brought back to him the scene with Lewis Coultas and the two "harpies," Minnie and Cora, and he burst into sobs.

Emma Lou had never seen her husband weep, indeed had never seen a grown man in tears before, and possibly did not know that men wept. She was rendered speechless for a moment, and then fearful her husband might have overheard some of the intimate things she had been saying to the chauffeur, she took out one of her finest silk handkerchiefs and wiped Mr. Harkey's face free of tears. He clutched her free hand and brought it to his tired old lips. The vision of Lewis Coultas tearing up the telegrams and throwing the pieces in his face created another outburst of grief, and his palsied hand went into his breast pocket and brought out the pieces of yellow telegram.

"He struck me full in the face with these," he vented his anger, and he handed Emma the torn pieces of paper, and began blubbering again.

Emma studied the scraps of paper. "A child has been kidnapped?"

"Yes, his legal son, though an Indian," Wilbur told her. But his eyes just then caught sight of the kitchen door partly ajar, and he was positive he saw the chauffeur standing there listening.

"Would you have Hibbard step in here a moment," Wilbur told Emma.

Emma put down the pieces of the telegram. "Yes, darling, but may I ask why?"

"I have my own personal reasons, my dear," he explained.

Emma Lou now behaved in a rather peculiar fashion, though perhaps Wilbur Harkey paid no particular attention to this oddity. Emma Lou walked backwards to the kitchen door, and then still facing her husband, she whispered, turning her lips toward the opening in the kitchen door, "Come in here, you idiot."

Hibbard Grady, all six feet four, holding high his barrel chest, entered, approached his employer, bowed rather low for a chauffeur.

"May I look at your face, Hibbard," the old man inquired in his courtroom manner.

Hibbard bowed again and stepped even closer.

Putting on stronger glasses, Wilbur Harkey studied the swarthy, somewhat sweaty countenance (sweating probably from the exertions of blowing the cornet) of his chauffeur, and then spoke in his forensic manner.

"Either, Hibbard Grady, you have just washed your face, or I was mistaken in thinking I saw lipstick on your cheeks and lower lip."

At this accusation, Emma Lou, who, after all, was only nineteen, broke down into weeping, and when coming up for breath every so often, she could be heard to exclaim, "How can you doubt me, oh how can you, dear Wilbur!"

Emma Lou was as prone to these weeping spells as her predecessor, Gabrielle, so that Mr. Harkey barely took note of it. Indeed his mind now all but completely strayed from the goings-on in his front parlor, his cheating young wife, and the cornet-blowing chauffeur. His memory was fully taken up again with the indignities he had suffered that day with the two harpies and Lewis Coultas.

"They are a brace of abandoned harlots, both of them," the old man cried out loudly as he relived his humiliation, "and by Christ, I'll see them all in prison, the whole pack of them!"

"Who, who, precious Wilbur?" Emma Lou begged of her husband, and she gave Hibbard Grady a look of imploring desperation.

To her added terror she all at once saw that the chauffeur had not entirely closed his fly, and she tried to point this out to Hibbard by gesturing wildly at the open trousers. Wilbur Harkey came out of his fit of absentmindedness long enough to see this gesture.

Leaping up, he seized hold of the finger with which Emma had been pointing at Hibbard's trousers as if he had caught a malefactor in the very act of performing a crime.

"What is the meaning of that motion with your finger, madam?" he roared.

Emma made every effort to weep, but no sound issued from her rebuked countenance, and Wilbur, his eyes dry as a sand bar, slapped her smartly across her face.

"How dare you engage in lewd motions before the very eyes of your husband," Wilbur Harkey upbraided her, and he rolled his eyes from his wife to Hibbard.

"Now see here, sir," Hibbard Grady now stepped forward. "I cannot tolerate your striking a lady in my presence. I won't have it, sir, employer or no employer!" He advanced threateningly toward the old detective.

Emma interposed herself between the two contending parties.

"I can explain everything, everything," Emma begged her husband. "Give me just ten words, or at least the number of words in a telegram."

"Telegrams be damned to hell," Wilbur shrieked at her, and Hibbard put up his two fists.

Just then the front doorbell rang imperiously, and Wilbur

Harkey, perhaps suffering another of his lapses of attention from the very scene in which he was playing so prominent a part, walked off in a hurry to the front door, and opened it with alacrity on Minnie, Cora, and Lewis Coultas himself.

"My dear Mr. Harkey," Lewis Coultas began with effusive, sweet conciliation, "I am here to offer my deepest and most heartfelt apology to you, sir."

"Have you brought the four thousand dollars?" Mr. Harkey wondered, and without further ado ushered the threesome into his front parlor.

"No, Mr. Harkey, that I have not," Lewis replied, "but you shall have it very shortly. . . . Meanwhile I have a promissory note to the effect that I am in your debt for that amount of money."

Mr. Harkey's attention, however, had again strayed from the business at hand to the sight of Emma Lou and Hibbard Grady standing in a supplicating pose before him. Both had their hands clasped before them in an identical manner.

"Are your bags packed, madam?" Mr. Harkey thundered at Emma.

"Oh, Wilbur, Wilbur," Emma was begging him, and Hibbard Grady mumbled a string of apologies.

Mr. Harkey now turned to the Lewis Coultas party, and said, "I have caught this hussy and this strapping hulk of a chauffeur billing and cooing in my absence. He blows a cornet to disguise the sound of their lovemaking, I've no doubt. I am therefore turning them both out into the street."

"Oh, give her a second chance, sir," Lewis Coultas warmly defended the guilty parties, and Minnie and Cora stepped up to the old investigator and echoed Lewis's plea, taking Wilbur's hands in theirs and pressing each of his fingers warmly.

Mr. Harkey extricated his hands from the two ladies. "I had no idea, of course, they were carrying on together. It was the cornet playing which deceived me, I reckon. Got deafened to its blowing sound so I didn't hear her being kissed."

Mr. Harkey shook his head, and grinned wryly.

"Very well," he rather quickly agreed, "Emma, you may stay the night, and tomorrow I will talk over a settlement. Go to your respective rooms, now, Emma Lou and Hibbard, if you will be so obliging, and try to control yourselves when alone. I must take up the matter of the Indian youth's kidnapping at once!"

Emma Lou again went through her rigamarole of leaving the room by walking backwards, this time throwing kiss after kiss of gratitude in the direction of Wilbur. The chauffeur had already disappeared.

"I have seen that Emma Lou somewhere before, Wilbur," Minnie told the detective.

"I am positive I have seen her," Cora echoed her sister.

Mr. Harkey gave the two ladies a severe look, and then turned his attention to Lewis Coultas.

"Your boy will be found, Mr. Coultas, rest assured of that. I have spent fifty years in the courts and nearly twenty as a private investigator. I have never lost a case, never. Your boy may be in Indian territory as we speak, but he will be found and returned to you, even if he wanders as far as the coast of China."

Mr. Harkey was silent a moment as he examined the promissory note Lewis had handed him. "My question is, however, Mr. Lewis Coultas," he gazed steadfastly at the Indian boy's father, "my query, sir, is this: Is such a young hellion worth all the hullabaloo of being returned to you? Think on that, my dear Coultas, and think hard."

Everybody leaped up just then as if by a spring in the seats they were seated in, and shaking hands all around they all took leave of one another with gaiety and good humor.

Alone in his spacious lakefront suite hours later, Mr. Harkey, without warning, perhaps astounding even himself, all at once let out a reverberating roar, followed by cries of vexation, rage and incoherent choler. Seizing his wedding finger as if he had grasped perhaps the throat of the young chauffeur who had cuckolded him, he tore off the upper ring from his finger, leaving the ring with which he had married his long-lamented Gabrielle. Then falling back into the pliant cushions of a Parisian divan, he cried out like a bereaved orphan until the night maid came on duty and handed him his brandy and almond cookies.

In the wake of his exertions, however, a huge white strand of his still abundant hair untouched by the dyer's art came loose and fell over his eyes, and the sight of this hoary reminder of his age and dereliction caused him to give forth even louder lamentations. But gradually, sipping one brandy after another and munching through the entire assortment of cookies, his grief at last subsided.

Morning found Wilbur Harkey still sipping brandy, toying with the white strands of his hair not touched by the dye, muttering about the professional disgrace he found himself in, and occasionally still moaning over his second wife's infidelity. He was so bemused he did not notice in fact that Emma Lou had entered the room and was speaking to him. He ignored her. She advanced closer to him with a stealthy, hesitant tread, for she feared he might throw something at her as he had once before, causing her to have to go to a plastic surgeon for her torn lips.

Getting no response from her husband, Emma finally kneeled by his bedroom slippers and held his thin shanks in her embrace.

"Don't send me away, Daddy, please don't, I will be good."

"Why it's you, is it?" Wilbur Harkey looked down at her. "Poor thing, you forget, don't you, that I can see through every one of your wiles."

She cried easily and loudly, for a long sleep in Hibbard's arms had restored the flow of her lachrymal glands. Wilbur Harkey ran his fingers through her tresses.

"You won't send me back then, Daddy?"

"Back to where I found you?" Wilbur Harkey laughed his unmusical ominous laugh. "My precious sweetheart, perhaps even *they* would not have you now, rotten to the core though they were then and if alive still are."

"I will be a good wife to you if you let me stay, Daddy. Hibbard Grady means nothing to me. And after all, I gave him only a few sisterly kisses."

Wilbur Harkey had quit listening to his second wife and was studying himself in an elaborate looking glass which he always kept handy.

"I wonder if you could freshen up the strands of white hair Priscilla Edwards seems to have missed on her last visit." He gave Emma Lou a look of reprieve at that moment. "I have to see Mr. Lewis Coultas today, my dear, and I'd like to look at my professional best," he explained.

"You're not going to see the man who insulted you, my love, and threw your telegrams in your face? Oh, Daddy, please think twice before you do such a thing!"

Mr. Harkey smiled tolerantly and took Emma Lou's hand in his.

"Yes, I am, my dear." He studied her pretty face with a kind of rapture. "My professional reputation is at stake here. I promised Coultas sunset, and sunset came and went without his boy."

While Wilbur Harkey was explaining the ramifications of the Lewis Coultas kidnapping case, Emma had rung for Hibbard Grady, who now stood patiently on the threshold of the room.

"Mr. Harkey's hair-dye equipment, in the bathroom, Hibbard, the upper cabinet drawer. And some hot water and plenty of towels."

Wilbur Harkey nodded in approbation of his wife's orders to the chauffeur, who immediately went for the various articles in question.

Emma Lou took Wilbur's hand in hers. "You should always let me touch up your hair, Daddy. If I may speak openly, Priscilla Edwards is past her prime as a hairdresser. You see, she stinted on your eyebrows also and your beautiful lashes. The colors don't match. Oh, oh, so careless!"

Emma Lou raised herself up then and kissed Wilbur Harkey on those parts of his countenance Priscilla Edwards had neglected.

"Oh, we will be happy as larks if you will take me back, Daddy. I promise!"

"We shall see, my dear," Mr. Harkey smiled in spite of himself. "We shall see. Of course I have removed my wedding ring you gave me during our marriage ceremony." Here he raised his wedding finger for her inspection. "I have left on, of course, the ring with which I wedded Gabrielle."

"Oh, Gabrielle, Gabrielle!" Emma Lou cried with jealous rage, "that is all I have ever heard from you. No wonder our marriage has foundered. Gabrielle! Gabrielle!"

"Now, now, my little precious," the old man chuckled, and he pressed her to him. "I am pleased to see you jealous. It bodes well for a reconciliation perhaps, But we shall see. We shall see."

Meanwhile Hibbard Grady had brought the dyeing equipment, and Emma was soon busy at work. She had placed a hot towel over her husband's head and eyes, and every so often Hibbard Grady would give her a rather vigorous pressure on her behind.

Emma now began going over with thorough precision and elaborate, meticulous detail the work of Priscilla Edwards. After an hour of her ministrations, she drew back from her work, and cried, "Much improved! Indeed, very nice, Wilbur!"

Wilbur studied himself carefully in the looking glass.

"You have missed one little strand here, my one and only," Wilbur pointed out to her.

Emma Lou quickly and without resentment touched up his one remaining hoary lock. All parties then—Emma Lou, Hibbard, and Wilbur Harkey—gave out great sighs of satisfaction and relief.

"Now to see Mr. Lewis Coultas, my lovely, and thence to a long motor trip to Northern Michigan or who knows? Perhaps Canada where that damned Indian brat is in hiding. . . . Oh I have informers, spies, you may call them. There is very little Wilbur Harkey does not finally get wind of! Sunset may have come and gone, 'tis true, but I know where the brat is! And to think he's not even Mr. Coultas's son. A legal bastard, but a bastard all the same and a half-breed to boot!"

Hibbard and Emma Lou both listened with bated breath to the old man, but Emma had the courage to break in, "Why can't Hibbard and I accompany you, dear heart, on this wild goose chase—I mean this search of yours."

Wilbur Harkey was patting his enormous mound of hair with a fresh towel, and then gave a last look to see if any of the expensive imported dye (he procured it expressly from Budapest) had come off on the fabric. When none appeared, he smiled contentedly.

"Did you hear what I said, Daddy?" Emma Lou persisted.

Wilbur Harkey thought back on her words, then grinned unaccountably.

"A capital idea, my dear," he replied. "You and Hibbard accompanying me. . . . It will be a rugged journey, though, my pretty, and you will not be allowed to have a sick headache, mind you, as we will go down back roads and are apt to place our lives in jeopardy, for I think some of the Indian chiefs may be behind the brat's recent moves. This is a *deep* brat, mark my words, who is up to something that bears watching. His legal dad Coultas is a crook himself. But let me say something here of great import to you two young people. The war between the white man and the redskins will never be over! This is my firm conviction! Remember that, my precious, when I am gone, if you don't remember another thing I ever imparted to you. The white man, and the redskin. . . ."

"But, Daddy, I never want you to leave me," Emma Lou cried piteously.

"Yes, my poor dove," Mr. Harkey spoke with satisfaction, "What will you do without me? What did you do before I came on the scene?" Mr. Harkey looked triumphantly at Hibbard Grady, and addressed him. "I found Emma Lou in a room with thirteen other orphans, all nearly nude, without food or toilet facilities, and with only white mice for company."

Hibbard Grady now stared at Emma Lou with a look between misgiving and desire. Then he nodded vigorously to Mr. Harkey and said something which passed for the appropriate.

"We have been through a lot together, since she was an orphan without food or toilet facilities," Mr. Harkey went on. "Of course she can't hold a candle to my late departed Gabrielle. Emma Lou doesn't even profess to, do you, Emma?"

"Daddy knows I don't," she replied and gave Hibbard a wicked wink.

"Then let us be off to Mr. Lewis Coultas, the noted speculator who's kept out of prison more skillfully than Houdini slips out of chains. As I say, my professional reputation, indeed, my entire future is at stake. God, the humiliation of these last hours! The sheer declivity of it all! Wilbur Harkey having to eat humble pie to a Beau Brummel of a cad and a scoundrel! And that Minnie and Cora, sisters, you know. What are they but hired strumpets for Coultas's insatiable appetite for human flesh!"

"You might have had the courtesy to tell us you were coming!" Cora almost shrieked on opening the door on Wilbur Harkey, Emma, and Hibbard Grady.

"Why you've brought a regular delegation, haven't you, Wilbur," Minnie tried to soften Cora's ill-natured greeting, kissed the old investigator warmly on the mouth, bowed to Emma Lou, and gave Hibbard Grady a long and lingering look.

"Apologies are in order, of course, ladies," Wilbur agreed, and proceeded to the center of the front room, and began removing his outer garments. "But the matter between Mr. Lewis Coultas and me cannot wait! I am his representative until Chad Coultas is found, dead or alive, and in that capacity I will not shirk my duties, I will not resign my responsibilities, and I will not be gainsaid!"

Minnie began to applaud, and Emma, Hibbard, and Cora followed suit. Wilbur Harkey beamed under the sound of approbation much as he had when, as a prosecuting attorney, he had concluded a speech to the jury urging the death penalty.

"But see here," the detective cried, softened by the applause, "I don't believe you ladies have been introduced to my present spouse, Emma Lou, have you?"

Cora and Minnie embraced Emma Lou warmly and made many compliments on her good looks. They also shook hands lengthily with Hibbard Grady.

"Emma Lou," Mr. Harkey began, still in a jovial mood, "is my wife in a temporary sort of way, one might say, for we've only been man and wife a mere year, but we've settled our ups and downs for the present, haven't we, my pretty. Yes, for the present!"

Minnie now cleared her throat in so forceful a way that dead silence descended on all present.

"You are wondering of course, Minnie," Wilbur Harkey began, "what is the meaning of so early a call on you here in your elegant privacy!" Here he looked about him appraisingly, and smiled, Minnie thought, in an unpleasant, cunning way.

"We are, dearest Minnie," he continued despite the sudden iciness coming from Cora and Minnie, "off in a few minutes on a special search-and-find expedition. Yes, we are on the spoor! But before we go on our safari, I must say a few words to my client, Mr. Lewis Coultas. I cannot depart without consulting with him!"

"Mr. Coultas is not feeling so well," Minnie explained. "At the moment, also, he is soaking in the bathtub, and can't therefore be consulted."

Mr. Harkey gave Minnie a look of contemptuous dismissal.

"Would you kindly conduct me thither at once, Minnie," he raised his voice from its usual bass to a fairly high baritone.

"Mr. Harkey," Cora interposed, "Lewis would be greatly aggrieved if you intruded on his privacy."

"Privacy, my dear lady, when my time and reputation are at stake. Privacy between a client and his representative! What folderol are you talking, my dear? I pity your ignorance, madam, I do indeed. Do you not know that sunset has come and gone and I have not fulfilled my professional commitment to Mr. Coultas? Privacy indeed! Will you now kindly conduct me to the bathroom or shall I find it myself?"

When neither Cora nor Minnie offered to move, Mr. Harkey stalked off, followed by Emma Lou and Hibbard, and rushed in a dead heat to the very bathroom in question, flung open its door, and exposed to everyone's view the naked soapy body of Lewis Coultas himself frolicking in a bath large enough for a grown seal to splash about in.

Though taken off his guard, Lewis Coultas looked on the whole pleased to be viewed totally in the raw, and one could perhaps see why. Ever since he was a young man he had practiced body building, beginning with Indian clubs, the horse and the rope (the Great Sandow was his idol), and going on to the boxing ring, and though no longer in his prime, his physique still caused heads to turn wherever he presented himself.

With a graciousness lacking any condescension, Lewis invited Mr. Harkey, Emma, and Hibbard to seat themselves on the high stools arranged about the tub, and he went on splashing and soaping himself.

"By the by, Harkey," Lewis Coultas finally inquired, after staring at Emma fixedly, "who is this young girl, may I ask?"

"Ah, yes, Emma Lou," the detective glanced at her as if he had long since forgotten she was in his party. "Well," Mr. Harkey sighed, "you might call her I suppose my morganatic wife. No, she is not my granddaughter," he put an edge in his voice as he thought he caught Lewis pronounce this phrase. "We have been married only a year, but married we are, and if Dame Fortune allows it, we may be in days to follow."

"I often wondered what morganatic meant," Lewis Coultas remarked, beginning to towel himself. "Now I can use the word and know what I'm talking about."

Then without any warning whatsoever, Lewis Coultas rose from his bath in order to reach a large Turkish towel, and both

Emma and Hibbard Grady let out cries of shock. Emma Lou covered her eyes and Hibbard looked to Mr. Harkey as if awaiting instructions.

Mr. Coultas had soon tied a towel as large as a small rug about his middle, and preceded by Coultas the party now walked out into the front parlor. On the way Lewis had thrown a magenta bathrobe about him and slipped into some fur carpet slippers which caught Mr. Harkey's envious glance.

"We have come at what is perhaps an unseemly hour," Mr. Harkey began, "but we are on our way to what is probably Indian territory. Northern Michigan and beyond. At least it was called Indian territory when I was a boy," he mused.

Mr. Coultas scowled nastily on hearing the word Indian repeated.

"We believe without a peradventure of a doubt your boy is in the Upper Peninsula."

"Doin' what?" Mr. Coultas all at once appeared to be in a bad humor despite the luxurious refreshment of his hour-long bath.

Mr. Harkey looked aghast, but managed almost to coo, "You do want him back, sir, don't you?"

"Yes, of course, or I can never see my wife and family again in Yellow Brook. . . . But at what price, Mr. Harkey? Bankruptcy? Four thousand dollars, by George, that's a lot of greenbacks when you consider the country is not yet totally recovered from the Panic."

"Look here, my dear Coultas," Mr. Harkey was suddenly benevolence itself, and he took from his breast pocket a familiar piece of paper. "Here is your promissory note back. I cannot accept it because sunset came and went without my bringing you your boy."

"The devil you say!" Coultas cried, and examined the promissory note with amazement and then grinned broadly.

"All I ask at the present is you pay perhaps the expenses of the gasoline and any long distance phone calls or telegrams."

Although the mention of telegrams caused Lewis's face to cloud over, he was in general agreement with the old investigator's proposal and smiled in the direction of Minnie and Cora who sat stiffly on as if at a prayer meeting.

"But, Mr. Coultas, before Emma Lou, Hibbard and I leave

on our voyage of search and discovery, I must ask you for the last and final time one paramount question, and you must reply to it with the utmost veracity."

Mr. Coultas waited a long moment on the word "veracity," and then said in a muffled but audible voice, "Shoot, sir!"

At this moment Minnie and Cora, resembling titled ladies who had been forced to co-mingle with the lower orders, excused themselves frostily, and left the room.

"I am sick to death of those two floozies," Lewis broke out in intense irritation before Mr. Harkey and company. "They don't give me a minute to myself, for one thing, and Minnie bosses me more than Eva did back in Yellow Brook. I am drained to a frazzle, Mr. Harkey. By God, women are a workout, I can tell you!"

"Mr. Coultas," Mr. Harkey was insistent. "I demand your undivided attention as to the question I just posed."

"Well, didn't I say *shoot,* God damn it, and *shoot* I meant. Fire away."

Mr. Harkey had taken out his gold pen and his tiny notebook and rested them both on his pathetically thin legs.

"Mr. Lewis Coultas, tell me, is this boy you are hunting your own boy?"

Lewis let out a great volume of air from his open mouth so that some papers and flowers on an adjoining table moved under the breeze.

"What a jackass of a question coming from a famous trial lawyer," Lewis roared. "By Christ, ain't the boy's name mine on his birth certificate? Don't it say in bold Gothic print, 'CHAD COULTAS'? Haven't I thought he was my own flesh and blood boy these fourteen years or more? Don't everybody in Yellow Brook think he's mine? So what more am I expected to swear to today? God damn it, Mr. Harkey, it's too late for him not to be my boy, and I want the little . . . ."

Here Mr. Lewis Coultas employed a word of such indescribable obscenity that both Mr. Harkey and Emma Lou let out cries of surprised shock and pain, followed by an echo of total amazement from Hibbard Grady.

"I want the little son of a bitch," Mr. Harkey amended the offending word with this milder one, "I want the little bastard returned to me, and I don't give a wooden nickel if it's sundown, starlight, or broad glaring moon. But I want Chad Coultas back so I can take him home to my wife and my relations in Yellow Brook!"

Mr. Harkey leaped up with the alacrity of a man sixty years his junior. He was smiling, he was beaming, he was very happy. Unaccountably, he stooped down and kissed Emma Lou as if they had just won first place at a horse race.

"Your boy will be returned to you!" the old man cried in a kind of rapture.

Everyone now shook hands all around.

"Mr. Harkey," Lewis Coultas said on ushering them out of his suite, "may I say you have a very fine taste in ladies. Mentioning of course no names," he added, and to everyone's surprise he blushed faintly, and then winked roguishly at Emma Lou, who bowed and mumbled something indistinct.

"All right, ladies," Lewis Coultas shouted once the door had closed on the old investigator and his party. "Come on out, Minnie and Cora! I know where you're hiding, and what you're thinking!"

All at once he sat down with the promissory note in his hand and burst into loud guffaws.

"Are you coming out, or shall I leave without you?" he roared.

Minnie and Cora appeared then, pouting and surly, but not acting quite so grand as they had when they stalked out of the room.

"What's amiss with my sweeties," Lewis leaped up and began kissing them with simulated zeal.

"Why can't you behave, Lewis, for pity's sake!" Minnie cried, close to tears.

"If I behaved, precious, you know you wouldn't care a hang about me. But we've no time for spats, do you hear. Get your duds on, because we're leaving."

"Leaving for where?" Cora appeared outraged.

"We haven't a minute to lose, ladies. We've got to get out of here at once, and tail him."

"Tail him?" Cora now spoke in her high society voice of dismay and disapproval. "What on earth are you talking about, Lewis Coultas!"

"Ladies, ladies, listen. We can't let that old skinflint and mountebank out of our sight. Though he is way past his dotage, he might find the boy before I can, if we let the old rip out of our sight. Don't you see he will collect a big fat reward from Pauline and Eva if we don't stop him? We've got to follow him, and then find the boy before old Wilbur can get his paws on him. Then I'll be home free!"

"Are you sure you're not dead drunk, Lewis," Minnie wondered, but she began putting on her outer coat and scarf.

"We can't just up and leave, like this," Cora pointed out. "We haven't even paid the hotel bill."

"I have a little piece of private information for you ladies," Lewis spoke in his raffish manner. "We're not going to pay the hotel bill, or the broken window, or the wear and tear on the mattress and bedstead. We're not paying, hear? At least I'm not, on account of, girls, I ain't got any more money to pay with. Now if one of you ladies want to put your diamonds in hock, that's another matter. . . . So let's put on our wraps and get the hell out of here. I tell you, we've got to follow old man Harkey."

Lewis had already got dressed and opened the door and given the women an indication that if they didn't follow him, they had seen the last of him. With a look, therefore, of utter horror at what they were doing, Minnie and Cora followed after him.

"We are slaves to this scalawag, Minnie," Cora whispered to her sister as they descended dizzily in the elevator.

"Lady Luck is smiling on us today," Coultas said. "Look there, sweethearts!"

Just a half a block away they caught sight of Wilbur Harkey, Emma, and the chauffeur consulting a road map in a mammoth touring car, and all busily engaged in conversation with one another, probably as to which road to take.

As they watched the investigator and his party, from under the awning of a florist shop, all at once Lewis gave out a whistle that could easily have stopped traffic, and he bounded toward an expensive but battered Studebaker. He shook hands energetically with the man at the wheel, and finally more or less embraced him, and handed him something from his billfold.

Hurrying back wreathed in happy dimpled smiles, Lewis explained to his two scowling lady companions that he had just run into his old business partner of some years back, who was—can you believe such a coincidence—looking to find someone to take his car off his hands.

The ladies were bitterly unenthusiastic concerning the proposal, but Lewis went on with his good news and did not notice their lack of zeal.

"Cyrus will also drive us as far as the state line, girls, he says, and then he'll catch a train for somewhere. So we not only have a good car, but a driver!"

Cora and Minnie exchanged looks of desperation, but then what could they do? They expected any moment a house detective from the hotel to take them into custody. They were furthermore, as they knew Lewis must know by now, in possession of stolen diamonds. A jaunt across state lines seemed then the practical and indeed the only sensible thing to do.

"And don't coquette now with Cyrus just because he is a good-looking bruiser," Lewis joked.

As Hibbard Grady was not a particularly fast driver, Cyrus, driving his more powerful engine for Lewis and his ladies, was able to easily follow after the party of Detective Harkey.

"Keep a safe distance, whatever you do," Lewis cautioned his new-found friend. "We don't want the old lawman to see us up close."

"Cyrus," Cora reassured the driver, casting warm glances at him (though a bit on the dark side, Cyrus was considerably younger than Lewis and had fetching sideburns), "you need have no fear of getting too close to Wilbur Harkey. He can barely see six inches ahead of him even with binocular-powered glasses."

"But how about his driver and the driver's lady love?" Lewis wanted to know. His fears about flirtation, however, were being fulfilled, and he could see Minnie wink at Cyrus.

"Ah, well," Cora replied. "Emma Lou and Hibbard will be too busy blowing kisses to one another to know or care who's behind them."

"So we're off to the wilds of Michigan," Lewis Coultas chuckled, settling into the shiny leather back seat with the two ladies. "I've never been in the wilds up north, have you, girls?"

Chad Coultas put as much distance as possible between himself and the fracas at the Resurrection Pentecostal Church by shouting and even occasionally lashing his poor mare to go faster. But nothing he did would make the beast go any more quickly than she already was. To add to his misery, the sky was now almost completely overcast so that he could not find any trace of the sun to guide him eastward.

He had almost forgotten about the humiliating outrages he had suffered at the hands of the churchpeople, when he saw two spectral figures emerge from a clump of shrubs growing at the side of a wide ditch. As he approached, the two strange white figures threw up their arms as if flagging for help. But then all at once the apparitions, as he drew closer to them, turned their backs on him and began limping away towards the shrubs from whence they came.

"Stop! Come back!" Chad shouted, for he thought they might be able to tell him if he was proceeding east in the general direction of Yellow Brook.

One of the white figures now stopped, and faced about. Then slowly the shape advanced and came closer to Chad and his wagon.

"You don't recognize your handiwork, you rotten hellion!" the taller of the figures screamed out, and Chad saw he was armed with a great stick which he brandished wildly.

Coming still closer the specter shouted, "Look at us! All your doing, you imp from hell! We are ruined because of you, you dirty mongrel!"

It was Brother Phineas with Silvester who stood before the astonished boy! Chad recognized them now largely by their being still at least partially tarred and feathered, for nothing of their original appearance was recognizable.

The two former deacons stood there immobile as snowmen, only their eyes glaring wrathfully at Chad.

"Tell me at least which way is east, if you'd be so kind," Chad spoke penitently.

"We would not tell you which way the wind blows even if we were to be tarred and feathered all over again, and then hanged in the bargain," Brother Silvester now spoke up, though some feathers still clinging to his lips prevented his words from all coming out distinctly.

"Why boys like you are allowed to run loose," Silvester went on, "is beyond all human understanding. And look at your poor horse, half dead with fatigue and probably starved to death in the bargain."

At the end of Silvester's speech, Brother Phineas picked up a large clod and threw it at Chad. It hit him on the head, and stung fearfully. Raising his whip, the boy threatened the deacons, and the horse, perhaps hearing the angry "swish-swish" sound, began to rush away as fast as her poor condition would allow.

Looking back after a while, Chad could see the two men still throwing stones in his direction. Then to his considerable surprise—since after all they had been churchmen—he heard them shouting filthy and vile names at him, some of which he had never heard before, despite his being accustomed to the general foul-mouthedness of Bess Lytle's pupils.

The rain now became heavier, and Chad realized he had no notion in what direction he was headed. He had spied a great old blanket in the back of a wagon, and he stopped the vehicle now since he was well out of danger from the two tarred and feathered churchmen, and folding the blanket properly, he threw it over the mare. She whinnied and neighed most piteously. She had such handsome eyes and eyelashes that Chad could not help kissing her on her damp forehead.

"We'll soon find shelter, my dear friend," Chad encouraged the mare. "I wish I knowed your name—it would make us even better companions for what we're going through."

They had only gone a few miles when a weatherbeaten and broken sign was visible by the side of the road. It said:

YOU ARE NOW LEAVING
THE UNITED STATES OF AMERICA

A skull and crossbones had been drawn under the words.

Chad stopped and thought a moment whether to turn back or to proceed. But then he recalled the unpleasantness at the Church of the Resurrection, and the lurking presence of the tarred-and-feathered deacons, so catching sight of a bit of light on the horizon he decided to go forward, for in his own troubled mind he felt he had left the United States of America a good many days before.

Again Chad must have dozed off despite the unpleasant and persistent downpour, for all at once the horse came to a full stop, waking him. Chad rubbed his eyes, and saw the horse had brought him to a large and isolated farm house. From its roof a huge chimney was letting out a graceful and comforting stream of white smoke.

The door to the farmhouse opened, and a raw-boned woman with very black hair, skinned back over a forbidding cast of countenance, came out on the wide porch.

"So you got here, after all, did you." She spat at one side of the porch. "And the poor beast I see, as usual, is half dead."

She began leading the horse and wagon toward a barn situated in the back of the farmhouse.

"What is the horse's name, ma'am," Chad thought he would say something by way of conversation.

The woman turned around from unyoking the animal, and stared at the boy. "Don't you know his name after living with your great-grandad all this time?" she shouted. "Have you been drinking on the road? You look as deadbeat as the horse."

Too puzzled to continue the conversation Chad now followed the woman inside the farmhouse, where he was ushered to a seat by the fireplace which was roaring noisily and was of course the source of the white smoke coming from the chimney.

"You'll have to take off all those sopping wet duds or you'll come down with pneumonia and die on my hands," the woman told him.

She waited.

"Go ahead, I'm not going to watch," she scolded when he did not obey. "After all the men I've seen from tiny squawling infants to hoary old lechers, you don't think I'm going to learn anything seeing you stark in your birthday suit, do you?"

While he was undressing, the woman brought him a suit of long underwear and some moccasins to put on.

"You're to spend the night here, your great-grandad says, and then the chief wants to see you tomorrow."

"What chief?" Chad gazed at her open-mouthed.

"Do you still have your adenoids the way you keep your mouth hanging open?" she scolded on. " '*What chief,*' he says." The woman appeared now to be in a perfect fit of rage. "You're comin' down with somethin' ain't you. Then we'll get out the whiskey before you've tasted a mouthful of solid food. God, are you in awful shape, and if that poor horse lives till morning it will be a miracle to tell your own great grandchildren about."

The woman stood over Chad until he had drunk a good deal of the whiskey which she had heated and laced with nutmeg, cinnamon, and other spices.

While she was hanging up his wet clothes in the little room adjoining the big dining hall where Chad was seated, he suddenly heard her let out a great series of screams. Before he could go in to see what was wrong, she had rushed out, carrying two small bags filled with gold coins and bullion.

"Have you murdered someone on the highway to have these in your possession? Answer me!"

She pushed the two bags into his hands.

"Ah," Chad muttered. "No wonder that blamed scarecrow outfit weighed so much if these were in the pockets."

The woman had folded her arms and was studying him cautiously. Then when she decided his own astonishment and surprise was genuine, she bent over the two sacks of the yellow coins intently.

"Well, open them, innocent-eyes," she barked at him.

But as Chad was about to open the larger of the two money sacks, a thick stiff envelope which they had not observed before fell out in front of them. It had written on the outside:

FOR THE FINDER AND THE FINDER ONLY

"That's you of course," the woman spoke now in a more mollified voice. "So open it, why don't you, instead of mooning over it."

With trembling hands, after helping himself to a few more sips from the whiskey, Chad brought out a discolored piece of thick paper from the envelope.

"Read it, on account of I don't have my spectacles handy," his hostess scolded on.

"Ah, well, then," Chad began, but all at once the sheet of paper dropped from his shaking grasp, and he rubbed his hand across his brow.

"Is that nasty-looking cut you have on your forehead bothering you?" she wondered. She came closer to the boy, and looked at the place where the deacon had struck him with a hard clod of earth.

"Let me tend to it," she said disgustedly, and she poured some whiskey on a cloth and began cleaning out his wound.

"Don't you dare pass out on me now, you little scamp," she railed.

"You know the tarred and feathered deacons?" he wondered. "They did that to me." And he pointed at where the clod had hit him.

She looked rather pityingly at him, and finished cleansing his wound. Then without another word, she went to a drawer in a china closet and drew out her spectacles. Slapping them across her eyes as though they were unbreakable as brass, she snatched the letter from his limp hand and began, "To the Finder and the Finder only, yes we read that, I know. . . ," she spoke under her breath. "The finder is of course you, as we also know." Then she began reading the contents in a monotonous, lugubrious monotone:

> My three boys died in the electric chair, but before they departed this life, they left me a fortune in gold. Yet this fortune has brought neither me nor them solace from my grief over their unjust executions. I do not want the State to have this fortune, for I brought my three boys up not to respect or obey the State, and what they done in the way of a few robberies was only getting back what the Banks and the Government was robbing the People of in the first place. I want this here fortune, for it is just that, to go to the young man the Indian chief White Cloud told me one day would go down this road and claim it. Let him put this fortune to better use than my sons and me have done. And may God return this land to the Red Man, for the White Man ain't worth the powder to blow him up with. Signed, Sussanah K.

"Sussanah K.," the woman mused, and put down the sheet of paper. "Why I knew her mother." She shook her head. "They were Ojibwas. Do you realize what you are in possession of?" Chad's hostess cried. "You can thank God Viola Franey is an honest woman," she repeated her name twice, "for most people seeing all this fortune would probably have murdered you! Do you realize, Chad Coultas, the value of what Sussanah K. has given you in these two small bags?

Chad stared uncomprehendingly from the bags containing the gold and bullion and then back to Viola Franey. His lack of enthusiasm for such a windfall and his general air of incomprehension nonplussed her even more perhaps than these same characteristics had nonplussed Bess Lytle.

Overcome by Chad's fortune, Viola Franey sank back into one of the soft armchairs, and then after attempting to say something several times without success, she finally gasped out, "See that big old bottle atop the kitchen range over there. Go get it like a good boy, and uncork it, and bring it to me on the double. Don't bother to fetch a glass. I'll drink it right from the lip of the bottle."

Chad was about to hand her the bottle but he came close to dropping it on the floor, for to his surprise he saw entering the room two young women who resembled so closely Minnie and Cora that had Viola Franey not screamed to him to watch out, he would certainly have dropped her medicine.

Still staring at the two young ladies who had entered the room so quietly and who made no motion to greet him or speak to Viola, Chad handed the woman her bottle, and she drank thirstily from it, wiping her mouth on a pot holder lying near by.

The two young women now came forward as stealthily as they had entered and sat themselves at the table.

"I would introduce you to these young persons—they are my daughters," the woman began in a less disagreeable tone when she had recovered her breath from several swallows of the medicine, "but the pitiful truth is, they cannot speak. Identical twins, they were mute from birth. They have cost me more sorrow I do believe than Sussanah K.'s own sons caused her by going to the electric chair."

"I would swear they are Minnie and Cora," Chad broke in, "though they're a good deal younger."

"Don't interrupt me when I'm explaining so important a matter as their being born deaf and dumb," the woman grumbled. "I hadn't half finished when you chimed in."

Chad mumbled an apology.

"They are spirited away every so often," Viola Franey continued, looking at her daughters now without her spectacles on, "spirited away by some crazy traveling salesman or carnival owner . . . as I told you my name is Viola Franey and these are my daughters, Sunny and Twiley . . . and you're Chad Coultas from what your great-grandad said."

Chad rose and expressed his pleasure at being introduced.

"You need not speak to them, Chad," Viola Franey reminded him. "They're deaf as adders."

Viola shook her head now and stared critically at her two girls who were, Chad realized, much more beautiful than Cora and Minnie could ever have been even in their prime.

"I must say I was very offended you mentioned Minnie and Cora just now," Viola brought the matter up.

"Why, do you know them, ma'am?" Chad was stupefied.

"Well, I'm sure if they're identical twins like mine and named Minnie and Cora they must be the jewel thieves I've been reading about in the Canadian papers. But describe them, why don't you."

"Well, they're rather plump with their clothes off." Chad said absentmindedly.

"Now see here," Viola bridled, "you watch your lip. Just because my daughters are deaf as posts doesn't mean you can talk like that under my roof."

"I was only trying to give you a good description," Chad mumbled and colored violently.

Despite his apology, Viola Franey appeared to become more and more indignant over what Chad had said, and helped herself now to another long swallow from the dust-covered medicine bottle.

"I thought you were a gentleman," she complained. "I don't think Sussanah K. would appreciate it that her fortune has gone to a young man who sleeps with jewel thieves."

"It was my dad who did that, Mrs. Franey," Chad defended himself earnestly.

"Your own dad is a companion to such women!" Viola Franey shook her head as if she had at last heard the final blasphemy. "Poor misguided Sussanah K.! That's all I have to say on the matter."

"But Lewis Coultas, it may turn out, is not my real dad after all, you see."

Viola Franey frowned, meaning of course she did not see.

"There has been a sharp mixup all the way around, Mrs. Franey," Chad tried to explain. "I was kidnapped, you see, as the sheriff called it, by my flesh and blood dad, who's . . . an Indian." The boy blushed a deep beet color.

Mrs. Franey was staring holes through him and nodding as she stared.

"Which explains, I suppose," she spoke rather softly now, "*explains* if any of this can be explained, why Chief Silver Fox wants to see you. Well, if you *are* one, then you are one, and the chief will know it the minute he sets eyes on you. Well, go on with your story," Viola Franey spoke more conciliatingly since she saw he was perhaps losing the thread of what they were discussing.

"All right then," he began and he felt he was in a similar position to the one he had occupied in the pulpit of the Resurrection Pentecostal Church. "You see after my *Indian* dad and me came back handcuffed by the sheriff and I was turned over to Eva, my mother, I was put under the third degree by the lawmen."

Chad's attention, always his weak point, however, began to stray now from his narrative to gazing at the two mute daughters, who were making faces at him.

"Yes," Viola Franey snapped, bringing him back to the present, "and then what occurred—do you remember?"

"Ah, yes," Chad spoke as doggedly as when Bess Lytle had made him do a problem in long division over again. "Lewis Coultas, my legal father—he's a white man—took me on the sly to Chicago unbeknownst to Eva or Pauline, my mother and grandmother," he added at an impatient scowl from Viola Franey, "where he spent the night with Cora and Minnie in the big hotel facing the lake. They bought me lots of new suits at a fancy haberdasher's."

"Then your legal father is a crook."

Chad swallowed several times, and to his own surprise, found himself nodding.

Viola stared at her bottle of medicine accusingly as if it were the source of her having to hear this improbable story.

"We'll have a little something to eat," Mrs. Franey then announced, and stood up and made motions of putting something in her mouth with her two fingers to her daughters. "We can all stand a little nourishment, I'm sure, and then, Chad, I will show you to your room. You'll need a good night's sleep before visiting Chief Silver Fox."

The supper meal was almost as good as the fare in the Pullman car or the hotel dining room. It consisted of fresh roast venison with a spicy rich gravy in which tiny little wild mushrooms were floating, roast squab, pheasant pie, and for dessert, lattice blueberry cobbler.

"I won't give you coffee, Chad," Viola said at the end of the meal, "because you might be up all night and miss your appointment with Chief Silver Fox. But I will let you have just a small glass of dandelion cordial which I make myself."

All during the lengthy supper, Chad's enjoyment of the victuals had been somewhat diminished by the almost violent kicks given him under the table from time to time by the two daughters, and whenever Viola went out of the room for something, he was belabored by both of the girls kicking like mules, until he was sure he would be black and blue all over his legs and thighs on the morrow. They also, when their mother was not watching, stuck out their tongues at him, and winked so that he would almost have sworn they were Cora and Minnie.

Viola now returned from the wine cellar covered with soot and cobwebs, and produced two bottles of the dandelion cordial. While Viola was uncorking the bottle, the kicking and winking from the two girls became even more frequent.

"It's too bad you're deaf or I would give you both a piece of my mind," Chad spoke to Sunny and Twiley.

Chad was also horribly bewildered and upset at the things Viola Franey had told him about Cora and Minnie, and of course Lewis Coultas. The thought his dad was a crook and that Minnie and Cora were jewel thieves came near to breaking his spirit.

He had just given out so deep a sigh as Viola entered the dining room that she came over to where he sat and said rather maternally (for her), "Now, now, it won't do, Chad, to be sorrowful over what can't be helped, will it?"

She poured him a small glass of the dandelion wine.

"We none of us ever get the parents we feel we deserve," she said, tasting her own homemade wine and making sounds of approbation with her lips. "My own Daddy tried to kill me fourteen times until I could stand it no more and ran off to Toronto while still a girl. What happened there is so terrible, I could not tell my dearest bosom friend. But I lived through it, and, Chad, if you quit shaking like an aspen leaf and sighing like the winter wind, you'll live through it all too, maybe . . . at any rate the gold from Sussanah K. will get you back to Yellow Brook, Chad. Let's hope Chief Silver Fox has something worthwhile in mind for you. And now, children, it's bedtime!" Viola cried, and as she was following Chad out of the room he was stupefied to hear her all at once slap both her daughters across the face—for what reason he was never able to determine.

Mrs. Franey ushered him into a room every bit as large as the bedroom his Dad and his two lady companions had spent the night in. The wallpaper looked new, and the rugs on the floor were very clean. But the bed in the room was, if anything, even larger than king-sized. It took up nearly half the space.

"Your pajamas are laid out here," Mrs. Franey pointed to garments hanging over the rung of a ladder leading to a trapdoor in the ceiling. "And your bathrobe is on the chair here."

She gave him a long doubtful look then, and sighed heavily.

"Good night, and pleasant dreams. . . . Remember at five o'clock, you're to be up and on your way to the chief."

She surprised him by kissing him wetly on his upper lip.

Chad was wakened some time later from a deep snoring slumber by two simultaneous movements on either side of him. Jumping up with a start he saw—how can one say he was stupefied or surprised again, after what he had been through, but certainly he was unprepared to see—the two deaf and dumb daughters lying in bed alongside him. When they saw he was awake, they smothered him with lingering kisses, and soon had removed his pajamas and thrown them on the chamber pot at the far side of the bed.

Memories of Minnie and Cora and his dad descended on him as the two girls worked him to such a pitch of excitement that they must have felt their kicking and banging him under the table had borne fruit.

Five o'clock came indeed just as all three of the occupants of the huge bed were sinking into a sodden sleep, with most of the bedclothes torn to ribbons, and the pillow cases mangled almost beyond repair.

Wilbur Harkey was perfectly aware that he was being followed by Lewis Coultas and his party, but he was so occupied with gathering evidence as to his wife's infidelity that he put the problem of their pursuit aside for the moment. Seated in the luxuriant cushiony back seat of his touring car, Mr. Harkey was better able to see Emma holding hands in the front seat with the chauffeur. A tiny imported camera, held almost invisibly by the old detective, was snapping one incriminatory photo after the other in his trained hands.

"What are those queer sounds, Daddy?" Emma finally inquired, and turned her ivory neck to discover her husband fast asleep.

"I would have sworn he was clicking something, Hibbard," Emma spoke *sotto voce,* and keeping one eye on her slumbering spouse she kissed Hibbard passionately on one of his sideburns.

"Oh, if we were only free, honey," Emma muttered.

"A good job don't come along every new moon," Hibbard spoke bluntly.

A ferocious snore came from Wilbur Harkey at that moment.

"He's taken some sleeping pills again, snorting like that," Emma remarked, and she laid her curls against Hibbard's ample bosom (he belonged to the German Young Men's Gymnastic League), and told him all over again how much in love she was with him.

"Gosh dang it, I believe Mr. Harkey is right as usual," Hibbard slowed the car down. "We *are* bein' followed."

Mr. Harkey pretended to regain consciousness and with one final and ferocious snore, he opened his eyes to their full width.

"Sleep well, Daddy?" Emma Lou smiled with sincere benevolence.

"Deeply, my dear," Wilbur grinned deceitfully in return.

"Hibbard," Mr. Harkey raised his voice to its forensic volume. "You will find in the glove compartment, or perhaps under the seat, a pound or more of ground glass mixed with spikes, brads, and various assortments of nails."

"I hear you sir," the chauffeur replied worriedly.

"Have you located them?" Wilbur Harkey spoke in his most severe tone so that Emma Lou shuddered violently.

"I have found the bag of nails and ground glass, yes, sir."

"Excellent. Now put full speed ahead for a mile or more so that we can outstrip them—they are driving a broken-down stolen car—and then we'll spread the spikes and ground glass in their path and be rid of them."

"Daddy is so clever," Emma Lou simpered, but a look of

deep worry marred the beauty of her otherwise snow-like forehead.

Hibbard stepped on the gas to such an extent that they lost all sight of their pursuers. The chauffeur then leaped out with the box of disruptive materials and sprinkled the entire assortment of sharp objects across the road.

"Now put on the gas again to make them chase us with all the power they can muster!" the detective roared between gales of laughter.

Wilbur Harkey's intense pleasure at what he was doing plunged Emma still further into worried gloom. She felt that her time with the old detective was nearing an end, and she was suddenly afraid. For some irrational reason she also wondered if he might not have put her in prison, for all at once she was certain he knew *everything*. Her early life of degradation and extreme poverty rushed back to her in a flash, and Hibbard Grady's ample bosom and athlete's forearms all at once seemed less appealing.

At a new adjuration from Mr. Harkey then, Hibbard slowed down and came to a stop. And presently they heard what sounded like a bomb going off. Looking back they saw that Lewis Coultas's car (at least it appeared to be his car) had not only blown all four tires, but appeared to be shooting flames from the engine.

"Drive on," Mr. Harkey guffawed, but his laughter was so ferocious and loud that Emma Lou broke into weeping.

"Now, now, my little lady," Wilbur Harkey stopped his laughing long enough to scold her. "Don't tell me you're coming down with another attack of headaches and heartburn and have forgotten to bring your peppermint drops."

"No, Daddy, no," Emma Lou turned about and penitently faced her husband. "I only fear you don't love me, Daddy dear."

"I never loved you," the old man spoke without a trace of humor.

"Never, Daddy, *never?"*

"It never crossed my mind that I loved you."

Hibbard Grady sank his massive chin into his chest and attempted to look small and inoffensive.

"I loved Gabrielle," Mr. Harkey recalled, "though she cheated on me constantly. But she cared for me in all other aspects, tucking me in at night, keeping my hair of a good natural sheen and hue, and always seeing that my toenails were properly trimmed . . . I always did my fingernails myself—can't abide the damned manicurist in our building. Has breath like a dead moose. . . . But as to you, Emma Lou, my dear, no, I never thought of love in connection with you!"

"But, Daddy, dear!" his wife protested.

"Will you stop calling me with that appellation, when you know I'm not your dad, your grandaddy or your great-grandad. Would you mind slapping her if you will, Hibbard, and bring her round. This is a command, my good fellow," he ordered the chauffeur when he saw him hesitate.

Without warning Hibbard struck Emma Lou half-heartedly full in the face, and she burst into an uncontrollable tempest of sobs ending in a kind of spasm of the hiccoughs.

"Pay no attention to women's tears, my boy," Mr. Harkey advised his chauffeur. "They can weep and pee at will, and it means nothing. They are born with a full-flowing conduit of liquids whereas men are born on the whole dry and spare. And if, Hibbard Grady, you run away with Emma Lou, as the low slut would have you do, know sir, that you will both starve to death, even if you don't end up in prison in the bargain. No one fools Wilbur Harkey. Now I have said my piece and can go back to sleep until we reach the farm of that old rip Viola Franey. I sent her a night letter so she should have our rooms aired out and ready for us."

Prior to settling back into the soft recesses of the back seat for another catnap, Wilbur Harkey drew out a large beribboned box of chocolate-covered cherries, and handed it to the sniveling Emma Lou.

"Have a bonbon, my dear, it will get you over your fit of lachrymal effusion."

He shoved the showy box of sweets in her face. Emma Lou reached inside, took several chocolates, and asked pitifully, "Can Hibbard have one, Daddy, though he's driving?"

"Can and may, princess. Stick one in his mouth so his hand won't leave the wheel," the old man acquiesced.

Emma Lou did not need to be told twice, and she placed one of the larger sweets in Hibbard's mouth. He bit her finger playfully as he accepted the chocolate-covered cherry.

"No one fools old Investigator Harkey for long," the detective droned as he sank deeper and deeper into the cushions of the back seat. "But, by George, let me warn you. Old Viola Franey is a tough customer. She's the matron of our sleeping quarters tonight. She's mean as a whole forest of pickaxes, has two deaf mute daughters who are strumpets and pickpockets, and her place is where my informants have telegraphed me the Indian boy has been hiding out. . . . But what have we here, by the side of the road?" Wilbur Harkey cried and sat bolt upright looking out the window.

A man in clerical garb was flagging their car excitedly.

"Stop, sirs, I bid you come to a halt!" the minister cried between cupped shaking hands. "I entreat you to stop!"

"Very well, Hibbard," Wilbur told the chauffeur, "you may put on the brakes, and we'll see what this man of the cloth wants with us, though be on your guard. Many crooks today wear the collar!"

Coming out of the car with his gold pencil and notebook, Mr. Harkey strode majestically up to the cleric. The man who had flagged down the Wilbur Harkey party was Brother Averil of the Ressurection Pentecostal Church, looking a bit unkempt since the appearance of Chad Coultas, and with one of his eyeglasses broken.

"If there is one thing a man learns in the courtroom," Wilbur Harkey began addressing Brother Averil at once, "it is this, sir. Do not repeat words again and again. You said *"stop"* at least fifty times, when if you had your eyes about you you would have seen my chauffeur, acting on my orders, was coming to a full stop. You preachers are all alike. Wasting words is your forte and probably your only talent. Repetition is death to argument, sir!"

As Brother Averil could think of no rejoinder to this speech, Wilbur Harkey went on, "Let me introduce myself, sir. I am the internationally-known investigator Wilbur Harkey, and I would desire you to state with precision and in as brief a space as possible why you have stopped our party on the public highway."

Brother Averil took Mr. Harkey's hand warmly.

"You are the right man then for this piece of information, sir," the preacher almost cried out with relief, crushing Harkey's hand so fiercely it caused the detective excruciating pain.

Wrenching free of the handclasp, Wilbur Harkey cried, "My fee, I must warn you, is considered by today's standard steep.

And I am already on a very pressing case. A kidnapping, at least a sequestration. . . . But what would you have me do, my dear cleric?"

"I would have you turn back for your own safety, Mr. Harkey," Brother Averil advised him, swallowing spasmodically between words.

He then produced from his breast pocket photos of Brothers Phineas and Silvester, taken prior, of course, to their being tarred and feathered, plus a number of pamphlets on anarchism and the lives of Emma Goldman and her paramour. Wilbur Harkey put on his thickest pair of glasses and studied, with curled lip, this evidence.

"And?" Mr. Harkey wanted to know, loftily staring at Brother Averil.

"These men, it is my firm belief, are Bolshevists," he began. "They were members of our church, the Resurrection Pentecostal, until they brought into our midst another member of their subversive society, a mere boy, who addressed the congregation in gibberish, and caused a riot. They were all agents."

Mr. Harkey handed back the documents and photos.

"And what is it, my good churchman, you would have me do. . . . Remember my fee now!"

"I told you, sir, I am advising all motorists who go past here to turn back for their own safety. The former ministers of the Resurrection Pentecostal Church are throwing bombs at passing cars, at least rocks."

"Well, which is it, bombs or rocks?"

"Rocks, sir, rocks, so far as we know."

"So far as you know," Mr. Harkey harrumphed. "May I say you would make a very poor witness in court, I fear."

Brother Averil gave every indication then of losing his temper, but Mr. Harkey went on, "By the way, churchman, you haven't seen by any remote chance a young Indian boy in a horse-drawn wagon. Has one blue eye and one black eye, and wears a stolen mantle."

Brother Averil gave out a cry of such intolerable pain and rage that Mr. Harkey went directly up to him and held him by both his arms. "Now, now, sir, this is no way for a grown man to give vent to his emotions. Brace up!"

"See, here," Brother Averil now spoke with all the fury of long accumulated rage, "it is the Indian brat you just named who brought everything to a head at the Resurrection Pentecostal Church!"

Brother Averil broke loose from Wilbur Harkey's straightjacket embrace at this moment. "He was in cahoots with the two Bolshevists, Brothers Phineas and Silvester. That is our opinion."

"Your opinion has no basis in fact," Wilbur Harkey said coolly. But he took his pen again with its accompanying notebook, to write down a few *aperçus.*

"All right, my dear cleric, I am waiting for your version!"

"Version be damned," Brother Averil cried. "Look here. That Indian boy you say you are seeking delivered a sermon which contained improper and incendiary material, and incited our congregation to riot, which is what the anarchists Silvester and Phineas wanted. The Indian was put up to it of course by these sub-deacons."

"And where is this Indian boy at the present time, since you seem to know so much about him?" the detective wondered without bothering to look up from his notebook.

"Why, I suppose he is throwing bombs, or rocks, with the two deacons, at passing cars up yonder."

"I am afraid we are in for a very exciting ride, then," Mr. Harkey turned from the churchman at this point to address Emma Lou and Hibbard. "Perhaps," he came back to Brother Averil, but Harkey saw that the cleric was so overcome with some kind of violent emotion he was not listening at all. "My dear friend," Wilbur Harkey took the arm of Brother Averil, "are you quite all right?"

Brother Averil replied by groaning deeply and nodding that he was.

"Then listen to me, my friend. Since you have warned us of the danger in store for us, perhaps you would shelter my wife Emma Lou here until we capture the Indian boy in question."

"No, Wilbur, no," Emma Lou gave out great cries of disagreement. "I will not be left behind in this dangerous region. I will run the risk of the bombs and rocks first, do you hear?"

"But my dearest, it might result in our injury or death," the detective said with the relish of anticipation. "We may all be dead by nightfall!"

Brother Averil nodded in agreement.

"Well, since my wife is as fearless as her husband," Mr. Harkey went back to speaking with the cleric, "we will be on our way. Thank you, sir, for all the information and advice you have given us this day. You can rest assured the guilty parties, if they are guilty, will be brought to justice."

"*If* they are guilty!" Brother Averil shrieked with vexation. "What are you talking about? Haven't I just given you the facts, and warned you, yet you are about to go blithely on and risk your own life and that of your wife, and that thug of your chauffeur. If so young a person *is* your wife, of course," Brother Averil added nastily.

"Now see here, my good fellow," Mr. Harkey raised his voice and all at once he clapped his hands as if summoning an attendant. "Out of my concern for you and your church, I have charged you no fee today for listening to your series of complaints. And hear how you repay my kindness and my benevolence!"

"YOUR KINDNESS," Brother Averil shouted as if from the pulpit itself, "when out of the *goodness* of my heart I warn you you are in mortal danger. If any fee is to be mentioned it should be mentioned by me. You lawyers are all alike, aren't you? You'd charge a man for even looking at you! And why, may I ask, are you so interested in this Indian boy?"

Wilbur Harkey gave Brother Averil one of his most eloquent looks of pity and contempt. "Because, my dear man of the cloth, I have been hired to rescue the boy, and bring him home to his mother and grandmother in Yellow Brook. Pauline has paid me to accomplish this."

"Pauline be damned to the hottest flame in hell!" Brother Averil was now completely carried away. "Rescue and bring home a confederate of an anarchist! What kind of lawman are you then? Why, sir, you must be one of them yourself! I see it now. You yourself are probably an anarchist disguised as a lawyer."

Mr. Harkey smiled again his pitying lofty smile.

"As I said a moment ago," Wilbur spoke quietly to Brother Averil, "you would make a very poor witness in court even dressed in your clerical robes. You should stick to Bible classes and Sunday school, for you are obviously an idiot of the first water."

Mr. Harkey tipped his hat and leaped quite agilely for a man of his years into the back seat.

The astonishment of everyone in the car increased when

they heard stones pelting against the back of the car. It was Brother Averil himself who was throwing one great rock after another in their direction, and calling after all of them imprecations couched in foul language and indecent insinuations concerning Emma Lou and Hibbard Grady.

"Never, never again. Absolutely never!"

Chad Coultas was awakened by the sound of his own voice uttering these words. He started bolt upright. He found himself again holding the reins and the patient uncomplaining mare was drawing him forward, but it was such a dark day he had no idea in what direction he was going. According to scolding, bossy Viola Franey, however, she had put him on the right road for his meeting with Chief Silver Fox.

Chad began to wonder if he was not perhaps still asleep, and had been asleep ever since Decatur appeared in his home town and began waiting for him in front of the school house. Was all that had happened since Decatur's appearance actual fact? Had it all taken place? And if not, when would he wake up and find himself again Eva and Lewis's son, and Bess Lytle's pupil?

Then remembering the gift from Sussanah K., he felt anxiously in his cloak. Sure enough, there were the two bags containing the gold coins! He drew them out cautiously, and stared at them skeptically. At least the deaf and dumb daughters and ranting Viola Franey had not taken even one of the coins, for they still filled the bags to the very top.

Ahead was a little copse and he guided the mare thither. He decided he would count the gold coins, but his head ached fearfully and his entire body was sore from where the two girls had lambasted him all the night through, and his mouth was actually bleeding from their incessant kisses.

All at once he remembered that he had brought from Eva one of her little vials of medicine, to be taken, in her words, "whenever you feel bad, dear heart." Under the mantle he searched through his good suit and found to his relief a fresh unopened little bottle of the "elixir."

He drove his horse and wagon near a great number of arrowwood shrubs, with some of their leaves still clinging to them. Most of the shrubs appeared to have been cleaved by lightning.

Here he drank sparingly of the elixir, for he remembered its strange power from when he had testified before the sheriff. In only a few minutes he felt like a different young man. His eyes cleared for one thing, and he saw by reason of the sunlight now struggling through the overcast sky that he was indeed heading northeast. In his outstretched palms he held the two bags of the yellow coins. He cautiously opened them and began counting.

It was a good thing he had tasted some of Eva's nostrum, for the more he counted the gold coins, the more there seemed to be waiting to be counted. And each coin was of a large denomination, all minted by the U.S. Treasury. He finally dared count no more, and looked about apprehensively to see if any robbers or cutthroats were observing him. The coins, he saw, if he lived to bear them home to Yellow Brook, would be enough to buy, if not the entire town, at least the Opera House, the Court House and the jail.

Whether owing to the medicine he had imbibed or because it had taken so long to count and recount the coins, he saw that the day was dying and the first shadows of evening were creeping about him.

He put the bags of coins carefully back under his cloak, and began driving in a slow deliberate way in the opposite direction of the setting sun on the road which looked more traveled than the one which had brought him to the copse of arrowwood shrubs.

"Oh, if Decatur had only not come back!" Chad mumbled. But at the same time he would have given all his gold, he knew, to be with the man he once thought he despised and hated. This strange contrariety of feelings puzzled him so much that he took another tiny swallow of Eva's nostrum.

"But Decatur *had* to come back!" Chad spoke aloud. "Just like, I guess, I have to see Chief Silver Fox. For I am, God help me, yes I must be, an Indian!"

Chad cried then so hard that the mare came to an abrupt standstill, and turned her head around and gazed at him.

Darkness had now enveloped the road, and the sky was a heavy black without benefit of any colors from the disappeared sun. Then in the not-far-distance Chad caught sight of what looked like bonfires, rising up now all at once, and then dying down. There were also audible shouts and laughter that struck fear into his heart for the cries were not unlike those he had heard coming from the procession of worshippers at the Resurrection Pentecostal Church.

He went on doggedly nonetheless, and as he got nearer he saw a circle of young men on horses who were defiantly approaching great circles or hoops whose outer edge were aflame. One after another the horsemen were forcing their uneasy mounts through circles of fire. As each horseman leaped through one fiery ring after another he gave out a "halloo" which was echoed from the surrounding black hills.

Now on the very edge of this strange pageant of daring and showmanship, Chad drew in his breath for all the young horsemen were practically naked, and wore headdresses of bright-colored feathers. They were, without a doubt, Indians.

"Here he comes, another one of us!" one of the fiercer and taller of the Indians cried on seeing Chad. "Well, get off that wagon, why don't you, and let's see what you can do."

Chad stumbled out of his wagon, and walked up to the speaker, who was all at once joined by another dark-skinned youth, carrying a rifle. Unaccountably the latter fired the weapon into the air, and both Indians let out great drunken war whoops.

A third Indian now brought up a horse without a saddle, which was pawing the ground and whinnying wildly.

"Jump on," the first dark man commanded Chad, "and you've got just five minutes to get your ass through every one of those hoops, or by the Great Spirit, you'll be scalped to your brains." He then gave Chad a fearful kick on his behind, and the boy jumped on the horse.

To Chad's dazzled eyes, it seemed he had fallen into a burning pit of a thousand flares, with countless tongues of blue and red flames. He felt his hair and his mantle being singed and set afire. But the horse, as he held desperately to its frayed bridle, leaped with a kind of dreamy fearless precision through one hoop after another, and then as if carried away by the beast's own perfect courage and skill, Chad rode unbidden through all the hoops again.

As Chad and the horse leaped through each burning ring, cries of ferocious "hosanna," war whoops, and gibbering laughter rang out so that one would have thought all the demons from the pit were watching Chad and waiting to claim him in some deeper pit of fire and burning flesh.

Then Chad dismounted, and leaning heavily on a palisade nearby, saw himself surrounded by the crowd of gleaming, naked savages. They embraced him and even kissed him on the mouth, and put a new kind of crown on his head in place of the old diadem he had taken from the scarecrow.

The naked Indians then raised bottles of something to their lips and drank, after each swallow letting out more ear-splitting war whoops, and making obscene gestures across their bare behinds.

Then there was a strange quiet. The first, the most stalwart and ferocious of the Indians and the one who had greeted Chad while he was still seated in the wagon, now addressed the circle of savages.

"And now boys," he began in a strangely inappropriate and calm tone of voice for a naked redskin, "let's call it a night, and take off our damned war paint and our headdresses!"

With this adjuration, all the young men in unison tore off their wigs of long hair, and walked over to three vats of steaming hot water. They then and there began cleaning and scraping themselves off—so it appeared—of their very skin.

As they bathed themselves in the hot water and soaped themselves with a kind of pumice-like substance, Chad observed with a growing terror that the redskinned savages were all turning into white men with very fair skin, and without their wigs, had hair like corn silk, and sky-blue eyes.

Then, just as in one of the plays Chad had seen performed at the Opera House, they all at once formed a circle around Chad, their perfect white teeth gleaming at him in the firelight. The original leader pushed Chad toward the steaming vats of water, while helping him remove all his clothes.

Then, without ever taking his eyes off the circle of fair-skinned white men with blue eyes and corn-colored hair, Chad dispiritedly, helplessly began washing his body and combing out his long black hair. Several of the young men now came forward and touched Chad's skin here and there, and then looked at their fingers.

Then there was a murmur, rising to a shout, and again the simulated war whoops of savages, as all the men came closer, enveloping naked shivering Chad.

"But he's a damned redskin himself! A dirty dyed-in-the-wool Indian, boys!"

And as they cried out, they laughed with fiendish, insane cries, and lifted the bottles of liquor to their lips.

"Take off his crown," someone urged, and several hands ripped off the chaplet of victory from Chad's head.

"A dirty Indian boy!" the cries of pretended outrage and loathing now rose up on all sides, followed always by choked laughter and more sounds of drinking from the bottles of liquor.

Some of the youths then picked up burning branches and advanced toward Chad. They struck him with the burning boughs. Chad scarcely felt the fiery sensations on his dark skin for all he could be aware of at the moment was his terror of being called *Indian* from so many white savage throats. He felt they meant indeed to kill him.

After burning him with the branches they struck him with their open fists, kicked him with their feet, and several spat mouthfuls of liquor at him. He was finally able, after going through the gauntlet of burning branches, fists and feet, to regain his wagon. For some peculiar reason they stopped at the paved road, and watched him.

He raised his whip above his head, and a low murmur of hatred, contempt and loathing came from their throats. One raised again a last burning branch.

"Dirt dirt dirty Indian," came the cry, but drunkenness was taking over and they fell back. A few lay down on the ground and yelled and kicked.

Then there he was again in stupor and deepest silence, not daring to draw rein, urging on the mare, but while he held his breath in sudden renewed terror, he saw that naked as he was he had had the presence of mind to grasp hold somehow of his old mantle and suit of clothes. Feeling inside its ample folds he found both the bags of gold and the panacea of Eva's nostrum.

But for a long time he could still hear the white men who had worn the warpaint of his own race crying out, "Kill him! Scalp the filthy redskin!"

As their voices grew faint, Chad's own sobs came now to his ears, which like his body seemed to have been afflicted with the burns from the fiery branches.

"I have never had any use for preachers," Mr. Harkey commenced another of his harangues after coming out of a fit of dozing off. "My own dad was one, before he left the ministry for the lumber business. But the memory of his interminable sermons and prayers is still ineffaceable in my memory. I suppose I get my forensic talent from him, if not the content of his mind!"

Hearing the old man sounding off again after his sleep, Emma Lou and Hibbard Grady left off holding hands, and straightened up in the front seat.

"I'm rather surprised, Daddy," Emma Lou spoke brightly, "that you think so badly of ministers of the gospel." As she spoke she pushed her hand against Hibbard's very substantial calf muscle. "Don't you have any good to say of them, my dearest?"

Mr. Harkey cleared his throat on hearing himself called *dearest.*

"Well, for one thing, to answer your question," the investigator began and he noted the body pressures being exerted by Emma Lou against the chauffeur's lower parts, "preachers are home all day doing nothing and as a result have little to occupy their thoughts with except other people's sins."

"But don't preachers visit the sick and infirm and perform other good deeds?" Emma wondered, and was not able to resist the temptation of sliding her palm under Hibbard's heavily muscled buttocks, which caused the chauffeur to let out a little squeal.

Mr. Harkey was fumbling with his pocket camera, but he feared the two young people might see him preparing to snap another shot of their billing and cooing, and so he let his hand rest for the moment on the lap robe over his knees.

"You certainly saw what an imbecile that deacon, Brother Averil, was," Mr. Harkey went on, for he knew that if he kept talking the guilty pair in front of him would be apt to engage in their surreptitious groping of one another.

"I have, even when I was younger, been fool enough to take preachers as clients," the investigator went on with assumed indignation.

He then snapped a few poses with his camera of Emma Lou resting her left hand on Hibbard's groin. At the sound of the clicking both Emma and Hibbard turned around nervously. But even as they turned their gaze backwards they caught sight of something which engaged their full attention, and to such an extent that Grady brought the car to a full stop.

"Mr. Harkey," the chauffeur cried breathlessly, "I'm afraid we are being followed again!"

"By whom, for good heaven's sake?" the old man wondered, and he too craned his neck and looked out of one of the side curtains.

"By the Almighty," Wilbur Harkey now shouted, "don't tell me it's Lewis Coultas in a different car from the one we blew up! And all alone at that! No sign of those painted jezebels he runs with. . . . Wouldn't put it past him if he's murdered the two trollops for their jewels."

"Shall I put on the accelerator and get him behind us, then, sir?" Hibbard asked, while looking down at Emma's dress which had gone far above her knees in the sudden coming to a halt of the automobile.

"No, Hibbard, my boy, we'll wait this time and see what the mutt wants, though it's against all my principles to allow a client to snoop around at what I'm engaged in."

The auto came to a full shrieking halt then, and Mr. Harkey flung open the door of the touring car, but as he went to alight, he tripped on the dilapidated running board and fell face downward on the road.

Mr. Coultas was already hastening on his way to greet the detective and was the first, actually, to help the old man to his feet, and proceeded to brush off the dust which had stained his jacket and trousers.

"You're not hurt, are you, sir?" Lewis Coultas inquired while Emma Lou and Hibbard looked gravely on.

"I've never been hurt in my life," Wilbur Harkey chided. "I am indignant, however, that you are pursuing me as if *I* were the runaway, and you were the investigating party. You are one of my most unsatisfactory clients, may I say, along with the damned preachers."

Mr. Coultas tipped his hat and replied, "I am sorry you think so ill of me sir," and more or less unconsciously his fists began to move nervously upward around his rib cage.

Ignoring the threatening gesture, Wilbur Harkey went on, "I wonder, too, what has become of your lady companions, if I may mention them in decent society." Mr. Harkey bowed sarcastically in the direction of Emma Lou, who lowered her gaze.

At the mention of the ladies, Lewis Coultas hung his head sheepishly.

"The news about the ladies is, I'm afraid, sir, bad."

"Hardly a surprise, Coultas."

"Will you let me finish, Mr. Harkey. You interrupt a client damned brusquely, if I may say so. . . . The ladies, as you call them, have been taken into custody. In fact, the car preceding mine blew up, and riding in it at the time were two Chicago policemen, who emerged from the wreck unhurt, and then took Minnie and Cora into custody."

"I am surprised, Mr. Coultas, they did not arrest you at the same time," Harkey sneered.

"I think they would have done so, but I told them you were representing me. They were very impressed, may I say, at the mention of your name."

The detective could barely restrain a broad smile, but then, catching himself, he knit his brows fiercely, and shook his head.

"What were the ladies in question arrested for?" Harkey wondered.

"They were taken in on suspicion of grand larceny and several other counts—blackmail, impersonating law officers," Lewis Coultas spoke brightly like one announcing something meritorious.

Mr. Harkey nodded appreciatively, and was about to take out his notebook and gold pen when Lewis Coultas boomed out, "Well, while we waste our time on two highway strumpets, have you any news of my runaway boy?"

Wilbur Harkey gave Coultas a look of patent disgust, but managed to reply, "I'm afraid we have too much news where your boy is concerned."

"You've located him then?"

"We might already have had the chap in tow, Mr. Coultas, had you not engaged in this senseless pursuit of us. You are interfering with my solution to this case. I suggest you return to Chicago or wherever you are checked in at the moment, and let me work in my own unimpeded fashion."

"But what the deuce," Lewis Coultas cried, and spat to one side of the road. "Why can't I accompany you if the case is nearly wrapped up?" the aggrieved father complained. He looked desperately overwrought at that moment, and his jocular manner was nowhere in evidence.

"Do you realize," Coultas went on, a kind of whine in his deep voice, "that the boy's mother has alerted the law enforcement agencies of half a dozen states! See here, I must find that boy, and return him to her, or my marriage and all its benefits are in imminent jeopardy!"

"I will have to raise my fee then, sir," the old detective spoke openly of the donative.

"Raise it to what?" Lewis Coultas's fists now began moving in a kind of menace of accelerated tempo.

Mr. Harkey stepped up to Coultas and slapped his fists downward with his small notebook in hand.

"Very well, sir," Wilbur Harkey spoke with concession, "despite your unprofessional behavior, the fee will stay where it was. But if you follow us on our search-and-find mission, you must do just that, follow, not *lead.* And when I rescue your boy and render an account of my stewardship, as I shall of course, you must make no overtures to him until I have questioned him thoroughly. Otherwise I will leave the case this instant."

To the considerable incredulity now of the Wilbur Harkey party, and perhaps to Lewis Coultas's own astonishment, the father of the runaway boy burst into a succession of choked sobs, such as none of those witnessing it had ever heard before. Emma Lou was especially moved, and began sobbing herself.

"Now, now, Mr. Lewis Coultas," the old detective finally stepped in and put his hand on the grieving man's shoulder. "It won't do at all, this blubbering."

There was now no trace of Lewis Coultas's manly and carefree demeanor, or any bravado from his nervous fists. His hands hung by his sides like wilted branches.

"I have always wanted a son, Mr. Harkey," Lewis spoke almost in a falsetto. "And now, confound it, there is doubt he is mine. Strong doubt. Those whores I've been sleeping with, excuse me, ma'am," he addressed Emma Lou here, "while I'm half beside myself with grief, those trollops were constantly at me, harping that the boy could not be mine owing to his dark complexion. But, you see, sir, there is, as I believe I mentioned in a previous confab with you, there is an Indian strain on the boy's mother's side."

Out came the tiny notebook again and the gold pen, and

Mr. Harkey was busy writing down whatever he felt was incumbent on him to indite when he felt a strong hand seize both objects.

"Will you quit putting down damning evidence, you gooseberry-eyed old dog when I am talking to you man to man! Damn you for the old skunk you know you are!"

Mr. Harkey was so astounded by this gross rudeness on the part of his client that he put his little notebook and pen away, almost contritely, and sat down on the broken running board, and began to make sounds not too dissimilar to the sobs that came out of his client Lewis Coultas a few minutes earlier.

Emma Lou now came to the rescue of the quarreling parties, and patted her husband tenderly on his cheek, and entreated Mr. Coultas to come over and ask her "Daddy's" pardon.

After more sniveling and whining on the part of the antagonists, both parties were reconciled and agreed to go with Hibbard and Emma Lou in search of the runaway boy.

"It is my settled belief," Mr. Harkey told Lewis Coultas as the two of them sank into the back seat now together, "that the boy is legally, if not absolutely, your son. You can rest assured, sir, on this point of law, or I am not Wilbur Harkey, the renowned investigator."

"Music to my ears!" Mr. Coultas retorted, and he took the detective's lean trembling hand in his and caressed it almost as daintily as Hibbard was now holding Emma Lou's hand in his massive grasp.

The car Lewis Coultas had been driving, which was in Wilbur Harkey's opinion stolen in the first place, was left at the side of a ditch under a sycamore tree for possible reclamation by its owner.

The four now all drove off in a kind of edgy amicability for quite a few miles, when Mr. Harkey sat up stiffly and said in his firmest courtroom voice, "I want to warn one and all of you at this time that we will have to spend the night under the roof of Viola Franey and her two deaf mute daughters. I have sent ahead a telegram, which God knows whether she will receive, living in so remote a habitation. But watch your valuables! Better to keep them always on your person. And lock all doors behind you if we are lucky enough to get rooms with locks on them. And ever be wary! Best not to sleep at all while guests of Dame Franey!"

"But surely, Daddy, there must be a good hotel somewhere in the vicinity," Emma Lou disentangled herself for the moment from Hibbard Grady's thigh.

"Listen to little Miss-Born-Yesterday, will you?" Mr. Harkey turned to Lewis Coultas for sympathy, but found his companion looking more lackluster even than before.

"My dear Emma Lou," Harkey turned his eyes toward his wife. "I thought I had made everything clear to you before we left our suite. That we were going to Indian country! I warned you from the start not to come with me on this jaunt as 'twould be full of bad surprises, perils, contretemps, and possible death. Yet you would risk it, wouldn't you, because you are partial to folly, that's why, infatuated with risk, and thereby, my sweet, throwing into the scale all our own lives and fortunes. Yet you would come, wouldn't you, intrepid darling?"

"For cripes sake, Harkey," Lewis Coultas's partiality for the fair sex asserted itself, "will you let up on the poor kid? Can she help it if she's not got all her buttons? And what do you mean we're in Indian country," he carped, for the word Indian did not go down too well with him anymore.

"I repeat, Mr. Coultas, we are in Indian country, as any glance at the topography will tell you! And another thing I'd have you bear in mind. I will reprimand my wife in my own fashion. Is that clear?"

Mr. Harkey then raised his voice to its greatest volume in his spouse's direction, "You must always have your way, Emma Lou, and see where it has got you?"

"I only thought, my dear," Emma Lou spoke tearfully, "I naturally *assumed* that hotels were plentiful everywhere."

"Well, then, you are a bigger goose than even I took you for," Harkey snorted. "We have actually left civilization as we know it behind us." He glared at Lewis Coultas on saying this.

An uneasy silence fell on everybody then.

Mr. Harkey again spoke like a stentor, "Remember, all of you, what I told you about Viola Franey and her establishment. Bear it in mind. I have known her for years. She has always been helpful in giving me information, most of which proves useless, but every now and again she will give out a clue or an inkling of a fact which comes in handy. Since we've traced this brat, excuse me Mr. Coultas, traced your boy this far, Viola's bound to have had commerce with him. There's no place else to stay for one thing in this Godforsaken wilderness. And Viola will know where he's headed, whether it's widdershins or deasil to which he's departed!"

"Widdershins or deasil, my foot!" Lewis Coultas exploded in wrath, and removed his hat and waved it threateningly. He caught sight of more leg-pressing in the front seat again, at which he sighed, and drew from his breast pocket a small tin, and from it tossed a small lozenge into his very red and handsome mouth. Whatever the lozenge was, it filled the car with a strong medicinal scent, so that both Hibbard and Emma Lou released their hold on one another, and looked to the back seat concernedly.

"As I said earlier," Mr. Harkey spoke rather malapropos, "my fee can always go up, don't you know, so kindly watch your speech, sir!"

"Have a cough drop and keep your eye on the road," Lewis said and forced a lozenge into the hand of the investigator. "And pass the box, while you're at it, to your chauffeur and his ladylove. By Christ, I've never seen two such love birds off their perch before!"

Mr. Harkey gave Coultas a look of such withering loathing and reproof that the former pugilist and devotee of Indian clubs finally subsided into a prolonged and deep silence, and slouching down in his seat helped himself to another cough drop.

Viola Franey always said she could tell when it would snow or when she would have guests overnight, from the pain in her bunions.

Her bunions had pained her unmercifully all that afternoon so that it was no surprise to her at all when Mr. Harkey's touring car pulled up in her front yard in the midst of a heavy snowfall.

"How many will there be spending the night this time, Mr. Harkey?" Viola said, having sauntered out to the touring car and drawing back the side curtains on Harkey's side.

"You mean to tell me my telegram to you has gone astray?"

the old man began his complaints at once. "Well, we require rooms for everybody in this vehicle, my dear Mrs. Franey. You can count them, there are four of us."

"Are the two in the front seat married?" Mrs. Franey inquired worriedly.

"Mrs. Franey, my dear," Harkey warned the innkeeper by tapping with his gold pencil. "Kindly pay me mind! The young person in the front seat is my wife. And the gentleman beside her is my chauffeur."

Viola Franey gave everybody a look of consummate contempt, and then putting on her other spectacles she stared at Lewis Coultas, until he straightened up and took her hand in his, and pressed it heartily.

They all now hurried through the driving snow into the front room of the Franey domicile.

"I'm afraid I'll have to put you all in the same room," she explained as they seated themselves around the roaring fireplace. "The telegram Mr. Harkey speaks of did not reach me, and meantime a whole raft of ice fishermen has dropped in on me and filled up every room in the house. As a result of this overflow, my daughters and me will have to sleep here on the floor in front of the fireplace. We're glad to do it, nonetheless, for the convenience of wayfarers."

"Mrs. Franey, before you begin cooking supper for us, for supper was mentioned in my telegram," Mr. Harkey got down to business, "the purport of this expedition of ours is this. We are in search of a runaway boy who, I've been told on good authority," here he consulted a sheaf of papers, ". . . . have been told on very sterling information, was seen lately in this vicinity."

"See here, Mr. Harkey," Viola began in a tone which meant she did not take kindly to his drift. "Be advised, sir, that if I asked every boy who stopped under my roof if he was a runaway or not I wouldn't be patronized by the people I am patronized by. I don't ask questions of my transients, never have, and never will." As Mrs. Franey said this, she gave a lofty stare at Emma Lou and Hibbard. "I am not a policewoman, Mr. Harkey," she finished and folded her arms.

Mr. Harkey threw up his hands.

"I wish people would learn to answer a simple question with *yes* or *no*," the detective complained. "It is the one thing I never ceased being surprised at when I was a prosecuting attorney. People simply cannot say *yes* or *no* to a question."

"I feel I have answered your question perfectly and forthrightly, Mr. Harkey, and I think you know I have so answered it. You asked about a runaway boy, and I told you I didn't ask any boy if he was running away. So that's your answer. Maybe you were into one of your dozes when I replied to your query."

"Then you have testified, Mrs. Franey, that you have not sheltered under your roof a runaway boy. Is that what you mean?"

"See here, sir. I do not know if the boy is a runaway or not. But I do know he is crazy."

"Now who are you speaking of, dear madam?"

"Why, the Indian boy of course, who raped my daughters. Who else?"

"Would you describe him to us, dear madam."

Mrs. Franey paused. "I don't know whether I like that *madam* or not, but since you're so stuck on direct answers, I will tell you. I'll describe him, that is, you stickler for particulars as I remember from your other visits here. Well," she let her memory work for her, "he'd be a good-looking young fellow if he wasn't so woebegone and worried and half starved to death in the bargain. He is an Indian, no question about that, save for one small particular."

"And that particular is, Mrs. Franey," Mr. Harkey inquired, writing very quickly with his gold pen in his notebook.

"His one eye was a rich, deep pool-like black whereas the other was roving lovely sky-blue. It made him look two boys in one."

"Two boys in one," Mr. Harkey repeated, writing down the comment, and then catching himself he crossed the last statement out hurriedly, as more opinion than fact.

"That was my son," Mr. Coultas now spoke as if coming out of a reverie. "And see here, ma'am, he's not considered an Indian back home in Yellow Brook, I can assure you. This is all a recent thing, his being charged an Indian."

Despite her first good impression of Lewis Coultas, Mrs. Franey now gave him an even more suspicious and distrustful glance than she had directed toward Emma Lou and Hibbard.

"If I were the parents of that boy," Mrs. Franey gave her opinion, "I would keep him at home until he knows north from south, or until at least he has learned to follow his own nose home." She drew in a great mouthful of breath, having said this.

"But he's been abducted, the poor tyke," Mr. Coultas expostulated and he slumped down between two cushions of a dilapidated davenport. As Mr. Coultas sighed, everyone from the party of Mr. Harkey wondered if Lewis was going to become maudlin again, and embarrass the life out of everybody in the presence of the harridan Viola Franey.

A dinner bell now sounded and they all marched into the dining room.

"As I told you at our supper table tonight," Mrs. Franey was booming away, after the meal was concluded, "I can only offer you people my big front room for sleeping all of you tonight. As you can see we're having a real snowstorm, you'd be fools not to take it. As I said earlier my good rooms are all occupied by ice fishermen and the curling team.

"But beds I have, beds for all. And now let me put in a word of warning. This is a decent house I run. I will have no carrying on here when the lights go out, no hanky-panky." Here she paused at a fierce look being given her by Wilbur Harkey. "And no lighted tobacco of any kind, and absolutely no topsy-turvy." She finished her speech in some sudden confusion and abashment at the severe countenance of Wilbur Harkey now bearing down on her.

"You should be the matron of a reformatory, Mrs. Franey, not a hostess for well-bred gentlemen and ladies," the old detective adjured her, and though Mrs. Franey attempted to interrupt him at this point, he raised his hand for silence. "Furthermore, madam, your use of the word topsy-turvy is inept, irrelevant, and in wretched taste since we are the helpless fugitives from a snow blizzard. But I wonder if indeed you know what you mean, my poor dear."

"Don't you dare to *dear* me after the way you've just talked and after the way you have been staring holes in me. You'd do better to keep an eye on your young wife—if she is your wife!"

The old detective interrupted her with some forbearance. "Let me warn you, Mrs. Franey, I am in constant communication with the entire continental and international network of surveillance. I am kept apprised every hour and minute of the day and night. You are therefore under suspicion, unfortunate woman that you are."

"I under suspicion, you say! Look who's talking, will you! Bringing to these premises three such suspicious characters as ever I laid eyes on, that snip of a girl you palm off as your wife and the two bruisers in your company are, it's clear as daylight, throwing her in the hay every time your eyes are closed shut, which at your age is most of the time!"

"I warn you, you impudent virago, all of this is being recorded in my brain, and shall be used against you—in *court* without any doubt."

"In court, my eye! For speaking my own mind under my roof, you low, pettifogging humbug! I'd have you remember, sir, that a woman's house is her castle, and you'll obey the rules here tonight or out you go, you and your legal jargon with you. And how do I know that you're not a white slaver yourself, appearing out of the blue with this girl, not far from a child herself, and hunting this young Indian boy. And to what purpose, I ask, to what purpose indeed! No, siree, I won't be criticized in my own home by the likes of you, Wilbur Harkey, and your flock of ill-assorted birds can depart into the raging blizzard unless you come to your senses!"

Mr. Harkey was about to respond to Mrs. Franey's accusations and calumnies at great length when a hammering at the front door silenced their altercation.

"Well, supposin' you answer the door, Mr. Wilbur Harkey, since you're in charge of surveillance, law and order, particulars, and arrest and detention. Go on, see who's banging out there at this time of night and in such weather!" Mrs. Franey could barely keep her hands from throttling the old investigator, so forthright was her anger at that moment.

"I think that is exactly what I shall do, my dear Mrs. Franey," Wilbur Harkey meekly replied. "And when the door is opened, perhaps we'll see just what kind of a house you are opening your doors on tonight, and if you are all you claim to be, speaking as if butter would never melt in your mouth!"

"Am I to be brought to trial under my own roof by that old drag-tail of a rooster!" Mrs. Franey cried loud enough now to be heard by all the ice fishermen, the curling team, and of course the party of the old detective.

There were cries of surprise and unbelief, and perhaps even joy, when Wilbur opened the door on the persons of Minnie and Cora, their hats and clothing nearly buried under thousands of wet and now dripping snowflakes. The two ladies embraced Mr. Harkey, covering him with snowy kisses, and swearing he was the most welcome sight in all the white-blanketed world.

"That will do, Minnie and Cora, enough is enough," Wilbur cooed, as he extricated himself from their close hugs and cold kisses, and began brushing off the great quantity of snow such close contact with them had bestowed on him.

Lewis Coultas, unaccountably, was somewhat restrained in his welcome of Minnie and Cora, though, after the embraces showered on the old detective, he felt he could hardly do less than kiss both women with something of his old ardor, and hold them to his breast.

"And where, my dear Mr. Harkey, do you expect me to sleep these two arrivals?" Viola Franey demanded.

"I will give up my bed, and sleep in the touring car," the investigator volunteered with a low bow to Minnie and Cora. "You can't in all conscience, dear Mrs. Franey, send them out in that blinding blizzard, can you."

"No, no, Wilbur, dearest," Emma Lou now stepped forward. "Hibbard and I will sleep in the back of the touring car, never you fear. You must have a good bed tonight to be fresh for your morrow's investigation."

They would have been arguing until dawn probably—which was not many hours away—had not Viola Franey promised to bring in two additional cots and place them all in the room where the entire company of Wilbur Harkey was to pass the night.

While Hibbard Grady did the actual work of fetching in the additional cots, Mrs. Franey clapped her hands for attention, and very red in the face now, she delivered her formal speech of warning:

"My livelihood, ladies and gents, depend on my being known as the proprietress of a decent rooming house. That reputation has been smirched earlier in the week by the behavior of an obnoxious and wayward Indian boy, him with the one blue eye. . . ."

"Now see here, Mrs. Franey," Lewis Coultas broke in at this

point. "I resent that aspersion on my son, and you know in your heart you are bearing false witness against him and me, his legal father!"

"I bear false witness!" Viola Franey cried as if Lewis had stuck her with one of her own hatpins. "Let me warn you for the last time. If you want to stay the night you will have to obey the rules, and that includes not sassing and contradicting the proprietress of this establishment, who is, Mr. Coultas, the woman now speaking to you. I shall be respected or you shall go out into that blinding snowstorm now!"

Too weary to argue, too bone-tired indeed even to utter another sound, Lewis Coultas opened the door to the communal sleeping chamber, and laid himself down with all his expensive Chicago clothes still on, including his pure silk cravat almost hidden under his stiff white collar. The others in the party of Wilbur Harkey, taking a leaf out of Lewis's book, also came into the room, yawning and rubbing their eyes, and soon everybody had followed suit after Coultas, and were lying down each in a separate bed.

"The center light in this room stays on," Mrs. Franey gave her final warning. "And remember, I will be only a stone's throw away—listening!"

She then slammed the door violently and perhaps owing to her closing the door so vigorously, the center light dimmed considerably, then went slowly out, leaving all the party of Mr. Wilbur Harkey in a cave-like inky darkness.

Long before the first cock's crow, stooped and stealthy, Wilbur Harkey closed the door of the sleeping chamber behind him and began tiptoeing out toward the front entrance of the Franey mansion when he came directly against the seated glowering figure of Mrs. Viola Franey herself, holding a rifle in the crook of her right arm.

"And what are you doing up in the dead of night like a tomcat snuffling at a crack?" she wondered loftily, keeping her voice very low, however.

Mr. Harkey gulped the cold pre-morning air, then swallowing hard, managed to get out, as he produced his camera from his billowing outer coat, "I've got enough evidence here on all of them to put them away for an eternity!"

"Just stand there a moment," Mrs. Franey threatened him, and she stood up to her full height, barely under four feet. "Don't move!" she cautioned him, and she advanced to a closed gray door and opened it with the forceful heave of someone who expects to behold a murder in progress.

Mr. Harkey peered into the room and saw stretched out on a large bed Mrs. Franey's two daughters, strapped firmly across the gutted mattress, gags about their violently moving mouths. They attempted to wave their pinioned arms on seeing their mother before them.

"Though dumb as fence posts," Mrs. Franey commenced, "they can make sounds like a congregation of Holy Rollers when they get started." She scoffed now at the girls' plight. "I had to know if they were still safe and tied down in here, Investigator Harkey, or whether they'd sneak into the room with your lolly-gagging chauffeur and that whoremaster Lewis Coultas."

She nodded with satisfaction over the predicament of her daughters. "These girls," Mrs. Franey pointed to her two daughters, "walk in their sleep." She spoke in a stage whisper which carried, however, as loudly as her blaring alto. On saying this she slammed the door shut on her daughters and turned to the detective, "And now, my fine stickler for the particulars, where are *you* off to like an escaped convict at this hour?"

"I will be forthright with you, madam," Harkey began, "but for God's sake put down that flintlock, will you, or we're apt to be blown to bits."

A contemptuous smile moved briefly over Mrs. Franey's white lips, but she put the gun in a corner.

"Now," he began. "Look here, I'll level with you. I've *got* to find the boy before *they* do, if you follow me."

He went speaking inaudibly as he fumbled in his pocket for his purse. After an interminable wait, he drew it out and pulled out of it some bills of very high denomination.

"All right, sir, before we talk terms," Mrs. Franey said coolly, looking at the fistful of greenbacks, "what exactly is going on in that sleeping room, do you mind telling me? Or better still, what have you photographed?"

Mr. Harkey snuffled the air again, and looked almost cute. Mrs. Franey cleared her throat, implying that her forbearance, always thin, was going.

"My dear Mrs. Franey, my last grain of patience has run out

with my second wife Emma Lou, who of course never could hold a candle to Gabrielle in the first place . . . I refer to my first spouse. Emma Lou has not only worn out my chauffeur with her concupiscent lust, she finally got her mitts on my client Lewis Coultas at least four times in succession according to my count before I got up my strength to put on my suspenders and get out of there."

"Thank God my daughters were bound and gagged," Mrs. Franey spoke in an almost civilized manner now, in contrast to her usual clapperclaw tone.

"The two men are worn to the thinnest of frazzles, for while my wife was enjoying the retired prizefighter—that's Coultas of course—Minnie and Cora were taking turns with my chauffeur Hibbard Grady, who (I've got to hand it to him) lasted the full fifteen rounds before passing out on the hardwood floor."

"There goes the reputation of my house, Mr. Harkey, thanks to you and your retinue! Yes, thanks to you." She affected now to bawl and wiped her tears with the back of her hand.

Wilbur Harkey pressed one of the high denomination bills in her hand, and patted her gently on a tear-stained cheek.

"Ah well, that's a woman's life," she shook her head, and pocketed the bill.

"My considerate friend," Mr. Harkey began now in his public manner, "I am in need of information, information which I believe you and only you, esteemed lady, are in the possession of." As he pronounced these words he waved the remaining bills in front of the landlady.

"Oh, Mr. Harkey, you are a regular ferret, you are!" She winked at him, and then lowered her eyes like a small girl. "Yes, you have the nose of a pedigreed hound, no question about it."

Mrs. Franey was all at once actually coquettish, and as he stared at her, Mr. Harkey could see some faint traces of a long-vanished beauty.

"Then, my dear, between you and me and the gate post, what is this talk about the Indian boy going to see Chief Silver Fox?"

Mrs. Franey's eyes kept straying to the rest of the greenbacks as if in fear they might somehow be withdrawn and put back in one of the detective's many pockets.

"It all comes from the terrible old man," she whispered, and one would have thought by reason of her confidential tone this terrible old man was also occupying one of her many rooms, perhaps tied and gagged to a mattress.

"I mean," she went on irascibly when Harkey showed no indication he knew who she meant, "I refer to the great-grandfather of the brat in question . . . you know, the Indian brat with the one blue eye. That's his old grandad's horse he drives—probably to both their deaths."

"I must warn you, call no client of mine a brat. I won't warn you again."

"Now see here, Mr. High and Mighty, if you want the information you will not correct my speech, and that's gospel. You may be a great ferret, but you don't always behave like a man in his right mind."

"The particulars—how many times must I say it—the particulars are all I am after, Mrs. Franey."

"Particulars, my fanny!" She sneered and looked again at the greenback. "Well, ask me a particular then, and if I can I'll tell you." She looked again indignantly at some more bills the detective had all at once produced and was holding in his fist.

"Where is the Indian at this moment then? Speak up!"

"All right, all right," she capitulated. "His grandfather or his great-grandfather, or maybe even his great great-grandfather—you know Indians live forever—has sent the horse to take the boy to Chief Silver Fox."

"Clear as mud," the detective complained.

"I'm telling you all I know . . . but we must keep our voices down or the crowd of fornicators in there will be up and about, and then your strategem will come to naught."

"So you feel the horse, which you say he got from his great-grandfather, is, by some sort of plan, taking the boy to this Chief Silver Fox, or whatever his name."

"That's your particular for you, Mr. Harkey. That's it, and that's all I know. I'm no medium after all."

"Very well. One last question, and I'm done with you. . . . Where in the nation is Chief Silver Fox, and who is he?"

"You mean to tell me with all your continental and intercontinental network of communications you neither know who the Chief is nor where he is!" She laughed nastily and then gave him a look of deepest pity.

When the detective was silent, she gave out with her information. "Well, Mr. Harkey, Silver Fox is the last of the great chiefs. The very last."

She moistened her lips generously before continuing. "Now for the directions, and pay close mind. If you take the little road that leads to the right of my house here, and follow your nose, so to speak, you will come to what's left of the reservation. About thirty miles from here. Maybe a little more, maybe a little less. The old man, Chief Silver Fox, who is over 120 if he's a day, lives in a kind of fortress-like structure with a tower on top of it. Be careful though of the Indians guarding the fortress. They don't like white men, especially old white men, and they would just as soon shoot a detective as peel an apple."

Mr. Harkey handed Mrs. Franey the rest of the bills, which she seized like a drowning woman a rope.

"And don't let them know where I've gone." He jerked his hand in the direction of the sleeping chamber. He handed her a few silver coins on saying this.

"And bend your ear down, dear, for this last bit of information," he advised her. "Beyond the shadow of a doubt," he whispered, "the authorities will take Lewis Coultas into custody at any time. Grand larceny. But he's booked a passage, I'm told, for Australia. . . . The two ladies turned him in in exchange for their freedom. Now, mum!"

"You'll recommend my rooming house, nonetheless, won't you, Mr. Harkey, when you get back home," Mrs. Franey begged. She did not seem to have taken in the news of the imminent arrest of Lewis Coultas.

"I'll give you four stars whenever your establishment is mentioned," he spoke with hearty encouragement, and hurried out the door.

She waited without moving until she heard his car start, and then she rushed into the dining room to prepare something fortifying after her sleepless and grueling night holding the gun.

Chad took generous but not too prolonged sips from Eva's tiny vial, which seemed at times to the boy to have a way of replenishing itself. Probably from his tears he thought. For he did nothing at times but weep, and only the sips from the tiny bottle kept him going. His mind was so confused, his heart so broken, his direction so misguided and misplaced, that he didn't know or maybe care where he was or whither he was going.

He observed at least that it was daylight, and the sun was hiding somewhere behind black and purple clouds, when all at once his patient horse came to a stop by a small mill surrounded by a silo.

"About time, too," a very dark-complexioned man spoke to him. Chad saw that the horse had drawn up to a kind of loading platform. The man, without further words, began throwing large sacks of something in the back of Chad's wagon.

"I don't suppose a lazy good-for-nothing like you would give a man a hand now, would you?"

"A hand, sure!" Chad leaped down, letting the reins fall where they would. "If you would tell me the best road to Chief Silver Fox."

The man stopped loading the sacks and watched the boy narrowly.

"There's no best road where Silver Fox is, my lad," the man finally informed him. "Chief Silver Fox, my boy, died a year or so ago, and so you all but got here in time for the funeral now, didn't you?"

Chad helped load the wagon with the heavy bags. Somehow he felt even more lost than usual at the thought Chief Silver Fox was dead, though he had never looked forward to meeting him, and he could not recall at the moment why he was ever supposed to meet him in the first place, except of course, and he pronounced the following words for some reason aloud: "Except we was both Indians."

"And right you are on that score," the man spoke with less surliness. He studied Chad now closely.

"You're not only an Indian," the man went on, "but you're due for a bath if ever I saw an Indian due for one. When you get to Wilma Trowt's, tell her to give you a soaking in her third-story bathtub."

"But if there's no Chief Silver Fox," Chad spoke his thought out loud, "why bother to go anywhere else?"

The man considered his words.

"Well, maybe Wilma Trowt could arrange for you to see Chief Harvest Moon, if he is still among the living, for he must be crowding one hundred and thirty."

As Chad helped him load the last of the heavy bags, the

man, as if taking pity on so grimy an Indian boy, said, "You can ask Wilma Trowt about your itinerary. . . . She's the head of the reformatory, if you don't know what all these sacks of flour are for."

"And so I'm supposed to follow my nose again, if I'm to get to her."

The man with the flour bags looked both weary and disgusted. "Since there's only one road here that leads to everywhere—to Wilma Trowt, and to Chief Harvest Moon—I don't think even *you* will get lost," the man sneered, "unless you can persuade that half-dead animal to take you backwards, which I wouldn't put it past you to try."

Chad switched the horse as gently as possible while the man was talking on, and horse and driver went off at a fairly brisk pace straight into the rays of the invisible sun.

Every few feet, for his elucidation, was a large sign, with the same words each time:

THE WILMA TROWT HOME
FOR RUNAWAY AND INCORRIGIBLE BOYS

The last sign he saw on the road read merely:

WILMA TROWT'S HOME FOR BOYS

Chad now saw in the distance a structure that appeared as large as a castle in one of the geography books in Bess Lytle's classroom. The horse, as if she knew (as she always seemed to) where he was going at least, drew up in the rear of the building. Two boys, about Chad's age, came out and began unloading the sacks of flour. Both boys were Indians, and behind their left ears each of them wore bright cock feathers.

"The man at the mill said I could have a hot bath in the third-story bathtub," Chad addressed the two boys.

The Indians exchanged looks, and a faint trace of a smile played over the lips of the taller of the two.

"When you see Mrs. Trowt about the flour," the taller one began, "in her front parlor, you can ask her about any bathing."

Mrs. Wilma Trowt was a person Lewis Coultas might have described unfavorably as too thin and raw-boned for a woman. She was at least six feet four in her stocking feet, but she insisted on wearing high heels, perhaps to give her charges a feeling of still greater authority, and as none of them were anywhere near reaching their full growth she succeeded in thus quelling them by her very towering appearance.

"You want a receipt for the flour, I suppose," Wilma Trowt said to Chad without bothering to look up from her desk and papers.

"I would like to have a hot bath in the third-story bathroom," Chad volunteered.

Wilma Trowt looked up then. "Why you're not him!" she exclaimed. "What is this?"

Chad felt an almost violent need for his mother's vial, but bore the scrutiny from Wilma Trowt with stoic resignation. She made clucking sounds with her tongue.

"As to a hot bath, great heavens! We've not had a drop of hot water in this house for twenty-five years, if then." She again studied Chad closely. "Are you going back to the mill from here?" she wondered.

For answer he sat or rather collapsed on a little settee which was fortunately handy or he might have passed out right then and there.

"I was to have seen Chief Silver Fox," Chad began after getting control over himself.

He heard Wilma Trowt tapping angrily with a pencil, more angrily even than Bess Lytle at her most severe.

"Have you committed a crime?" Wilma Trowt narrowed her eyes.

"No, no, ma'am, I have not."

"Well, see here. There is no Chief Silver Fox." Wilma Trowt took off her glasses and looked out the window.

"And no Chief Harvest Moon?" the boy wondered.

"Oh, well," Wilma Trowt considered the last name, just as Bess Lytle might have considered one of his wrong answers in long division. "The Indians up there do nothing but drink, you understand. They're always having a funeral or choosing a new chief. But there never was, so far as I know, any Chief Silver Fox. I don't think any respectable Indian would call himself that in the first place."

"But did they give him a funeral, ma'am?"

"Funeral? Oh, they have funerals up on the hill all the time. Most of the Indians are over 100, so what can you expect?"

Chad had been fumbling as Wilma Trowt spoke, with Eva's

little vial, and he quickly pressed the bottle now to his lips. Wilma Trowt was silent as he sipped.

"Let me say this," she began in a hushed voice. "You are in bad shape for a young boy. And you haven't committed a crime as yet? Well, if you haven't, then you haven't, and this is therefore no place for you. Crime is like chicken pox—catching."

Aided by the elixir from his mother, Chad began a rather excellent recital, he thought, of his three kidnappings, his escape from his great-grandfather in his great-grandfather's wagon, the night at Viola Franey's, and finally his search—in vain, as it turned out—for Chief Silver Fox.

"Yes, Chad, I can see you have been through a good deal for a boy of your years. What has happened to you should never have happened to anyone. But then, that is life, isn't it? We don't choose our parents or our destiny."

She shook her head long and solemnly and kept her eyes averted from him. "I'll tell you what I advise," Wilma Trowt spoke after her long cogitation. "Since the wagon is your great-grandfather's, and you are certainly an Indian from your every appearance—except as you've pointed out for your one eye—why don't you leave your wagon and horse here, and we'll buy you a ticket back to what was the name of the town you hail from? Ah, yes, Yellow Brook. I didn't know there were any Indians residing that far south any more, but you ought to know if you come from there."

"Well, there's Decatur," he sighed.

"Decatur? I see." Wilma Trowt indicated he could tell all he knew about Decatur.

Chad stumbled, almost choked, but finally got out the story of how one day coming down the staircase he had met the dark-skinned man who claimed him for his boy, and how the man had nearly had a stroke when he laid eyes on him at the top of the staircase.

"Would you care for a sip of my mother's elixir, ma'am," Chad finally suggested to Wilma Trowt when he saw her sink into a kind of prolonged meditation after his story had been told.

"No, I will have to decline that offer," she said, still deep in contemplation perhaps of his narrative. "If you didn't have two fathers, a great-grandfather, a maternal grandmother and of course your mother, sister and the uncle who has a glass eye—

according to your story—I would recommend wholeheartedly that you stay here with the other boys for a good year or so. But your trouble, Chad, if you don't mind my saying so, is you have too many people looking after you already, and you've had to be—to use your term—kidnapped again and again to satisfy their need for you. My, oh my, I wish just one of my boys here had parents who cared enough about them to abduct them even for an hour! But these lads have nobody! No one who cares a straw if they live or die. Nobody would kidnap one of my boys if they were paid a fortune to do so. And the sad thing is, after my boys leave here they all come to bad ends. I should not be saying all this, especially to you. What has come over me? The one exceptional case, however, was that of Jonas Leppingwell, who went on to be a prize fighter in Duluth, Minnesota, but then was murdered in a box car going to Portage la Prairie. Dear dear Jonas Leppingwell!" She sighed and wiped her eyes.

A bell loud enough to be heard all the way (Chad thought) back to Viola Franey's, now sounded, announcing dinner, which was held at the hour of noon. Taking Chad by the arm as if she had known him for years, she ushered him into a dining room almost the size of the main floor of the Opera House in Yellow Brook. Seated at twenty-four big tables young men of all heights patiently waited, but everyone had complexions dark as the cloudiest sunset. They were waiting for Wilma Trowt's arrival. She took her place now on a high dais overlooking the dining hall so that she appeared to be ten feet tall.

"Sit over there in the northwest corner, if you will, Chad," Mrs. Trowt spoke to him through a small megaphone. With some trepidation he hurried to obey her.

"Ready!" Wilma Trowt shouted now through the megaphone. "Sit down!" (They had risen upon her entrance.) "Begin putting on your napkins. Say fifteen seconds of grace. Eat!"

There was immediately the sound of forks and knives going lickety-split over the big ironstone plates.

Chad had followed Wilma Trowt's instructions and found his plate heaped high with venison, sweet potatoes, cabbage, and different kinds and colors of squash. The only unappetizing thing, a small one, was that there were pieces of deer fur throughout the baked venison, but the taste was not harmed by this oversight in the kitchen.

The next thing Chad could remember was Mrs. Trowt giving him instructions as to where to go to "surrender" the horse and wagon.

"Your trek and your voyage of discovery are coming to a close," she told him, and stepping down from her great height she kissed him goodbye.

"If there should be another funeral in progress where you're going," she advised him as a kind of afterthought, "give whoever is in charge this piece of paper. It will probably be the young man they used to call Black Lynx, though sometimes he like to call himself White Wolf. Whatever he is called these days, be sure to hand him this piece of paper."

"And Black Lynx or White Wolf is an Indian, ma'am?"

Wilma Trowt shook her head, and held her arms akimbo.

"My dear young man, I am the only white person there is for two hundred miles around. Keep that in mind. So of course Black Lynx is an Indian, and for mercy's sake, don't please ask around from now on if *somebody is one or not.* And don't use the word redskin as I heard you while you were eating your venison stew say to somebody. You have a long way to go, and an awful lot to learn, so keep your mouth buttoned tight for the most part."

With that, Mrs. Trowt could not resist giving him another prolonged and rather slobbery kiss on his forehead, and then slammed the door of the front parlor after him until he could almost swear he heard all the ironware dishes in the dining hall rattle and threaten to fall into pieces to the floor.

Waking up with a start, Chad looked about him. He saw by the light struggling in the sky that he must have traveled all night over impossibly rutty roads, impeded by fallen tree trunks, boulders, and huge pit-like declivities in his path. He marveled that he was still moving onward. And near every ditch he passed he read one sign after another:

ROADS UNSAFE: TRAVELERS BE WARNED!
BEWARE OF ARMED BANDS OF MEN!

Under the lettering were the usual drawings of skulls and crossbones, which had now become familiar to him. Indeed, he reflected, almost nothing now made much of an impression on him. Every so often nonetheless he would think he was back in Eva's house, or was in his grandmother's upper chambers with all the medicine bottles and herbal tinctures. Or that he was out riding with Decatur under a full moon.

Then there occurred what later he would think of as perhaps his "final awakening," for he was pulled out of another nap by someone shaking him violently, and then slapping him somewhat gently. He opened his eyes and saw the face of the darkest man he had ever beheld, at least so he appeared in the peculiar light drifting down from the sky at that moment. So dark was the man's complexion and so very long his black hair falling almost in braids, that one felt there fell from this newcomer pieces of his own blackness, as soot falls from heated chimneys.

"Chief Harvest Moon?" Chad wondered, and then looking about him, seeing neither horse nor wagon, he cried, "Where is she?"

"Your horse is dead," the stranger said. He put his hand briefly on the back of Chad's neck.

Chad began to make a kind of moaning sound, and then looking about him saw he was sitting in the front seat of a rather spiffy four-seater automobile with a very expensive shiny dashboard with a big ticking clock on it.

"There's an alert out for you," the man informed him, and when there was no response from the boy, he turned a set of wonderfully white and rather sharp teeth in a gesture of encouragement. The gleaming white of his teeth made his face all the more midnight dark.

"I'm Shelldrake," the man said, keeping his teeth still exposed, and moving close as if he felt the boy was deaf.

Chad kept looking about him and feeling in his pockets for something.

"How long is it you've been gone from home?" Shelldrake wondered.

Chad shook his head. "Quite a long while." He smiled when the man grinned at his remark. Chad kept searching in his pockets.

"Are you looking for something in particular?" Shelldrake inquired.

"Never mind," Chad said dispiritedly.

Reaching behind him Shelldrake held up the two sacks of gold coins and the little vial Eva had given Chad.

The boy's eyes brightened when he saw his possessions.

"Everything's there," Shelldrake told him. "And now I'm going to drive you home if you're ready. We'll beat the posse to Yellow Brook."

"But what about all the Indian chiefs I was supposed to see, Harvest Moon and the rest?" And Chad looked more closely at Shelldrake's braided hair.

"Oh, Chad, who put it into your head there are Indian chiefs waiting to see you! I don't think there's an Indian chief around here for five hundred miles—unless you count me!" He grinned, and Chad gave him another of his faint smiles.

As Shelldrake smiled back at him, Chad felt he should be frightened, for the countenance before him was so ferocious in appearance, and the white teeth so very beast-like and close. Yes, Chad would have been frightened, he reflected, at one time, but hardly after what he had been through ever since Decatur had appeared and stared up at him from the foot of Eva's staircase.

"Let me try to tell you again, Chad," his new companion began. "There is this alert out on you all over this part of the country. They are *looking* for you, Chad. And your dad, Mr. Lewis Coultas, has busted out of jail, and they say is on his way to Australia. Anyhow, you won't be seeing him for a good long age. . . . Did you hear what I said?"

Chad tried to hide the fact some tears had come into his eyes, but Shelldrake put his own hand to the boy's face and wiped the tears away.

"I didn't know he was ever in jail in the first place," Chad spoke bitterly. As he spoke his eyes fell on Shelldrake's hands. They were enormously large and swollen, with little cuts on them everywhere, and a few deep scars showing white against his dark flesh. Even Decatur's hands would have looked small and of little account alongside Shelldrake's.

"I've got a lot to figure out," Chad mumbled.

"You've been asleep for quite a few hours. I found your horse and wagon in a ditch, with the poor beast dead, and the wheels off the vehicle. So I up and took charge of you. Now do you want to sleep some more or shall we get going for Yellow Brook?"

Whether it was because the man who called himself Shelldrake had pronounced the name of his hometown, or what, Chad found himself unaccountably taking one of the stranger's hands in his and pressing it hard.

"Does that mean I can drive you home then?" Shelldrake wondered.

Chad nodded, for his heart was too full to speak.

"Are you cold, you're shivering like that?" Shelldrake wondered.

"No, I ain't cold, sir."

"I wish I had a son just like you," the man said all at once in his throaty far-away voice.

Shelldrake picked up Eva's vial and looked at it. "I tried some of this concoction while I was counting your money," Shelldrake said hesitantly. "It's way and again too strong for a boy like you. No wonder you was such a sound sleeper when I found you!"

Then Shelldrake gave Chad a look the boy did not quite understand. The expression in those deep-set ebony black eyes seemed to be that of a deep hurt or outrage. All at once he drew the boy's head toward his lips, and kissed him slowly on both his eyes.

The strange kiss such as had never been bestowed on him before gave him a kind of quiet throughout his entire body which he had not ever felt before. At that moment Shelldrake started the motor of his car, and they went off almost at once at a killing speed.

Then his companion was talking all at once on the subject of the chiefs. "Even if they ever saw people from outside," Shelldrake was explaining, "they would not have been of any help to you. But take me, I'm one of them, and I have hardly ever set eyes on one of those chiefs since I was a young boy like you. So you've been on a wild goose chase."

Then without warning Shelldrake brought the car to a full stop, and after a pause took Chad's left hand in his and pressed it.

"Chad, listen to me. In this life, there are no guides. There are no chiefs waiting to tell us something. Understand?"

Chad's eyes met then the burning black eyes of his friend.

Shelldrake started the motor again and if possible the wheels moved even faster over the winding road before them.

The hurt and puzzled look that had persisted over Chad's countenance for so many weeks began to relax a little. He kept looking at Shelldrake from time to time as if to reassure himself he was really there. On one of these furtive glances he noticed that the man wore a kind of feather of many shades behind his right ear. The thought crossed Chad's mind that maybe he was after all one of the chiefs himself.

Then Chad fell back in the seat in a manner that seemed to express either that he had given up trying to figure anything out, or that perhaps he had found an answer to everything in Shelldrake's presence itself.

"As I told you, Chad," Shelldrake was speaking again, "I would give the whole world I think to have a boy like you. So why don't you think about it while we're on our way to Yellow Brook. If you ever need a real flesh-and-blood father I will try to be him."

"I believe you mean that," Chad spoke in a peculiar tremolo.

"I don't think I ever said anything I didn't mean," Shelldrake looked straight ahead as he spoke. "I need a son more than I need air to breathe, and I've known that for some time. So you be thinking it over too before we get to Yellow Brook."

What actually then occurred was "too terrible" to happen to a boy of scarcely "fourteen summers," to quote Mr. Wilbur Harkey's phrase.

Shelldrake was driving faster than any ace among the racers of that time, with one hand resting from time to time on Chad's shoulder. He was still speaking about adopting him now that Lewis Coultas had skipped the country. If Shelldrake had not talked so much and promised so much he might have noticed that a car was coming from behind, a car that, if this was possible, was speeding even more swiftly than Shelldrake's, and someone, with the aid of a bullhorn, was calling out to Shelldrake to stop.

Then there was a peculiar quiet from the pursuing car.

Without further warning, the first shot came, going right through the gleaming windshield. Shelldrake stopped the car.

Chad heard his friend say something in another tongue—

Chad remembered that, for Shelldrake spoke several sentences in this unknown language to him.

Then Shelldrake swore in Chad's own language and helped himself from the back of the vehicle to two guns—or perhaps actually some kind of sawed off rifles—and handed one methodically to Chad, and held the other on his lap. Then giving out a piercing yell he turned again into an ace of a racer.

"Even if you say you don't know how to handle a gun, you can pull a trigger if they come up on us," Shelldrake encouraged him.

When they had outstripped the pursuing car, Shelldrake without any warning (it seemed he had turned into another man altogether—stiff, hard, cold as the sky at sunrise, and all at once looking more like a white man to Chad, by reason of his new coldness and fury) veered dizzily to one side of the road, leaped a ditch, and turned into a vacant field. The wheels crunched and screeched as they passed over what felt like the remains of corn stalks. Some kind of large birds flew up as they passed and screamed as the car came crashing into them, and then as they were struck, feathers flew everywhere, and drops of red.

"So this wasn't in the cards!" Shelldrake cried.

Then coming to a partial stop, he took Chad's left hand so tightly in his right one that Chad could hear his bones crack, as Shelldrake mumbled, "You must be worth it, why I don't know, but guess you just are. . . . And if they blow my head off I'll say the same thing from the other side. . . . Chad, trust me, I ain't a bad man, I'm just an unlucky one."

They drove or rather bobbed up and down like a boat in high water until Chad heard Shelldrake give out a whistle. It was a whistle that would have waked the dead—a whole acre of dead men. It was a whistle Chad never thought could come from a human being's lips. They had stopped at a kind of vacant storehouse.

Shelldrake rushed to the trunk of the car, fetched a can of something, opened it, and then advanced to the storehouse. Then he came rushing back to the car which, still in gear, he drove off then putting as much distance between himself and the warehouse as he could.

After a queer silence, Chad heard something even more terrible than Shelldrake's whistle. His eyes pained all at once from the sudden light following the explosion in the storehouse behind them, and turning around he saw the whole earth and sky aflame.

Shelldrake laughed uproariously, but his laughter resembled screaming more than joy, and the engine of his car echoed his cries. The whole car gave off sounds as if it too was about to explode into fire.

Directly ahead now Chad caught sight of another kind of structure. It turned out to be a large house, with at least four stories.

"Now keep your head down as we go in here, Chad. They are probably still behind us, and they don't want to take me alive and breathing, do you hear."

They slunk with heads down into the dark house, and Shelldrake closed and bolted the door, then hurried to the rear entrance, and bolted it also.

Shelldrake hesitated a moment, then he took Chad's gun away from him.

"Supposin' you go back into that bedroom there, do you hear? And lie down on the floor and keep laid down."

But as he said this, he hesitated. He all at once gathered Chad into his arms, which trembled. He held the boy against his ribcage so hard that again Chad felt the sound of bones cracking, and then Shelldrake leaned down from his great height and kissed him on his blue eye. Then as if he had caught the true color of it for the first time, he kissed him there again.

"Drink some more of your ma's liquor, why don't you," he advised him, and then he closed the heavy door between himself and Chad.

Chad drank off nearly all of the remaining elixir. He was trembling like the mulberry leaves at home in a summer thundershower, and then when he heard the gunfire right outside the house he peed his pants.

Then he heard what sounded like two cars driving right up almost to the wall behind which he stood, and the firing began in earnest, and presently bullets began coming even into his room, the glass of windows was busted to smithereens, and he heard men talking through bullhorns, or maybe from the flames of hell (there were flames shooting now from somewhere outside). Chad's room had no windows, but the fire was visible through the cracks of the walls.

Chad remembered Shelldrake's warning to lie down, but as

he fell on his knees like at prayer, he found he could not move another inch, not even to lie down, and so he remained there on his knees waiting.

After all the time that passed with the sounds of countless guns and the spitting of flames and the bright explosions as something else again caught fire, the door behind which he was hidden came open, and for a minute he thought it was Chief Silver Fox who had come to see him. Why he thought it was him he did not know for he had certainly never set eyes on him.

But it was a chief of some kind. Most of his upper garments were gone, but his body did not need garments now for it was a moving cloth of its own, a cloth of blood from his scalp to where even his trousers had been cut by bullets and the very dark flesh had opened up to pure red. His hair had come fully down. Chad had never realized any man had hair that long and that beautiful, and the top of his head looked like a light had been kindled there.

He could only walk as far as Chad, and then he fell against him, holding him now until the boy felt he would suffocate to death from the pressure. They fell together to the thick comforters and torn sheets of the bed, and from suffocation by reason of Shelldrake's wounded bare frame, they held one another. The hands that were too strong even for a man, even for an Indian man, the hands must be, Chad saw, the hands of some spirit, some true Chief; and the blood then came from him like it was a hailstorm from above, the strong hands holding Chad, the blood—he had never known how much blood a man's body holds—Chad was floating, smothered, drowned in Shelldrake's blood.

"I will hold you like this forever," Shelldrake told him. "Remember it, won't you," he went on. "I am holding you forever."

His lips, curtains of blood, or fire, closed over Chad's face and sought his lips. "This is me, your friend forever," he called. Then a great thrilling movement went through Shelldrake's body, as if he was falling with Chad from a high eminence like the cliff at home that overlooks Yellow Brook from a height of five hundred feet. Chad felt himself being carried over that height and then floating below with the tremor that floods have at their crest, and he had all but fallen with his friend into the torrent when a strong blinding white light reached him, and a voice called, "If any of you are alive in there, come out with raised hands."

A gun went off, and then Chad could remember staring into the white blinding light, but his hands were at his sides, paralyzed, and not hands anyhow but flowing streams of crimson, scarlet, all the shades and hues of spilled Indian blood.

PART IV

WHEN CHAD COULTAS WOKE UP he saw almost at once that he had on brand new clothes, including a silk tie, and silver cufflinks, and he was riding again in a Pullman train, and turning round he supposed he would look face to face with his dad. But as he turned to see who was sitting next to him, his right hand was wrenched painfully by cold steel, and looking down he saw a handcuff held him to the wrist, not of Lewis Coultas, but a man who faintly resembled his dad but looked nearly a century older.

"My young friend," the ancient man began, "it's all right. Don't fret, don't cry any more than you have already for we're completely out of handkerchiefs. . . . The fetter you see on your wrist is not placed there because you have committed a crime. Far from it. Crimes have, however, been committed against you. You are handcuffed to my hand only because we certainly do not want you to be kidnapped, do we? Do we?" Mr. Wilbur Harkey repeated impatiently, for of course it was the old detective who was handcuffed to Chad's right wrist.

"But where is everbody?" Chad wanted to know.

"Everybody?" the old man quibbled at the use of the word. "You must learn to be more exact when you speak, my dear boy. *Everybody* is not a word that would have any merit in court. You must be specific when you speak. *Everybody* is meaningless."

"Well, where did Shelldrake go then, if there was a Shelldrake. And what am I doing here if there ain't one?"

"I'll tell you what I am going to do, my young friend. You remember your own name, I hope."

"I certainly do," Chad pulled on the handcuff energetically.

"I am going to take the handcuff off you, for I see it's very uncomfortable—but you must promise me not to run away."

"I don't see how I could run away on a train going this fast," the boy snapped.

"Right-oh," Wilbur Harkey nodded. "I see you have quite a saucy streak in you. I'm not surprised. I reckon without it you might no longer count yourself among the living."

Having said this, he unlocked the handcuff, and Chad pulled his right arm free, and began rubbing his wrist.

"To think you had a man shot to death on top of you. And an Indian at that!" the old detective muttered. "So covered with blood yourself we thought you were dead along with him!" Wilbur Harkey went on. "I was in charge of the search-and-find party, I may as well tell you. Directed the entire maneuver with local law enforcement assistance of course. *I* directed, *they* used the guns."

The old man appeared plunged in thought, then rousing himself, he took out his gold pen and notebook, and wet the nib of the pen with some saliva.

"I must now ask you, Chad Coultas, a very important question. Without a proper question my mission may simply fold and disperse into thin air."

"What is your mission?"

Wilbur Harkey laughed in spite of himself, until his gold teeth—and they all appeared gold—shone in the very feeble sunlight coming through the Pullman train windows.

"My mission is to bring you back to your mother and grandmother. I am the renowned investigator, Mr. Wilbur Harkey. Your loved ones sent out enough alerts to capture the lost Dauphin, or the Prince of Wales himself if he should disappear. . . . But you see," and here the old man began peering at one of Chad's eyes, "what puzzles us all is both your eyes are of a very dark color."

"Who is *all,* sir," Chad spoke up now, "since you have forbidden me to use the word *everybody.*"

The detective looked stung to the quick.

"I do not believe I should be insolent to my elders if I were you," he cautioned his charge. "I would avoid it."

But the detective's observation concerning the color of his eyes bothered Chad, and he kept touching his right eye.

"I have asked the lady in the next compartment to lend me her looking glass," the old man explained, "against just such a contingency." And he drew out quite a large, fancy, looking glass from under the seat.

"Now, my young man, will you kindly look at both your eyes and tell me their color."

Chad seized the looking glass, as if it was his property which had recently been filched from him. Giving Wilbur Harkey a reproachful look, he then held the glass to his eyes, and as he did so a slow moan escaped from his lips.

"I'm glad to hear you cry out like that. It denotes genuine surprise!"

Chad closed both his eyes, and silently handed the looking glass to the detective. His head bent over, and he gave out a few short sobs.

"I told you we have no more handkerchiefs!"

"Be quiet, why can't you," the boy almost roared. "Leave me alone."

"That is precisely what I cannot do. You are my ward, and if you don't behave I will put you back in handcuffs and maybe foot-fetters to boot. So think that over, my smart young charge!"

"My right eye has changed color."

Out came the notebook and the gold pen.

"And what *was* the color of your right eye, may I ask, if you won't chop my head off for asking."

"My right eye was blue, just like Lewis Coultas's and my mother Eva's eyes are. Now it's black as night, or maybe that damned looking glass is from the fun house!" And seizing the glass, Chad smashed it in front of Mr. Harkey's amazed countenance.

"You have destroyed the property of another person, do you realize that?"

Chad was so busy sniveling he probably did not hear Mr. Harkey.

"Where are you taking me now?" the boy said after a while as he watched Mr. Harkey picking up the broken pieces of the looking glass.

"I should be taking you to the reformatory, but we are, as a matter of fact, headed for Yellow Brook. . . . And as I am starving after the ordeal I have been through, we will now proceed to the dining room and have some sustenance. Rise, please, and precede me, for I don't trust you yet. Not by a long shot. So, march!"

Four lordly black waiters were expecting Mr. Harkey and

company in the dining room, and two of them immediately began slapping two chairs with their stiff linen napkins, while all four grinned encouragingly, showing teeth as gold as Mr. Harkey's, though Chad decided the waiters' gold teeth were of better quality than the old detective's.

"I have never heard of a chap's eye changing color," the old investigator said, reading the menu. "It has given me pause, let me tell you. You have always been identified as a boy of Indian features, but with one blue eye. That eye has held you to the white race. But no more. If indeed you are Chad Coultas!" At this, the detective threw down the menu as if he had read the boy's death warrant in the list of steaks, omelettes, and buttermilk pancakes.

"It will probably change back to blue," Chad said in a comforting tone.

"Your Mother will probably know if this is really you when we get to Yellow Brook," the old man brought the discussion to a close.

"And what will the young gentleman have this bright and sunshiny day?" the youngest of the four waiters asked Chad.

"I'll take the steak and potatoes and the pancakes and the corn fritters. Then," he paused, "I believe I'll have the hominy grits—and the gravy also."

Like Mr. Harkey, the waiter held a large gold pen with which he wrote down each word.

"And you, distinguished sir?" the waiter turned to the detective.

"I believe I had best follow suit, unless the young gentleman facing me forbids me to do so," Mr. Harkey told the waiter.

Chad stared at the detective out of both of his black-colored eyes and stringently tied his big napkin around his neck.

"This young gentleman," Wilbur Harkey began speaking while the head porter was seeing to their table being cleared after their meal, "this boy, here, almost a child," and the detective raised his voice seeing he had attentive auditors, and the head waiters and head porter gathered round the table, holding their napkins languidly over their arms and their eyes resting more or less nowhere, "this child, then, has been the subject of a nationwide search, and was rescued only in the nick of time from an Indian rebellion. He came within a hair's breadth of being scalped himself, although he persists in boasting he has Indian ancestry."

The waiters now moved their attention toward Chad, let their gaze linger there, and then, carried away by Mr. Harkey's forensic bass, their eyes fell to the thick tablecloth.

"He has been kidnapped at least five times," the detective went on, "the last time by a notorious desperado who had planned to adopt him, so the boy claims, but I happen to know he was going to murder the poor lad for the gold he was carrying with him. Anyhow, Shelldrake, so called, was wanted for murder in ten states and four territories."

Chad attempted to dispute this analysis of Shelldrake, but Wilbur Harkey, stung as only he could be at being interrupted forensically, shook the handcuffs threateningly at him.

The waiters all drew back at the sight of the handcuffs, but then at a movement of Mr. Harkey's head, they again gathered round to hear more of the investigator's yarn.

"We are now returning him to Yellow River," the old man summarized the story.

"Yellow *Brook,*" Chad corrected him somewhat vociferously, and the waiters suppressed a snicker.

"Have it *Brook* then, damn it all," Mr. Harkey complained. "Though I do wonder, Chad, my child, after what you have been through, that you even know where you're from let alone if you're sure of your own name or if your eyes are blue, black or hazel. . . . He's no more sure who his father is than I am," the old man addressed the black waiters.

All the waiters exchanged apprehensive looks with one another, and made stinging sounds with their handsome napkins as they raised and lowered them over their arms.

"His one eye has changed color, and you have no idea how that is a source of deep worry and vexation to me. I have always prided myself on particulars, and a sudden change in a particular like this is a most trying and, as I say, vexatious thing. I will require medical advisement on the subject of his eye of course. It was the blue one, or right eye, which has changed color without rhyme or reason. I would go to his legal dad with all this, but Mr. Lewis Coultas has been arrested on a charge of forgery and grand larceny, and has skipped the country in the bargain."

Chad Coultas stood up at this, dropping his heavy linen napkin and ring on the resplendently-shined shoes of the tallest of the waiters.

"You have no right to mention him—in the presence of strangers!" the boy cried out in a voice unrecognizable as his own. "I won't stand for it! I won't allow it! Whatever he did, he is innocent!"

Chad advanced at that moment so threateningly toward the old investigator that the youngest of the waiters suddenly took hold of him and held him back.

"Lies! Lies! Everything is lies," Chad shouted.

"Now, now, simmer down," the waiter advised him, and he held him gently by both his hands. "Anger don't mend no fences." He helped the boy now into a chair, and gave him a glass of water to drink.

"The lad is understandably upset," Wilbur Harkey droned on, and by raising his eyebrows indicated he would require the undivided attention of all the dining room personnel.

"Lewis Coultas had a devastating charm, and many winning ways, as you can see from the way his legal boy here has reacted to my merely giving the particulars of the case. Lewis Coultas was indeed Prince Charming, no question about it. None whatsoever! But Prince Charming, as Prince Charmings usually do, had another side to him. Alas for this poor boy and his mother Eva. And alas for Pauline too! She's the grandmother who lost her fortune to Lewis."

Chad sobbed on in shame and humiliation as the foibles, shortcomings and misguided conduct of his once-dad now were revealed to all who cared to listen.

"Lewis Coultas with his male charm and abundant good looks ruined all who so much as crossed his shadow. Minnie and Cora have been sentenced to twenty years each in the women's penitentiary thanks to their having known him. But I believe the final chapter in Lewis Coultas's career may have been written. We are not apt to hear from him if he is in the Antipodes. The Antipodes have a way of burying a man from sight!"

"Antipodes?" Chad spoke up now.

"That is what I said, sir," Wilbur barked at him. "I suppose misguided, trusting, foolish Bess Lytle (who permitted everything to get out of hand in the first place) has taught you *some* geography!"

Chad showed obvious surprise at Mr. Harkey's mention of his old seventh-grade teacher.

"There is very little, you see, that I don't know about you, Chad," the old man smiled painfully now.

Mr. Harkey had finished his visit to the dining room and he rose now with majestic deliberation, dropping as he did so his special traveling toothpick secured in a little gold container.

"No, no, gentlemen, I won't have it!" he waved back the waiters who attempted to retrieve it. "I will pick up the article myself. I am not that old yet, Wilbur Harkey is not. Old, but not that old!"

With great and groaning difficulty he managed to salvage the gold-encased toothpick from the carpet.

Mr. Harkey then proceeded to pass out shining big silver dollars to all the fine "Africans" as he called them, which evoked from the most inattentive of the waiters now complete alertness, broad sunshiny smiles, and many "Thank you's."

As if not to be outdone, Chad found in his own brand new suit of clothes a gold piece, which he assumed must have dropped out of his own collection, and he handed this now to the head porter, who bowed his head in thanks almost to the boy's knees.

For a moment Mr. Harkey was speechless at such profligate largesse. But he recovered himself in time to say, "That will do for now, my boy," and gave Chad a resolute shove out of the dining room.

After their repast in the Pullman diner, Wilbur Harkey suggested to Chad that the boy "slumber" a little while because they were in for an ordeal at the main depot of Yellow Brook.

"What do you mean by ordeal, sir?" Chad inquired a bit huffily.

"Is it the word which you do not understand, or the situation which the words stand for?" Harkey asked loftily, and tapped with his fingers on the back of the seat.

"Well, both, I suppose," the boy replied.

"Never suppose, Chad. Always *know.*"

"Well," Chad said after a silence, "what am I to expect, then, at the depot?"

"Good, that's a proper question now, shows you could endure cross-examination if it ever comes to that. . . . The ordeal I refer to, my boy, is the press. They will be waiting for us at the station. They will want to ask you questions and take pictures."

Chad curled his lip.

"I want you, when they ask you something, to try to reply by just yes or no. Nothing more. Don't go off now on one of your narratives, telling them about Eva and Decatur, your dad Lewis Coultas, and his ladyloves Minnie and Cora, now behind bars. That won't do you any good. Remember this, too—the press and the men who write for it have not the slightest interest in fact, particulars, truth, or the human race. They're out to invent everything from whole cloth, and the only reason they are not gangsters or outright bandits is they lack the talent and the backbone to be bona fide malefactors. They choose the path of lies and misstatement for money. But their intent is the same as that of the criminals they often write about: to cheat, lie, obfuscate and mislead in order to sell newsprint."

Chad's eyes had closed during this speech, and taking advantage of the boy's being "out" for the moment, Wilbur Harkey clapped his hands almost noiselessly in the direction of Ethelbert Graustark, the youngest of the Pullman porters.

Ethelbert strode leisurely over to the investigator and lowered his ear to the old man's cavernous mouth.

"Our young friend here," the detective whispered, "is in for being received by the press, you know, newspaper people, and I wonder if you could take him to the W.C. and spruce him up a bit. Since he's asleep would you mind just carrying him in there, he don't weigh more than a sparrow after what he's been through."

Ethelbert Graustark, who was stronger perhaps than most porters by reason of his having worked on the road when he was in jail for a time in Georgia, carried Chad off as if he weighed no more than a dead grasshopper, and was already at work sprucing him up when the boy came to.

"Try not to look so broody, young man," Ethelbert soothed him. "You're in good hands here all around. Good capable hands."

Chad gave a long look in the mirror at Ethelbert's fingers working away.

"Hey, do you know where you are," Ethelbert joked. "Tell me then if you do, why don't you?"

Ethelbert went on trimming Chad's hair.

"We passed Chicago an hour or so ago," the porter almost sang out the words. "You're a handsome boy, do you know it, under all the scratches and bruises and the busted upper lip. Don't tell me how you got so banged up. I don't want to hear about it."

"Wilbur Harkey is still on the train, isn't he, sir?" Chad wondered.

Ethelbert grinned over the "sir." He put away his scissors, and took out a package of Sen-sens, and put one of them in Chad's mouth.

"Wilbur Harkey, yes, he's still on the train. I'm telling you when we seen you get on the car with the handcuffs on, that was a red-letter day for us all. I knowed for myself you was no wanted desperado. But in these times and tides, you can't be too sure any more. And you was so dark and as I just said so darned cut up. We wondered, yes sir we wondered. . . . But you goin' to be all right now. Mr. Wilbur Harkey, he travels this road quite regular, and though he's about as amusin' as a stuck record, still he is a man of note and *press-tige,* and so you're goin' to be all right."

Chad smiled ever so faintly for his cut mouth pained him. And it was all he could do to keep his eyes open, as Ethelbert prettied him up some more.

All at once Ethelbert was whispering in his ear.

"Now if things don't turn out so good with Mr. Harkey and the detective business, Chad," he was saying, "and you ever need a friend in Chicago, you can call on me, hear? That's all I'm goin' to say at this time."

He handed Chad a printed card with several names on it, and a blurred address with the street, however, in bold letters: South Parkway, and under it in bigger letters, Chicago, Illinois.

For the first time since perhaps the times Chad had taken rides with Decatur, he smiled broadly, and comfortably lifted up his eyes.

Ethelbert pulled the boy up from his seat now, and made him stand straight up so he could see how he was going to look to the delegation that would be meeting him at the depot in Yellow Brook.

"You'll do," the porter said, and then looking dead serious, he poked Chad in the ribs.

"Yes, he certainly spruced you up all right!" Mr. Harkey

exclaimed on seeing Chad emerge from the W.C. "He has a fine touch, Ethelbert, especially when you consider he spent quite a bit of time in a chain gang in Georgia. He tells me most of the fingers in his right hand were broken, but he can still lift a tray of dishes, and can certainly handle a comb and brush. And now, for our ordeal, for we're coming into Yellow Brook at last."

Chad could hear the engine begin to slow down, and outside enormous clouds of white smoke blotted out the view of the depot.

"Remember," Mr. Harkey admonished Chad as the porters put down the step, and the old man handed out lavish tips. "Remember, Chad, what I told you when they ask you questions!"

But it was already too late. A crowd of newspaper men were surrounding the boy and Mr. Harkey, and the flash bulbs were going off.

The questions from the press came thick and fast, such as *Is it not a fact, Chad Coultas, that though your name and photo are circulating the globe you are so scholastically deficient you are repeating the seventh grade for the second or perhaps third time?*

A hundred other similar questions were yelled out as a heavy snowfall descended on everyone, but, as in Bess Lytle's class in advanced arithmetic, Chad found himself without an answer. He instead kept looking into the crowd for someone.

Mr. Harkey had been informed by a night letter that a torchlight parade would greet him and the runaway boy. He had not been misinformed, for once they were through the crossfire of the reporters, a crowd of at least twenty-five men bearing torches appeared. Owing to the heavy snowfall each torch kept sputtering a peculiar light and smell but miraculously retained at least part of its illumination.

Then as the torches were flickering and spitting moribundly, the town band arrived, consisting of several slide-trombone players, two cornets, three saxophones, a French horn, and a drum, with each instrument in almost as bad a state as the torches, at least out of tune. The string section of the band had stayed inside the Opera House to greet the returning "hero" there.

The mayor now came forward, but before he could say a

word to Mr. Harkey and Chad, Eva had broken through the cordon and seized Chad around the neck and was covering him with her kisses, made still wetter by the now almost blinding snowfall.

"You're taller, precious, by a good inch. But you're so peaked and meager, sweetheart. And what has happened to your eye?"

She pushed his head back gently so that the illumination from the police searchlight would fall a bit more evenly on his face.

"What on earth have they done to you?" Eva sobbed.

Melissa also now greeted Chad.

Bess Lytle and Todd came forward, and then Pauline, trying to extricate her hands from a sealskin muff to embrace her grandson.

"Mother, where is he?" Chad managed to free himself from all his loved ones to utter this one paramount question.

"He, darling?" Eva wondered absently, covering his face again with her kisses.

"Decatur, Mother, Decatur." Chad was, she saw, as usual, moody.

"He's been in jail, Chad," Eva spoke with hesitation. "But the sheriff assured me he'd be let out for the reception and ceremony."

"But I've got to tell him!" Chad cried, and looked around at the crowd surrounding him, the faces of whom were unrecognizable by reason of the heavy snow falling thicker and thicker by the minute.

"Tell him *what,* precious?" Eva wanted to know.

"The truth, Mother, the truth," Chad spoke to her.

"Chad, your cut lip has begun to bleed a little," she pointed out. "Here, let me put a little something on it, for it won't do to have it bleeding like this during the ceremony."

She extricated a small container of a salve of some kind and put it on his mouth. "That will have to hold it from opening for the time being."

"Tell me, Mother, what was Decatur put in jail for?"

Eva was still looking apprehensively at his cut lip. "Oh, well," she hesitated, "it seems he went on some kind of rampage." She stopped, and then when he tugged at her sleeve, she continued. "Got hold of the wrong kind of liquor, the police claim. He mashed nearly all the streetlights on Main Street, and all the store windows also. Oh, it was frightful. They blame it on his being across."

All at once Chad broke away from his mother and disappeared into the crowd of curiosity-seekers, just as Mr. Harkey was pushing his way through the select members of the mayor's party. Eva was prevented from following after her son by Mr. Harkey's taking her securely by the arm and saying, "I am the gentleman who rescued your son." Wilbur Harkey then introduced himself lengthily to Eva's family and to the mayor's aides.

Eva was still looking in the direction where Chad had disappeared, and then seeing the detective's face bearing down on her, she recovered herself enough to say, "Accept my heartfelt thanks, will you, Mr. Harkey, for finding my boy. Without you I am sure—"

The mayor now came forward, interrupting them, and urged everybody to get in the car waiting to take them to the Opera House for the ceremony.

"There he is—Chad!" Eva cried, and pushing her way past the mayor, she managed to seize her son and almost dragged him toward the limousine.

Inside the car, while Eva scolded and complained bitterly about Chad's running away, Mr. Harkey was holding forth at some length on the subject of Mr. Lewis Coultas, though Eva was hardly in a state to listen to him. "The last we heard of your husband, Mrs. Coultas," she heard the tail end of his speech, "he was in New South Wales and had, I know this on good authority, opened a. . . ."

The investigator's last words were drowned out by the sound of the band greeting them in front of the Opera House.

The delegation of Eva, Chad, Pauline, Bess Lytle, Mr. Harkey and the mayor's party had finally reached the stage of the Opera House. On either side of them were the band and the men's Glee Club.

Owing to the fierce snowstorm raging outside, the attendance was an extremely limited one. It was surprising, the mayor later commented, that anybody at all had come. But, he added, "everybody who was anybody was there," which may have been a reference to Judge Hebbel, the sheriff and his deputies, nearly all the town's lawyers, and a good number of the clergy.

After interminable outpourings by the men's Glee Club, a

soprano solo, and several generous selections by the band, Mr. Harkey was nudged by the mayor to go up to the rostrum and deliver his address.

Mr. Harkey for a lengthy while could not find his spectacles and the Glee Club therefore sang another selection which was vociferously applauded. A few of the audience began to slip out, for the weather report had now reached some of them that an electrical storm of severe violence was expected about midnight.

Mr. Harkey had barely, indeed, begun his address, when he stopped at the unprecedented sound of thunder, and a resounding crash from very close to the Opera House caused several persons in the audience simultaneously to cry, "Lightning!"

Mr. Harkey raised his hand for silence, and continued his address, but even the old detective's forensic skill was brought almost to a final halt by two phenomena. The first was a crash of thunder so loud that the great chandelier hanging over the assemblage moved dizzily and threateningly over everyone's heads, and then, when it had begun to cease its movement, the main door to the orchestra opened and a man of great height wearing a cloak, and with his black hair falling almost beneath his shoulder, entered.

Every head turned to look, even though his entrance had not been heralded by trumpets. But only one person rose to greet him. Chad Coultas stood up on the stage. Eva attempted twice to pull him back to her, but the boy was already going down the steps which led from the stage into the auditorium.

There was complete silence except for the distant peals of thunder and a kind of wailing, even further distant, of the wind.

Chad walked confidently, his hands moving with the palms slightly upward, in the direction of the latecomer who had come to a full halt and in direct line with the advancing boy.

When Chad had reached to within a few feet of the man facing him, he stopped as if astonished or indeed struck dumb. The sound of the wind rising again was audible, and the thunder pealed this time closer but with softer tones.

Then a few whispers of shock or surprise came from some of the spectators as the boy threw himself at the stranger's feet and held to them with a desperation and strength which now brought loud cries of disapproval, perhaps horror, from nearly all the spectators.

"No, Chad, no," a woman's voice came from the stage, and then the echoing sounds from that cry went over the entire Opera House.

The man in the dark coat and long hair, who was Decatur, lifted the boy up forcibly, and the two held to one another convulsively like men condemned by the spectators to death. They clung to one another indeed finally like prisoners already perhaps executed and holding to one another in the tight embrace of death itself.

Then Decatur took Chad by his arm and led him from the Opera House into the street now piled in snowdrifts above their heads, while above them the sky flashed with a kind of cerise fire.

A low murmur continued to follow after them from all the spectators, confounding it with the thunder in the background, a murmur compounded of shock, awe, perhaps even satisfaction and approbation.

Mr. Harkey made an adjuration for silence, but almost everybody on the stage and in the audience had risen and turned to look after the departing Decatur and Chad. And despite Mr. Harkey's continuing to speak from the rostrum, the band struck up a salvo of victorious sounds, and the mayor, bowing to the entire concourse, then led the way out of the Opera House.

PART V

WHEN IT WAS ALL OVER, and Decatur and Chad had left Yellow Brook, had left Eva, Bess Lytle and the schoolhouse, Eva tried to sort things out. She kept stiff little filing cards on which she wrote down her thoughts, like a person who is to give her own public address somewhere, yes, perhaps also at the Opera House, at some future unspecified date.

The night at the Opera House continued to haunt Eva like those dreams which recur from early childhood until old age. She had never understood why such a ceremony took place in the first place, and she could find nobody in Yellow Brook who seemed positive about it either. Certainly Judge Hebbel was not able to tell her—or the sheriff, or his deputies—what was being commemorated. The return home of a seriously mistreated and confused child, half deaf from exposure and neglect, and bleeding from his torn lip?

At the ceremony itself Eva felt she had been put on trial, and with all those faces staring at her, the jury had already brought in the verdict marked "Guilty."

Then the impassioned meeting of Decatur and Chad as she stood powerless to go to either of them, and Chad's prostration before Decatur, and Decatur's lifting him up finally to embrace and kiss him before all those spectators!

Eva, Pauline, Melissa, and Bess Lytle had finally been able to work their way from the Opera House, despite drifts of snow towering above them on all sides, but from behind them they could still hear Mr. Harkey's voice, carried by loudspeakers, giving forth with his famous forensic eloquence.

What it was he said escaped them. Days later, while Eva was speaking with Judge Hebbel, the oration of Mr. Harkey was mentioned, and the judge told Eva that the investigator had been speaking on the necessity of proper procedures in law, the maintenance of continuity through investigation, and the proper identification of particulars. Old Wilbur Harkey in his closing words that evening declared that his having found Chad Coultas alive was, in the old detective's opinion, the crowning effort of his fifty or sixty years' devotion to surveillance, and the maintaining of social continuity.

Eva was never to see Mr. Harkey again, but she was informed by Judge Hebbel that the old gentleman had waived his fee for finding Chad, and Eva would owe him nothing.

The return of Chad, the strange reception ceremony at the Opera House, and the shocking spectacle of Decatur and Chad's impassioned reunion blotted out from Eva's mind for the time the appalling scandal of Lewis Coultas's fleeing the country to avoid certain arrest for forgery, misuse of funds, and other crimes. Too much had happened for Eva to put anything in its proper perspective, and so Lewis Coultas appeared as far away and remote as he really was—Australia.

As the party of Eva Coultas was returning to her mansion from the Opera House they observed with relief that the temperature had gone up markedly, and the snowflakes were changed to raindrops.

Eva ushered everyone into the front parlor, and rang for the hired girl.

"Today," Eva began when they had all seated themselves, "I observed a real harbinger of spring, just before the big snowstorm."

Pauline looked at her daughter admiringly. She could not remember Eva looking so beautiful for quite a while, or so young.

"The crows were flying about the upper stories today," Eva went on, and she gave a nod to the hired girl that she was to bring in the refreshments. "Yes, the crows have nearly driven me mad with their cawing. They are always quarreling with the jays and sparrows."

"My great Aunt Ida had a pet crow," Pauline reminisced. "The crow had a partiality for jewelry and over the years had been stealing Ida's best jewels. It spurned her imitation ones. Ida was nearly frantic thinking a burglar was coming and going at will. . . . But some time later they found all of Ida's jewels neatly tucked away in the bell tower of her home."

"No, darling," Eva corrected her mother. "They found the jewels in the choir loft of the Presbyterian Church."

"Ah, right you are," Pauline recanted. "At any rate, the thief was a crow!"

Bess Lytle now fidgeted to leave, pointing out that it was long past midnight.

"It is out of the question," Eva told her. "You must spend the night here. I will not allow you to go out into such foul weather."

"But, Eva," Pauline now interposed, "where on earth are Chad and Decatur?"

"Oh, Mother, Mother," Eva spoke with weary condescension. "They are gone off together, don't you know that? Can't you remember their reunion together before all those eyes! We'll never see them again!"

"Eva, my dear, you are always acting in some play or other! What do you mean they've gone off together? What is she talking about?" Pauline spoke these last words to Bess.

"I'm afraid Eva is right," Bess Lytle now spoke up. In this subdued light Eva noticed that Bess's hair was going very gray, almost white.

"I could see clear from the stage," Eva went on bravely, "that Chad's cut lip was bleeding again. I hope Decatur knows how to patch that up."

Both Pauline and Bess stared at Eva, like participants in a reading who await the principal reader's next lines.

"Chad always used to get a nosebleed when he was upset. You will recall that, Bess, being his teacher for so long. But let me say this, if I am not repeating myself. Why on earth a ceremony was planned before the little fellow had had time to alight from the fast train, I will never know."

"Yellow Brook always greets people who have achieved something unusual," Bess spoke a bit falteringly.

The hired girl now entered with a huge tray of sandwiches, hot milk, and cakes.

"Oh, dear, how welcome refreshments are after what we have been through," Eva said gaily. "And our dear cook has outdone herself, poor thing, kept up at such hours. Well, she can thank her stars she has no children to worry her into an early grave."

They sat down to a small round marble-topped table, and Pauline and Bess claimed they were not hungry, but then after a few nibbles they attacked the sandwiches and the hot milk with good grace.

"Thank God Melissa has not deserted me," Pauline remarked. As she spoke she opened a small pillbox and swallowed something. "I have to have *one* of my grandchildren with me in my last years. And if Eva is right, which she almost never is, I wont't see my grandchild Chad till who knows when."

"I never said any such thing, Mother, and you know it. I merely said God knows when we'll see Chad again now he has seen fit to publicly show he favors Decatur over his own mother."

"I am sure Chad will walk in here any moment," Pauline contradicted her daughter. "Wait and see."

"But the boy has been through such an ordeal," Bess Lytle now spoke in her customary dominating manner. "One can't expect him to act as if nothing has happened."

"No, don't you see, Bess," Eva began in a calm and restrained manner unusual for her. "The ordeal was not what men did to him in Canada or in large cities, or where he went driving his horse and wagon, being attacked, humiliated, struck down, nearly murdered, oh I can't remember all that the old detective filled my ears with. That wasn't the ordeal at all, don't you see? Not at all! Listen to me. The ordeal he has been through was he would not yield to the claim, the . . ." Here Eva broke off and stared about her like one who has completely lost her way.

"You must finish what you were going to say," Bess spoke sternly.

"I don't know if I can," Eva faltered. Then bracing herself, she said, "His ordeal was that he had seen a light long before he was abducted by anybody, kidnapped or stolen or taken from his mother. He feared the light he saw, and that led to all the trouble. No one needed to tell him Decatur was his father, for Chad knew it almost from the start. Chad came back to Yellow Brook for only one reason, to claim his real father. That was the light that led him back. He came back for his father. Decatur. I saw that in both their faces when they embraced before all the spectators. I am only his mother, Decatur is his all. That's what their embrace meant and why it was so terrible. When Decatur came to me one day fourteen years ago, when I was so ill, coming up that long staircase, seeing my door open, all he wanted, then as now, was a son. Why, Decatur was barely older than Chad is now. He was looking for a son even then. What did I mean or matter in face of that—and I saw that on both their countenances when they held to one another in that desperate act of reunion."

"Eva, Eva," Pauline cried. "You do not know what you are saying!"

"In a minute, Mother, in a minute! Let me finish. I knew then that as soon as the snow melts, or they may not even wait that long, they will go away together. Chad's braved through too much to require schooling, Bess. It's too late for books. It's too late for me. And my fault was I gave the boy a father who was not his, I gave him Lewis Coultas. Chad knows that, so how can he trust me again? I gave him the wrong father, who could never be his. So you see, I am barred from my own boy."

Pauline had come over and knelt down beside her daughter.

"You must go upstairs and get some sleep," her mother said to her. "The ceremony has been too much for you. Tomorrow everything will be clearer."

Eva stared at her mother, and shook her head at her words.

"Nothing has ever been as clear as it is now," she said, and took her mother's hand and looked full in the face at Bess and Melissa. "Nothing is clearer! I always knew I would lose Chad because he was never mine. Melissa is mine, even Lewis Coultas was mine, but when Decatur stole in, took me, stole *me,* I knew then, ill as I was, he would be back. I always knew he would be back, and from the time Chad was a tiny baby, I knew one day he would be stolen by Indians. I was the only one who knew who the boy was. So you see though I loved him and do love him more than life itself, I knew from the beginning I had no claim on him. That is why I loved him as much as I did. Every time I kissed him I said farewell. . . . But there is another love that is greater even than mine. I saw it in his face when he returned. It is not a human love that Decatur has for this boy—maybe it is divine, I don't know—but it is immoderate like the lake in a storm, and the forest when riven by lightning. It comes out of the sky and the thunder. I can't vie with that. When I saw the changed color of his eye, and when I saw that Decatur saw I saw it, as he looked at me from where he held Chad in so close an embrace, I knew it was all over. I wanted to call out to Decatur where I sat in the Opera House, and say, *'He's yours now, so live for him then. Live only for him.'* "

Pauline put down her cup of hot milk, and Bess Lytle moved her fork over the hand-painted china plate, and picked up a last crumb of yellow sunshine cake.

"It's nearly three o'clock in the morning," Bess spoke at last. "I think I will take your invitation and go upstairs and rest, for I have to get up at five to open the schoolhouse, you know."

They all rose then, kissed one another tenderly, and began climbing the stairs to their separate rooms.

About the Author

James Purdy, one of the most distinguished contemporary American authors, was born in rural Ohio and educated in Ohio, Illinois, Mexico and Spain. He spent several years teaching English in Cuba before the Castro regime. His first book of fiction, *63: Dream Palace,* was published in England in 1957 to great critical acclaim. Since then Mr. Purdy has written numerous novels, plays, poetry and short stories, including *Malcolm, Eustace Chisholm and the Works, In a Shallow Grave, The House of the Solitary Maggot, On Glory's Course, The Running Sun, Color of Darkness* and *Proud Flesh.* In 1965 Edward Albee adapted *Malcolm* for the Broadway stage, and *In a Shallow Grave* will soon be made into a motion picture. James Purdy lives in New York City.